Secrets

M.A. McNally

This is a work of fiction. Unless otherwise indicated, all the names, characters, businesses, places, events, and incidents in this book are either the product of the authors imagination or used in a fictitious manner. Any resemblance to actual person's, living or dead, or actual events, is purely coincidental.

Created with Vellum

Also by M.A. McNally

The Broken series

Book one, *Broken*

Book two, *Secrets*

For Aless C, Tracey G, Kasia J, Lindsay H, Teressa W & Verity.
Thank you for reading the book and for all the feedback.
You are diamonds.

CONTENT GUIDANCE:

This novel explores aspects of domestic abuse and mental health and contains depictions of self-harm, alcohol abuse, animal cruelty, blood and gore, child abuse. Please read with care.

Part One

Chapter One
Patricia

When the world says, "Give Up," Hope whispers, "Try it one more time."

— *Unknown*

Sunday July 18th 1976

What am I doing?

Staring at my husband until my eyeballs hurt, I wish a miracle would happen and he'd spontaneously combust right in front of my eyes. My body feels like lead, glued to the pavement, watching his every move. *Thump, thump, thump,* I don't know what's louder, my heart or my head, both near enough ready to explode as I watch, contemplating whether I should just turn around and run the hell away with my children while I still can. As much as I want to, I know I can't. I have to go back to the monster I stare at who I know could, probably kill us all with one strike of his fist.

I hate myself. I *hate* myself.

My heart and head are so confused, so conflicted. My heart hates myself for putting my children's lives in danger, but my head knows I have to come back. I *don't* have any other choice. Jayden's killing - *again*. No one else will help me. What's worse, when James sees I have not one, but *two* children in tow, he'll explode. He'll explode like a bomb and kill us all.

What the hell am I doing?

Squatting down, gently stroking Jayden's soft cheek, the baby I clutch squirms, repositioning her so she is comfortable. Unusually, Jayden's olive skin is as white as a ghost, his face expressionless as two tiny tears race each other down his little face. I know why he's crying, what he's thinking, because I'm thinking it, too.

"I'm so sorry, baby. Mummy didn't have any other choice."

Hugging Jayden to me, our tears combine as we watch his father from where we are. James' movements don't seem to be in time to the music blaring from the house, him suddenly stopping and twitching, pointing to the sky like he's painting something invisible. I'd know those movements anywhere. He's drunk and high, which means two possible things.

Hospital or death.

What am I doing?

What the fuck am I doing?

When I left James six months ago, I thought that would be it. I thought I'd never have to see him again.

I left with only one child. How can I be back with another in tow?

He'll go nuts. He never wanted kids. Ever. How the hell am I going to explain away having another?

He's not stupid, he won't believe the baby I hold in my arms is his for one second.

The last twenty-four hours are such a blur. I really think I'm going mad.

The animals.

I'll never unsee those poor animals' heads inside the wardrobe.

The eyes. They'd all only had one eye. Why?

Looking into Jayden's eyes, it's like butter wouldn't melt. No one would believe he'd be capable of slaughtering one, let alone ten, eleven, twelve defenceless animals.

I can't control whatever resides inside him to stop and that terrifies me.

Those poor animals.

What did any of them ever do to deserve Jayden's wrath, his blade, his hate.

I had to run. I had no choice but to run to the only person I despise more than anything in this world.

Jayden is half of him, has the same evil flowing through his veins, so surely he will be able to stop whatever resides inside his son from killing.

I'm not sure who I'm more terrified of.

Whimpering in my arms, I bring the baby's cheek to mine, rubbing her soft skin with my lips, rocking her back and forth, shhh, shhh, shhhing in her ear.

Is she really mine?

It happened so fast.

One minute I was helping Gail, the baby's mother give birth. The next she was begging me to take her baby.

What could I do?

I'd met Gail, a homeless girl, months before, back at another train station. I never thought, not in a million years, that I'd ever see her again.

I never thought I'd end up helping her give birth to her child in another toilet at another train station.

How could I have imagined that?

In the blink of an eye she'd handed me her baby and a lock of her hair, and I'd walked calmly out of the toilet and walked onto the train with Jayden and her baby.

How could I have been so selfish, so stupid?

When Bill, a man from my past had thundered towards me on the train, I'd thought that was it. But he'd had other things on his mind. He hadn't even noticed the baby.

If I'm honest, I never thought I'd see him again, either. I *never* wanted to see him again after what he did. I still have nightmares of that night.

I dream of him driving off with my car that he won in a game of cards with James, and Jayden's in the back, thrashing his little hands against the glass, screaming for me to help him and I can't do anything.

I can't do anything to help my baby.

When I wake up I'm sweating, and Bill's sneery face is above mine, looking down into mine demanding the keys to my car.

After he'd told me that James had given him a choice of prize, the car - or *Jayden*, I'd really started believing what he was telling me was the truth. Thank God he'd chosen the car, but he said there were others who'd have chosen Jayden.

I'd run.

I'd begged Bill to drop us at the train station and had run to my sister, Ava's.

I can't go back to her. I wish I could, but Jayden made sure that can never happen again.

Ava will *never* have us back after what he did to her cat.

Beautiful Tiddles had never done anything to Jayden to make him kill her with such savagery.

What had any of the animals he's killed ever done to warrant such hate from him.

I have to protect them.

Jayden can't kill any more defenceless animals.

I can't believe I'm even saying that.

Looking into Jayden's anxious eyes, they are wide, not blinking, looking from me to his father. He knows why we're back. He knows that this is the only place we could've come. I only pray this works. I hope a miracle happens and James is able to tame whatever monster resides inside his son.

Stroking Jayden's soft cheek, pulling him and the baby close, I tell him to help with the suitcase.

"It's time, son. It's time to go back."

Chapter Two
James

"Shrooms are full of shit. That's the whole story. Grown in shit, it's their essence."

— A.D. Aliwat

Sitting on the deck, smoking a joint and sipping on a large JD and Coke, the stupid cars honking at two young women pointing at the beautiful sky asking their kids where they think the planes are going; they are pissing me right off.

"Shut the fuck up! Who gives a shit about the sky or where the fucking planes are going?"

Holding her hands over her kid's ears, one of the women looks at me like I'm a piece of shit.

"Hell, I already know I'm a piece of shit. Fuck off, you stupid bitch."

This is my favourite part of the day and I don't want any fuckers spoiling it, especially no women and kids. Why would I want any reminding of my wife and son? If I never saw them again it would be too soon.

The family two houses down start shouting like they do every night. Crying, the kids don't want Daddy yelling at their Mumma.

Slam. Bang. Screaming.

Stupid bitch probably deserves it. She won't leave, she ain't got the guts. Shame for the poor bastard.

Whatever they're cooking though smells good. Lamb chops, hamburgers? I could eat ten of them.

Barking, the dog joins in, the father telling it to shut the fuck up. The poor mutt probably smells the meat cooking the same as me. The only thing anyone will be getting in that house tonight is a fat lip.

I'm surprised my music hasn't drowned them out, it's louder than usual. That, or the mushrooms I took an hour ago are playing with my mind. Rubbing my arms, I'm cold. I hope that don't mean something bad is coming. Grabbing my hoodie from behind my chair, trying to put it on, the mushrooms ain't making the job easy because my arms don't want to help my brain. Sitting back, the birds want to join in pissing me off too, singing with their bird voices above me like they're in a bird choir.

"Shut the fuck up."

Shooting them with my finger, it's real hard not to focus on the blue, yellow, red, and orange of the sky. It's like it's been painted especially for me. The lady walking past wasn't wrong. I don't usually notice the sky.

Moving my arms in time to my music, '*Ain't My Bitch*' plays, waving my arms, pretending I'm an artist painting the sky. I love this song and can't remember how many times I've listened to it. Paintbrush quickly changed to an air guitar, suddenly the birds and sky disappear and I'm playing my guitar like I'm in *Metallica* itself.

Something disturbs me.

A scraping sound coming from the pavement up my drive. Who the fuck is it?

Two people, one big, one small are walking up my drive with what looks like suitcases. Who the fuck is coming at this hour? I'm not expecting anyone. Those bloody preachers wouldn't dare come to save my soul again, would they? I thought I'd scared them off well and good with my devil music the last time they'd tried to tell me I'd be one of the 166,000 saved. Hell, I don't need saving, especially by them. I know exactly where I'm going and it sure as hell ain't Heaven.

Pointing my left arm towards them, it suddenly detaches from my body and floats right to them in slow motion. Index finger warning them not to come nearer, they ignore it, watching as my arm floats back and reconnects to my body again, seeing the people have each quadrupled, and now they have halos around their heads, all eight of them.

Who the fuck are they?

'*That Ain't My Bitch*' is still playing.

Swaying backwards and forwards, squinting my eyes, glaring into the faces of my wife and son, six more of the same heads float around them, all staring at me.

"This is some strong shit."

Clicking my fingers, waiting for them to disappear, I fall backwards, grabbing the post to steady myself.

"Hello, James. We're back."

Lifting something out to show me, it looks like a baby?

"Meet your daughter."

What the hell? This ain't happening. This ain't real.

"*M e e t y o u r d a u g h t e r, m e e t y o u r d a u g h t e r, m e e t y o u r d a u g h t e r.*"

All my wives speak in slow motion, deep, like they're talking backwards, pointing four tiny people at me with halos.

Is it God?

Is God trying to tell me something?

"*Fuck off.*"

Stepping backwards, tripping, bending down, shaking my head, and banging it on the post, I count them, but they're moving real fast in a circle looking at me with the same halos, smiling.

The mushrooms are playing with my brain, making me see things.

I'm going crazy.

Whoever sold me these will fucking pay. This is not the buzz I wanted.

Pointing at the ghosts, telling them to piss the fuck off, they don't move.

"There ain't no baby, no wife, no son, no God. Now fuck off, all of you."

Backing into the front door, bumping into everything, I grab my JD and Coke off the table, stumbling to my bedroom, gulping it back before collapsing on my bed. The ceiling spins with the faces outside.

"That ain't my baby. You bitch! This is some strong shit."

Crash.

Waking the next morning, glass smashed all over the floor, my head feels as big as a balloon about to burst. Swallowing, it's like I've got dirt stuck in the back of my throat, nearly choking. Picking myself up off the bed and walking with two left feet to the tap in the kitchen to drink straight from it. That was some strong shit last night.

"Waaah."

Blinking a hundred times, rubbing my eyes to make sure I'm not still hallucinating, the newborn in the box stares up at me, half crying, half smiling.

The mushrooms weren't to blame.

"What the fuck? She's tricked me again?"

It don't make any sense. We only had sex maybe one time and that was only because I was desperate. This has to be a joke. It has to be someone else's baby, not mine. If she were pregnant when she left though, then that's the reason why she went AWOL on me. She knew I'd try and kill it, like the last one. But why'd she bring it back? It don't make any sense.

Gurgling, tiny blue eyes smile up at me; I'm sure I see my own eyes staring back. For a split second, I don't know why, but I smile back. I think it's a girl. It's too pretty to be a boy. Those dark-blue, almond-shaped eyes are nothing like her mother's, or mine.

I know those eyes.

Meet your daughter. That's what the bitch said to me last night.

She's mine?

She is mine. I feel it, more than I did with the boy. I don't want to feel it. What I want is to pick the thing up and wring its neck, end it right here and now, but something inside, a feeling I'm not used to, stops me. There's something about the girl that makes me stop. Touching my finger to her cheek, she grabs it, all of a sudden feeling warm, like an electric charge has bolted through my body.

I don't want it.

No. I won't let it happen, won't let any of that shit in.

Walking to the bitch and the boy in bed, I know she's awake; bending down to her face, seeing the twitching of her eyes giving her away. She don't fool me. I want to kill her, kill them all, but I don't because the feelings inside my body are making me feel like a pussy.

What's happening?

"Waaah."

"Fuck this shit."

Chapter Three
Patricia

"Family is supposed to be our safe haven. Very often, it's the place where we find the deepest heartache."

— Iyanla Vanzant

A hundred hummingbirds are fluttering inside my chest, waiting, watching as James stands over the baby, praying he doesn't harm her. I heard him come in and now my eyelids are fighting to stay closed, desperate to shield my child from his violent hands. All he has to do is wring her tiny neck and it's over.

Should I get up, stand guard over her?

Holding my breath, feeling like I'm buried - deep underground - trying to claw myself out, the earth keeps weighing me down, stopping me from breathing, stopping me from getting to my child to save her. The heaviness on my chest. I can't move, not even an eyelash; my whole body is stiff with fright daring to open one eye to a slit.

He's standing over her, looking at her, holding her hand. What will I do if he picks her up and wrings her neck?

Holding her hand?

Please God, spare the baby from his hands. Don't let him hurt her. My heart can't take it.

He's turning, moving towards us. Jayden is still sleeping oblivious to everything beside me. Please let him stay asleep.

Snapping my eye shut, his footsteps stop in front of me, watching me, watching Jayden, feeling his eyes boring into my face, smelling his breath up close to mine. What is he doing, thinking? Am I going to feel his hands on me any second?

"Waaah."

Walking back to the baby, standing over her, please God, don't let him hurt her.

Please God, please anyone?

"Fuck this shit."

Leaving, banging the bedroom door behind him, I listen to him grab his keys and slam the front door. Springing up, kneeling on the bed, and peering out of a slit in the curtain, I watch him get into a new car and start the engine, the gravel and dirt underneath the wheels causing a mini sandstorm as he revs up and drives off.

Someone from beyond has helped me again.

Quickly jumping off the bed and picking the baby up out of her makeshift bed of a box lined with blankets, I rock her backwards and forwards whispering to the ceiling.

"Thank you, Mum."

One week later, I've decided to call her Maxine Gail Rose after my father Maxwell, her birth mother Gail, and my own mother Rose, who, I'm sure, helped from wherever she was in the universe. This baby, another gift from God I thought I would never get, is something I'd only dreamed about.

I miss my mother so much.

She would've loved Maxine. She would've helped me make sense of everything. Knowing Mum, she would've walked me straight to the police and made me confess. She was like that, very moral, very into doing the right thing. Such a strong influence on me growing up. If she'd met James I know she wouldn't have liked him. I probably wouldn't have chosen him if she was still here, but then, I wouldn't have Jayden.

When I met James I'd already given up on myself, my sister, too.

How depressing I've ended up back with the bastard. Ava, my older sister, would be so disappointed in me, especially after everything her and her husband, John, did for me when I left James. I wish so much I could've gone back to them, but I doubt I'll ever see them again. Jayden ruined that. What he did to their cat, Tiddles, no one would forgive. I wouldn't if it was me.

Holding Maxine close to my chest, looking down into her beautiful tiny face, I can only hope my mother lives through her, makes her as strong as she was. If my baby turns out anything like me I may as well kill her now.

Walking her to the kitchen, opening cupboards to retrieve some bottles, I set about sterilising them and filling them with boiled water from the kettle. Grabbing one from the fridge that has already cooled, I fill it with a small amount of milk powder, shake it and submerge it in some hot water to warm it up. The pigsty of a kitchen has pots, pans, cups, glasses and burnt knives covering surfaces gasping for breath. The place looks like a tip, but lucky for me, I've found some money James must have forgotten he stashed behind some pots. God does indeed work in mysterious ways.

Falling asleep drinking her milk again, I'm worried Maxine's not getting enough.

Does she sense I'm not her mother?

Her cheek is so soft on my lips, walking her back to the bedroom seeing Jayden is still asleep. Gently placing her back in her box, waiting until I'm satisfied she won't wake, I tippy toe to the wardrobe, rifling through it, retrieving the placenta from its hiding place. Dried up and hard, I still can't believe I actually helped bring Maxine into the world.

Overcome with emotion, wondering where Gail is now, how is the poor girl feeling? This last week has been so full on, so busy. I've closely followed the news of another child, possibly Maxine's twin, left abandoned at the hospital, sure the mother in question was Gail.

Feeling the hardness of the placenta through the bag, I wonder whether Gail would've wanted me to bury the vessel which had kept her baby alive?

Straining my hand, taking the bag outside, I bury the placenta underneath a rose bush I've already prepared. It hasn't bloomed for many years, silently dedicating the bush to all my child's namesakes. Relieved to have it finally concealed, who knows? It might even encourage the rose bush to come back to life.

Creeping back to my room, throwing the bag in the bin, grabbing my box of newspaper clippings to hide back in the wardrobe. If this abandoned child, another girl, is Maxine's twin sister, then I want Maxine to know.

Reading through the articles, I can't help but wonder if Gail is ok? Alive? Stroking her lock of hair, thinking back to the day in the station toilet, I place it under my nose smelling a faint hint of apple shampoo. Gail must be going through hell.

I wish I could let her know her child is loved and safe... for the minute.

Packing the newspaper clippings and her lock of hair away, they must remain another secret. No one can see them. No one can know what I've done until I'm dead.

Jayden suddenly squeals, hurrying to him, seeing he is up and sitting where he always sits, close to his sister.

If only they both had the same blood flowing through their veins, how perfect it would be. It feels like they do.

Not leaving her side since we came home, he's besotted with her;

a shift I wasn't expecting. He is a different child, the sinister part of him completely gone, replaced with one who loves.

If I'd known how much of a miraculous change the baby would've had on him, I would never have contemplated coming back to James. I would've stayed at the flat with them both, but I couldn't go back to my old life. It might've encouraged whatever resides within Jayden to resurface again. I had to come back for his sake as well as Maxine's.

James still hasn't come home which has given us space to breathe just that little bit easier, but, I know it won't be long until he returns and everything will change.

Quickly preparing myself and the children, making sure all the documentation needed for Maxine's life to legally begin is ready, I catch a cab to the Registry Office and enter Maxine's birth, telling them I'm a single parent, making up some cock and bull story about getting pregnant out of the country. James will have no claim to any part of her. Giving them a random address in Australia, they don't ask for any proof and just like that, Maxine Gail Rose Warner now exists.

I wish Jayden had my maiden name, too. He will have to remain Rodgers, like his father. I just hope he forgives me.

Watching him play with Maxine's hand, there is a reason God chose me to mother this baby. I don't quite yet know what it is but what I do know is, the love I already feel for her is monumental, and knowing I had a hand in helping her come into the world already means she feels like mine.

The risks coming back have paid off, but I can't, won't be complacent. Finding a stash of James's money was just pure luck, having hidden it with the money Bill gave me in my secret box. I'll use it if need be to escape, but until James comes back I'll sleep with one eye open, both once he returns. Please God he's forgotten about the money on his return. What will he be like? The look on his face when he'd looked into Maxine's eyes. It was more than enough reason for me to stay vigilant. I'll pay one day for ruining his life again, but until then, I'll make damn sure the children are safe.

I owe them that much.

Returning two weeks later, surprisingly, James leaves us all alone. I don't dare ask any questions about where he's been or what he's been doing, and our relationship resumes from where it left off.

The only exception?

The baby.

There's something about her that freaks him out. He looks at her when I'm feeding her, changing her, bathing her. His eyes tell me he is hiding something.

What?

What could he know about the baby?

Very different from when I'd had Jayden, it worries me. What is he planning? The calm is making me panic.

Before too long, he is back on the booze and drugs and the beatings resume. Stupidly, I'm relieved. This is what I'm used to. This is what I know.

Jayden, throughout the last month, has been a changed boy. Besotted with his little sister, he protects her, and now that James is back, he is even more careful, watching for any signs that will alert him his father is about to turn.

As Maxine grows so does his attachment to her. I see it and know James sees it, too.

The green-eyed monster eats me, wanting the bond Jayden has with Maxine to be the same with me.

It is nowhere near.

James's constant angry face confirms he's not happy about the union either, but for other reasons. Frustrated he can't get near Maxine, he knows that if he so much as lays a finger on her, Jayden might turn. He senses it, and after I told him about the happenings at

Ava's with the cat, I'm sure James senses the evil in his son, beating him twice as much.

He leaves Maxine alone.

Six years later Jayden is as big as an ox, and in time he is able to turn things his way. Once he matures, his father no longer tries to control him seeing he has grown into a solid young version of himself. One time too many, James suffers, taken off guard by his son's left hook. He no longer touches him.

I'm not so lucky. Both my husband's and son's eyes watch me, berate me, blame me, hate me the same. I'm powerless and told I'm not worthy of anything other than what I get. Maxine protects me, loves me, and eventually dies for me.

Chapter Four
Maxine

June the 17th 1994—age seventeen

I've watched my beast father beat my mother and brother instead of me too many times to remember. My mother's face has healed over and over, having done nothing to protect herself, or us from his cruel hands.

I haven't been touched because Jayden has protected me, not her.

I hate my father. I wish he would die.

As for my mother?

I'm confused why she allows him to hurt her, have all the power all the time? Why doesn't she fight back? What hold does he have over her that allows her to let him treat her the way he does? Treat us the way he does.

Jayden suffers the most.

I've often wondered if our mother even loves him and have asked myself why I've protected her for so long?

She deserves everything she gets. I have no respect for her at all.

One thing's for sure. I will never be like her.

Ever.

If that happens, I'll kill myself.

I've dreamed of how my life would've been if I'd had a different mother. Someone I respected, loved.

Why did I have to have these parents?

There's no special bond, no connection with either of them, especially her. She is a stranger. There is no feeling of anything other than hatred where my father's concerned. He enjoys every minute he hurts us, seeing his grotesque face light up when he does.

I may look like him, but that's where it ends.

I hate him.

He is the devil.

Chapter Five
Jayden

The only time I've not seen my mother beg for her life from my father is the day she got up and left him for using me as a prize in a game of cards. He was prepared to use me, his son, as a prize to win a game of lousy cards.

I think that is when she finally realised the depths the bastard would be willing to sink to for his addictions. I was only six at the time so was too young to fully understand the impact, but that one act of my father's was when it all changed for me. I blame him for who I became.

I blame them both.

Living with a mother who promised to protect me from my father's forceful fists and never did, only added to my hatred of people. I didn't trust anyone, especially adults. When she left him, I thought it would all come right, but she took me to my aunts, forced me to stay in a place I hated. I, her beloved son, became more violent than she could ever have imagined.

The last thing I thought she'd do was return to my beast father, but she returned with not only me, but another child to add to the mix for him to intimidate and push around. I still can't remember my mother ever being pregnant with Maxine, but a lot of my memory from childhood has been blocked for good reason. All I remember was when we arrived back I was never going to let my father near my precious sister.

Ever.

I hated my mother more for that.

"I love you more than God loves you."

How could she have loved us more than God?

Lies.

All she did was lie. She'd never protected me, us. I'd protected my sister from our father's violent hands. Not her.

My father played with my mother like a ragdoll. He pulled every inch of her apart, and sewed her back together again and again with his false words and promises, only to rip her apart again. It was a game. I couldn't believe how stupid my mother really was.

Were women that dumb, foolish, imbecilic?

Was it that easy to control them?

I had to find out, have a go myself? I had to know what it felt like to dominate.

So, I started treating her the same way my father did, and we started taking turns beating her. He began to look at me with respect, pride. Our relationship took a U-turn.

Flashbacks of the animals, the domination, control increased. The animals were too easy, almost boring in comparison to how it felt when I beat my mother. This side of me enjoyed the savagery, the feeling of total control.

I was twelve when I took my first frenzied punch. I looked into my mother's pathetic pitiful face and saw eyes pleading much the same way the stupid animals had done before I'd plunged the knife into them.

I felt a little sorry for the animals.

I didn't feel sorry for her.

She was more pitiful than those animals ever were. At least they had tried to protect themselves.

Squirming, begging me to stop, she was useless, worthless. Who better to take this power out on than the woman who'd started it all. The woman who'd brought me into the hellhole I lived in.

My sister's eyes watched me, feared me. I didn't want her to be fearful, she must've known I would never have hurt her, the only person in the world I loved.

Dropping out of school at the age of fifteen, Maxine tried to talk me out of it, but I didn't listen. She loved school, I hated it. She was every teacher's dream whereas I was every teacher's nightmare. They gave up on me like most adults. I didn't care. I didn't give a fuck about learning anything.

The only thing I cared about was getting high, getting laid and playing Backgammon, my new hobby for money. Drugs heightened my senses, especially when I was getting laid.

Girls?

They didn't want a good boy. They wanted a bad boy and knew I was far from an angel. What was it about girls that made them go weak at the knees for someone who treated them like shit? The worse I treated them, the more they wanted me. I thought it was piteous and only reinforced my contempt for them. My teenage years were spent protecting Maxine from my father, getting stoned, getting laid and making sure my mother paid. My relationship with my father improved so much, he ended up hooking me up with a good dealer who made sure to give me the best shit he had.

"Any friend of Jimmy's."

Friend?

I'd never be my father's friend.

Hell would freeze over before that ever happened. It was hard enough admitting I was his son. I don't even think the dealer knew. It was hard not to know; I looked so much like the bastard.

Still, I couldn't complain, the dealer was good and provided me with class A shit which was all I cared about.

Loving the domination, loving that girls did what I asked of them without hesitation, I got bored with how easy it all became.

I needed more.

My mother became as compliant with me as she was with my father. It wasn't even a challenge anymore.

Maxine was more of a challenge.

She started trying to help the stupid bitch when she saw I was about to turn. She knew the signs and tried to distract me, but it never worked. She had no chance. There was no stopping it. Not even I had control over it. It needed, craved the release. Even I knew that. Why didn't she?

She was lucky my alter ego didn't turn on her. She's lucky I trained it to leave her alone. She's lucky it loved her and wanted her to stay safe.

She must have known that?

She must have known she was the only reason we stuck around. She was ours to love.

Ours.

Chapter Six
Maxine

1st July 1994

My mother's screams have increased. I'm scared my father and brother are going to kill her, kill me. There's so much blood. How is she still alive? She's so frail. I know my father won't change, but where has my beautiful brother gone?

It's like he's two different people.

He doesn't touch me. Ever. But I've seen his eyes question it many times.

The eyes tell all.

The inner turmoil he suffers makes me fear one day that the monster inside him will win and kill. I have to do something, get away before it gets me. Before it kills my mother.

I don't know why he tortures her so much. I know she's not the best mother in the world, but does she really deserve what he does to her? He's just a younger version of the barbarian we live with, and I'm not sure I love him anymore.

I once followed him to the woods and saw him digging what looked like a hole in the ground.

Was it for my mother?

I'd dared not even breathe, just in case he'd heard, seen me. What would he have done if he had? I hadn't wanted to find out. All I knew was I didn't know who I was more terrified of.

Jayden or my father?

Now? He is wild, untamed and I'm not sure I won't be his next victim. Will my mother be enough? His savagery towards her is that of the same as our father and what's worse, he's even joined forces with him. I don't know what she's done that is so bad to them both?

I don't know.

I want to know why they leave me alone. I don't love my mother, but I don't want to see her beaten to death, either. I have to run, find help before he and my father kill her - before they kill me.

I hate him! I hate them both.

She's screaming again for her life. I have to help her.

"Stop! You're going to kill her."

Trying to separate her from my brother, it's no use. Screaming, bleeding, begging him to stop, my mother is so fragile. Can't he see that? Jumping in front of her to give her half a chance, Jayden's eyes warn me to back off.

They scare the life out of me.

They aren't his eyes.

Whoever he is possessed by is in total control. His soul is so black. I have to get help before he kills her. Before they kill her. Who will he and my father turn on when it's done? Me? I'm not going to find out. It has to end.

Running for my life out the door Jayden follows, screaming with bloody fists.

"You fucking get back here! You'll be next, you fucking crazy bitch. You hear? I'll fucking kill you!"

I can hear my mother's screams.

I don't recognise my brother anymore.

It has to stop. I have to get help.

Chapter Seven
Jayden

"I miss you in ways I didn't know existed. You are a mental and physical ache."

—Jessica Katoff

The police find a body. There's a necklace with a pendant, M, wrapped around the victim's neck.

I bought Maxine a similar necklace for her sixteenth birthday. We'd gone to get matching tattoos, red and green hearts because she'd heard a song with her name in it, and the woman had a red and green tattoo. I'd thought it was a crazy idea, but she'd begged me, so we'd gone to get them done thinking we'd be connected forever. I'd bought her the necklace after she'd stood admiring it from a shop window. She'd been so brave having her tattoo, it was my way of rewarding her.

"Look, it has M on it for Maxine. I'm going to get that when I have the money. I'll put yours and my photo in it. It's so pretty. What do you reckon, J?"

Only she could get away with calling me J. Her beautiful fingertips had stroked the glass wanting so much to have it; her face had lit up like she was on the stage. I had to buy it for her. I asked her to run to the cafe to save us a table telling her I had business to finish somewhere else; she'd gone and waited for me, not having a clue I was lying. We ordered lunch and while we were eating, I'd surprised her with it, saying it was a little something for being so brave with her tattoo. Her screaming had made people jump out of their skin and I'd had to calm her down so I could help her put it on. I'll never forget her face. Her smile as she'd opened and closed it had filled the place like the sun had come down and walked right in. She'd called it 'her treasure' and had never taken it off.

Police reports confirm the girl who's been found has a necklace the same. There are no photographs inside the pendant but it's too much of a coincidence not to be her.

Is it Maxine? My beautiful, crazy, talented sister can't be gone.

The last thing she'd seen, the last words she'd heard from my mouth to hers, *"You'll be next, you fucking crazy bitch."*

Why? Why had I said it? Why had they been the last words she'd heard from me?

I don't even know how I remember. The blackouts usually didn't allow it.

I don't understand why my mind has allowed me to remember. Is it trying to punish me?

If I'd known the day I'd bought the necklace that I'd only have two more years with her, I'd have bought her so much more. I'd have bought her the entire shop.

It can't be real.

My beautiful sister can't be gone.

It has to be wrong.

Driving to the spot where they found the body, I lay flowers, the knot in my chest not budging. I need it to go. I don't want to feel - anything.

Everything hurts.

Even blinking.

Why can't I close my eyes and be with her forever?

I can't control how I feel.

Laying my flowers where others before me have done the same, I read through the cards, touched by how many people loved her, even ones she didn't know.

'Rest in peace my beauty, no more will I love you from afar. Wait for me. Jono xx'

Who the fuck was he? Love you from afar? What does that mean?

Lifting my head to the sky, the trees shake with my anger and birds are startled from their branches as a voice not even I know I have, roars in the stillness of the forest. Falling to my knees, not even bothered that the ground is wet and muddy, tears that don't seem to end these days fall from my face to the same patch of earth she was found.

"I'm sorry, Max. I'm so sorry. Please forgive me. Please? Forgive me."

Whoever did this will pay. I'll kill them. I'll rip them apart.

Chapter Eight

"Death leaves a heartache no one can heal; love leaves a memory no one can steal."

— Richard Puz

The body they found was not my sister's. The victim was older, with a tattoo, but not Maxine's tattoo.

The police, able to obtain CCTV from a pawn shop, see the back of the man who sold the necklace to them, but his face is hidden under a large, black, baseball cap. Huge, all they can see is one scarred, burnt hand handing over the necklace, but the owner of the shop informs them that he cleaned the necklace before selling it on, leaving no DNA to trace.

Could this man hold the key to where Maxine is? Is there a chance she could still be alive?

I need to know.

Every tissue, vein, organ screams to know.

. . .

Days pass in a daze. The drugs help a little to ease my pain.

Where is Maxine?

Why did she run off that night when every other night she stayed? Why that night?

If she'd stayed, she'd still be here.

The numbness. I need the numbness gone.

Another month passes, and my good for nothing parents think they'll help by arranging a vigil.

What good will that do? It won't bring her back. Nobody understands, especially them. Why all of a sudden are they pretending to care? They've never cared for her, for me.

It's all a show.

My pain is real.

No one but them knows how close we were. No one but them knows how much I loved, still love, my sister.

I don't want to go to the vigil or watch people who meant nothing pretend they are sad she's gone, but I'm curious to see who turns up, and I need to know if anyone has any information that can help.

Drinking and smoking for most of the morning, I arrive, throwing the doors to the Porirua Community Centre open. Unable to walk in a straight line, somehow, I manage to make my way over to a chair in the corner, all eyes on me, staring at me in slow motion.

I don't give a fuck.

I hate them all.

Floating outside my body, up above everyone, my aunt, uncle, and cousin surround my crying mother, comforting her. I fly to them, whisper in their ears, tell them it is her fault Maxine is gone, but they can't see or hear me.

Watching my mother's pathetic bruised face lap up attention from everyone like she is the one suffering the most, my blood boils with rage.

She'll suffer later; I'll make sure.

Who is the other man with my aunt? I don't recognise him. He doesn't look like the rest of the family. His thick, grass-like hair growing from his head, and spectacle-free face, stand out like a sore thumb. I don't trust his dark, shifty eyes. They're not focused on what is happening, instead watching all the people, scrutinising them, planning something. I've seen plenty of the same eyes through my daily dealings and know he's up to no good.

What though?

He nudges Anton, who nudges my Aunt Ava, who nudges my Uncle John, who finally nudges my mother. Below, my body snarls at them, baring teeth, making them squirm like frightened little lambs to the slaughter.

I know what they're all thinking.

I can hear them whispering to each other.

They think I've done it, that it's my fault Maxine is gone. They don't feel safe to be near me.

Keeping eye contact with them, laughing, mocking them, I love that they still don't know how to act around me.

"Meow."

Cutting across my neck with my left thumb, hanging my tongue out of my mouth, I shout at them.

"Pussies. Ha, ha, ha."

Everything in slow motion, others turn to watch me, roaring at them, hating them.

I hate them all.

None of these people loved Maxine. Not like me. None of them knew that without her I was already as good as dead.

Breathing, listening to the rhythm of my heart, it is beating ten to the dozen as I float back to my body regaining my senses. A thousand volts of electricity jolt through my body, and suddenly I can smell people's combined perfumes and perspiration. I can hear the mumbling as suddenly everyone's head, including mine, turns to the doors.

Stumbling through, clumsily bumping into tables and chairs, his turned-down mouth looks withered and more than a little drunk. His hair, greyer, unkempt, and greasy, hangs from underneath his 'I love potatoes' cap, and a green vest, dirty three-quarter length shorts and steel capped boots, don't exactly scream he is here for anything remotely attached to something as important as a vigil for his missing daughter.

Lumbering towards me, reading his cap, it reminds me of the many times Maxine commented and laughed that he even had it. Is he wearing it for her?

Sad droopy eyes that appear to have been crying, look red raw. Surely it's the booze, or does he genuinely care she is gone?

He never wanted her. He never wanted her born, for both of us to have never been born. Why is my father pretending to care?

It's all for show, to trick everyone into believing that she meant something to him.

Surely everyone knows just how he felt towards his kids?

Surely, they too are wondering what the hell.

Two of his friends call for him to go over to them, and not paying any attention to anyone else, except me, he nods as he passes, stopping to stare into my eyes.

Peering over to my mother, looking back at me, I know what he's thinking, confirming I'm right when he whispers, "later" in my ear. Nodding back, watching as he walks to his friends, he doesn't give anyone else a second glance.

Others turn up from school, one who I vaguely remember having sex with in the disabled toilet. Making eye contact with her, she tries smiling at me but I warn her off with a glare, not needing or wanting any trips down memory lane today. Taking the hint, she doesn't come near me for the rest of the day.

Other women I don't know turn up claiming to have worked with Maxine.

Work?

These women look like hookers. Sluts? Whores? The makeup, skimpy clothes.

One, in a painted-on dress, eyes me up a little too long. I'll have her by the end of the night and even better, will try to get some information out of her if I can. Two for the price of one.

Who are these women? Where are they from?

Teacher's, shopkeepers and one neighbour turn up to show their respects, but really, all I can see anyone has come for is the free food, booze, and a good gossip. I don't want to be with any of them.

Pictures of every stage of Maxine's life stare at me, smile at me, laugh at me. Her beautiful face spins around me, watching me, smiling at me, pleading with me to help her.

I hear her, calling me, begging me to come to her, unable to take anymore.

I want everyone gone.

I want the pictures and everyone gone.

Ripping them off the wall, throwing them to the ground, stamping on them, screaming, my head splits open, hitting the floor. The last thing I see before I pass out are translucent-blue eyes staring at me from the back.

Chapter Nine

The vigil brought nothing but confusion. I knew some of the people, but the ones who'd claimed to have worked with Maxine, and the last set of eyes I'd seen before passing out, were the ones that had confused me the most. From what I remembered the man was huge, and before I'd hit the floor, the girl with melons for tits was walking towards him, like she knew him. When I'd asked people who he was, no one knew.

"Probably just another one of Maxine's friends."

Another friend? Who was he? How could she have known him?

Another month passes.

Drowning myself in Jack Daniels and whatever drugs I can find, I use them most nights to numb the pain, but all I see is Maxine's beautiful face.

If I stay sober my mind does nothing but think of her, which I don't want it to do. But I don't want to forget her either, and my thoughts fight each other constantly, a battle I lose time and time again to my alter ego. Whatever resides inside me does whatever it wants. It doesn't care that my mother bleeds, beating her often just enough for her to recover so it can beat her again. It needs her to suffer, needs to punish her because it is her fault Maxine is gone.

My mother, weak as she is, has finally had the last laugh. She witnesses my suffering; sure she enjoys it. She more than anyone can see Maxine's death has hit me hard. She's well aware that if Maxine hadn't been protecting her from my fists that night, she wouldn't have had to run for help and would still be alive. My mother has to suffer. Until she is dead and buried, she has to suffer.

I'll make her wish she was already dead.

The hurt consumes me, eats me alive from the core of my stomach to every finger, toe, eyelash in my body. Why won't it go away? I'd be beaten a thousand times over if it meant Maxine could come back. I shouldn't have loved so much, given my heart to her.

Why can't I be with her?

She is still out there, and without a body, there is still hope. One thing is sure. I won't leave her to come back to our arsehole parents on her own. No way. I'll make sure they stay alive so she can face them, tell them how they forced her to leave that night. I want to be there when she tells them how much she hates them. I want to watch them squirm, and then I want to kill them with my own two hands and let Maxine watch. I want her to see how much I love her.

I'll wait until she comes back, but first I'll keep on playing with the bitch who started it all.

The drugs become stronger. Mixed with the alcohol, I turn into someone worse than my father. The thrill of killing the animals is long gone. I have an even bigger thrill now.

Women.

Dozens of them.

Why do they stoop so low, humiliate themselves for a man's pleasure? Just like my mother, they aren't worth pissing on. Just like her, they are useless, only good for one thing. Hell, they even look like they enjoy it. Why shouldn't I give them what they want? My mother is like all the rest of the women out there, pathetic as shit.

Pathetic as they are, I want them all. Every shape, size, and colour. Doing what I want, when I want, they need me, love the way I use them, control them, dominate them. They can't get enough, and then when I think I've got them where I want, they become needy and want more than I care to give. I tell them I only want them for one thing, explain I don't want any emotional involvement, that I just want to fuck them and then piss them off, but they always end up wanting more.

Why do they expect that I want more?

I don't.

It's the same over and over.

Using them and then rejecting them, they whine, ring me, follow me. They beg, asking where I am, and when I think they're gone, I suddenly pull them back to play with again like pieces of elastic until they snap. It's all just a game. I am in control, not them. Their pathetic faces when they don't get what they want makes me sick. There are so many out there willing to put up with anything to be loved.

But I'm still not satisfied.

I need to find the right one. I need to find a girl who I can keep, use, dominate. I need a girl who will become mine to own. I will find her if it's the last thing I do.

Weeks pass. Drinking, smoking, injecting myself with anything I can get my hands on to keep my mind numb, one day I push it a little too far. High on opium, my foot slams down on the accelerator, zooming down a road I think is unpatrolled, quickly finding out it is when an unmarked car hiding behind a tree pulls me over. I know I'm done for.

Ordering me to get out, one officer checks my licence and finds a warrant out for my arrest for unpaid parking tickets. Cuffing me, searching my car, they find a lot more than they bargained for. Tucked away in the glovebox is my stash of class A drugs. Why the fuck did I put them in there?

"What do we have here, Mr Rodgers?"

Snarling, kicking the back of the seat, my head hurts from banging against the window. What the fuck have I done? Hauling me back to the station, I'm charged with possession and sentenced to two years.

Nordsworth Prison proves to be a piece of piss. My childhood was way worse than the pussies they have in here. Joining forces with the biggest and most powerful prisoners, we terrorise and control the weak. Everyone bows down to us, even the screws. In return, they and their families are protected inside and outside of jail. They, in turn, protect our families on the outside until we are released. Not my family, though. My parents can rot in hell for all I care. The only person worth protecting is now gone because of them.

I wouldn't piss on them if they were on fire.

Most of the screws turn the other cheek, except one. Familiar, I can't pinpoint where I know him from. Undoubtedly evil, he is a hell of a lot bigger than the other screws, looking like he's been inflated with air; the muscles and veins taking turns to show off. Eyes that are too close together, the translucent-blue orbs stare, soulless as dolls, not blinking; his crooked flat nose looks like it's been broken too many times to guess. Lips like wax, they look to have been burnt as does his pockmarked skin covered in a fuzzy five o'clock shadow that you'd swear had been glued on rather than grown.

He's uglier than a baby parrot.

Ugly as he is, it's his eyes that give you a clue to how cold his soul is. Ice-blue, they warn you to stay at arm's length. If you do or say anything he doesn't like, they turn like a predator fixating on its prey. I've been told many prisoners haven't made it out of the hospital after one of his beatings, the Governor turning a blind eye, giving excuse after excuse. Every prisoner and guard watch their back when he's around and nobody knows his real name.

He is known simply as J.

I already hate him.

Feared by other screws and prisoners alike, even the biggest, most evil convicts, warn me to do as I'm told and not to mess with him.

This is one time I listen.

A night in the common room changes it all.

Sitting, strumming a guitar, I've learned to play *Romeo and Juliet*, my favourite Dire Straits song, softly playing it as Rod, a fellow prisoner, sits retelling a story he's heard. I usually ignore the bastard, but something he says makes my ears prick up.

Huge, with tattoos all over his body, including his bald head and the inside of one of his eyes, one of his gold front teeth shines bright reflecting off the lights as he announces with glee what he's heard.

"Said he smoked a cigarette over her body. Made sure her cute little ass was dead. Hee, hee, hee. Checked her pulse and looked into those pretty blue eyes one last time. Said he nearly laid her one last time just for fun. Hee, hee. Probably because he'd seen her titties up close at the strip club too many times. He said it was just pure luck he bumped into her that night. The poor girl was running from her good-for-nothing brother who she thought was going to kill her, and her mother, too. Shame she ran into someone else just as evil. Hee, hee, hee."

Rod's cellmate, Mac, sits opposite me. Dark hair and stubble, the scars on his face are pronounced under the light as he looks at me with confusion. He of all people would know if Rod was telling the truth. Raising an eyebrow to me, he shakes his head. I'm surprised he's even giving me eye contact. Glaring at him to stop, he quickly looks back at Rod. I don't think he believes a word he's saying.

"Yeah, she had a real funny tattoo. A red and green heart on her right shoulder. Said he nearly cut it off. Real shame. All he got was a stupid necklace. Yanked it straight off her pretty little neck. Hee, hee.

Pure gold. The letter M. Made sure to take her pictures out before he sold it, though. Pretty sure they found it on some other dead woman. Now ain't that a coincidence?"

Lighting a cigarette, laying back, looking straight at J who's standing in the corner, Rod points at him with two fingers, gesturing he's watching him. Smirking, raising one eyebrow, he blows a puff of smoke out of his huge mouth as J looks on.

I'm a volcano, simmering with rage, repeating what Rod has said in my head over and over. Is he talking about Maxine? Mac doesn't see me, instead looking backwards and forwards from Rod to the screw waiting for something to happen. He has no idea that I'm the one about to blow.

Trembling from my feet all the way to my eyeballs, I'm ready to erupt.

Roar.

Pouncing, ripping every part of Rod's body apart with my arms, legs, teeth, and head, I punch, kick and bite, hearing his last words over and over.

M.

Pure gold.

Red and green tattoo.

Five screws grab me seeing the same red and green tattoo Rod's just described etched on my arm. They know why I've attacked him. Dragging Rod off to the hospital, J grabs me by the throat marching me out to the courtyard.

I can't breathe.

Heavy rain thumps my skin which still pumps with adrenaline ready for anything the pig has to throw at me. If Rod is still alive, I'll kill him, rip him apart with my two hands. I'll sneak into the hospital and finish the job off. I'll fucking kill him.

Whack.

Out of nowhere J pushes me to the ground and handcuffs me.

"You fucking piece of shit, who gave you permission to be God? Up on your knees. Now."

Knees cracking on the stones, he bends down just close enough for me to see into his eyes.

"Your sister was delicious by the way. Poor girl was out of her mind with worry that you were going to kill her. Ha. Killing her was easier than putting on my socks. I knew I'd make you pay one day for what you did to my family. Didn't think it would be this easy, though. Just luck I guess. I've dreamt of finding you for so long, for making you suffer. I knew it was you who killed my cat, Sita, and I knew it was you who started the fire. Now I get to kill you and your slut sister. She was a bonus."

Blue eyes from my past stare hard into mine, seeing his black and white cat in the wardrobe, suddenly remembering the flyers and the boy who was looking for his pet cat. The boy was disfigured. His name was Jonathan. J? The house I set on fire was his.

"You'll pay for what you did to my family, and my cat, you prick. Your sister already has, now it's your turn."

Thud.

Chapter Ten
J

"And I crave you.
Not like an addiction.
But an obsession."

— Unknown

I knew where she lived. I'd followed her home every Thursday night after her shift. Her friend with the biggest tits I'd ever seen, and fellow dancer, always took her back to hers and waited in the car while my girl changed into normal clothes and washed away all traces of her makeup. Her friend would then drop her back to her house where her brother, or lover, waited for her outside. It was the same every week. What a sneaky little monkey she was.

I'd hunted her for months, hoping to catch her out on her own, but she'd always been with her huge brute brother or lover? I couldn't tell which, never having seen his face because he'd always had his back to me, and most of the time it was dark. All I saw were his hands as they'd draped themselves over her shoulder and around her waist, almost marching her inside, like he wanted no-one to see her. His hands made me sick.

Driving past her house one night on my way to work, my luck changed.

1st July 1994

I nearly miss her. Running out of nowhere right into my path. I barely have time to swerve, screeching to a halt, stepping out of my car, yelling at her, looking into her delicate face.

"What are you doing? I nearly killed you! Are you alright?"

She is even more beautiful close up; my frantic, frightened, fragile little bird.

"Please, help me. He's going to kill my mother. *He's going to kill her.*"

"Who's going to kill who? Just calm down and tell me everything. Shh. I'll take care of you now."

"My brother, he's going to kill my mother, and then he's going to come after me."

Jumping into my car without any thought, her brother must've been the man I'd seen clutching her tight.

"Shhh, I've got you. You're safe. Just breathe. Shhh."

She is finally mine.

"I thought I was going to die. My mother, she might be dead. Please call the police. Help her. Jayden might kill her."

Jayden? That's a name from my past I can't ignore.

"Jayden? I knew a boy named Jayden. He used to live in Tauhinu Road about twenty years ago."

Her eyes tell me everything. I've dreamt of killing him for so long. She can't be his sister. Not my little bird. How lucky I am.

Pulling on my gloves, driving away, I nearly give myself away. This is going to be so easy. She's so anxious about her mother, I have to keep her chatting, keep her mind off what has just happened at home. She has no idea what's about to happen to her. She doesn't even recognise me, her biggest fan. I'm a little bit hurt. Before she'd come along I'd been so close to never going back to the strip joint, had even contemplated trying a new place, but then she'd slinked onto the stage all young and gorgeous and just that little bit different from the rest, and straight away I was hers. She wasn't as confident as some of the other girls, but that made her more beautiful to me. A real diamond in the rough. I'd fantasised about her cute little ass ever since. Who knew she'd eventually be the one to reunite me with the person who'd ruined my life. God must've sent her to me to make up for what He'd let her brother do, the good for nothing piece of shit.

Turning off the road, driving down a long lane I know well, I can smell the fear in her voice. It's so hard for me to contain my excitement.

"A-a-are we taking a shortcut? I-I-I don't recognise where we're going?"

Her voice is so sexy.

Slowing down along the bank, turning left, I drive down deep into the trees and stop. She's already screaming when I open the door and order her out of the car. I can't help myself and grab her by the hair. It smells so good.

"What are you doing? Let me go!"

Pulling her deep into Mount Victoria Woods, I've only ever come here once before, and that was a long time ago with another love of mine. She'd betrayed me. I saw her by accident at a restaurant hand in hand with another man. She hadn't a clue I knew. I found her lover and beat him until he couldn't think anymore, and then I brought her to the woods, taught her a lesson, too. The look in her eyes when I'd let her know what had happened to her lover. I'll never forget it.

She deserved to die. She hurt me more than she could ever know. I don't know how many times my knife hit her skin but, just to make sure, I put both hands around her throat and watched the life drain from her beautiful body. I'd thought I'd never love again after that.

Until my little bird.

She's been sent to me for a reason. She even looks a bit like my other love. Maybe it is her? Maybe she is sorry and has come back to me?

Trying to run from me, it only makes me more excited. She has no idea how excited I am. Pinning her to the ground, covering her mouth with one gloved hand, I hold her neck with the other.

Her eyes.

The fear is such a turn on.

When one of her titties comes free, I can't help myself. I've never been able to touch them, and now, up close, bare and inches away from my face, I have to see how soft they feel. Struggling for breath underneath me, much the same way my love did all those years ago, I let her scream just a little, but the bitch catches me in the balls and manages to break free from underneath me. I can't let her get away.

"You bitch. I saw you with him. I saw you with the pig. You said you loved me, would never hurt me. You lied. Lied."

The stupid girl screams; it's so easy to find her. Pulling my knife out of my back pocket, I see her ahead, lucky for me she stumbles. Trying to run again, I don't give her any time.

It only takes a minute.

My little bird lays there, covered in blood. Nothing moves. Not even a finger. How many times did I strike her? I lost count after thirteen. Staring right up at me, her hollow eyes are beautiful. Those lips. I want to kiss them while they are still warm, feel their softness on my own.

My love.

My pants are damp when I get up, bending down and stroking her soft cheek with my gloved finger while the wind plays with her hair. She is my goddess laying on the ground, still, now one with nature again.

"My love. I had to have you again."

The cigarette tastes good. Smoking it over her body while she stares up at me with so much love, I don't want to leave, but I can't take her with me, so I cover her beautiful body with leaves. No one will find her. I've never once seen anyone else come here before.

Something around her neck glistens in the moonlight. Ripping it straight off her neck, I see it is the letter M. Pure gold.

Is that what her name starts with? M?

I don't even know her name.

Opening it, I see photos of her and her good for nothing brother.

Punching the ground, I'll get him if it's the last thing I do.

Checking her pulse, she has no signs of life, stubbing out my cigarette on her left thigh. My little bird's flesh smells good. She doesn't move, not one little bit. Looking into her eyes one last time, I nearly give her a kiss and bending down and whispering into her beautiful face, I tell her how much I am going to miss seeing her pretty little ass at the club and that her brother will pay for what he did to me, to my family...

Chapter Eleven
Jayden

"And now here you are, paying for what you did, you mother-fucker. I checked her pulse one last time, put my stubbed cigarette in my pocket, and walked up the hill to leave your precious sister to rot."

"Fuck you. Fuck you. I'll kill you. *You hear? I'll fucking kill you!*"

"Shhh, no one can hear you, pretty boy. You'll strain your voice. Shhh. I told that mother-fucker Rod to keep his mouth shut. Unless it was around my cock. The stupid prick just couldn't keep it to himself. That's what you get for letting someone suck you off, not that he was any good. You get what I mean? Your mouth, though? I bet it's real warm, eh? Just my luck I went back to the pawn shop the next day with a friend who bought your sister's necklace for me. It was too pretty not to share. How do you think they found it around some other woman's neck? She was a slut, too. I should've kept it, pretty boy. I could've wrapped it round your neck, seen you cry like your pussy sister did. Boohoo, your sister is dead. The insects would've loved feasting on her tight little ass."

Soaking wet, hitting my face, the rain feels like glass on my skin, ready to break it. Whack. A fist slams into my skull making me fall to the wet ground. Scrambling to get up, a foot kicks me in the stomach, groin, head, every part of me in pain, trying in vain to shield myself with both cuffed hands. Hearing the screws words replaying over and over in my head, I've never hated anyone so much in my life as I do now. Trying without luck to get to my feet, he is way too fast, pinning me to the ground with one of his huge feet. The puddles are red as I look into my distorted face, dying, tasting blood swimming on my tongue as I'm pulled from the ground to my knees. These might be the last words I ever speak. Eyeballing the screw, I scream over the rain.

"I'll fucking kill you! I'll make sure you pay for what you did to my sister, you fucking piece of scum. What a shame you didn't die in the fire. With a face like yours I bet you wish you had. Did you scream in pain like your darling little cat did when I stabbed its eye out? I bet you did. I bet all your family screamed. I'll fucking kill you. I'll kill you if it's the last thing I do."

Trying to breathe, I don't have time to protect my groin before he drags me to my feet, grabs my chin and screams into my face.

"*What are you going to do in here, pretty boy?* She had much prettier eyes than you. I looked into those beautiful blue eyes and watched the life drain from her just before she died. Family, eh? Ha. Aren't I the lucky one? I'm surprised you didn't come say hello to me at the vigil?"

Eyes widening, he knows I remember.

"Yeah, I was there. Don't you know everyone came for me? To see what *I'd* done. You spoiled it all by making a fool of yourself. You ripped all her pretty pictures off the wall so I saved one. See?"

Placing his right hand in his back pocket and retrieving a picture, he unfolds it, holding it up to my face. Maxine smiles into the camera, poking her tongue out, pointing to her necklace. I remember the day I took it. She was so happy to have it. I can't look at it. Grabbing my chin, J turns my head, making me look at two tiny photographs he's retrieved from his top pocket. They are the ones from Maxine's necklace. Smirking, placing them back in his pocket, he makes me watch his tongue as it caresses Maxine's picture, licks her lips as a sudden clap of thunder above booms from nowhere.

"I kiss it every night. She was my favourite dancer. I can still see her cute little ass on stage. Some of the girls she worked with were there, at the vigil, too. Surely you saw them. Big tits, tiny dresses? I tried to get you alone after that, but you were too hard to pin down. I think you took a shine to one of them. Ha. I even left a note at the site where they thought they found her body. Didn't you see that either? Signed it to my love, from her Jono? You were too thick to put two and two together. You were always so dumb, weren't you? I knew you'd end up here. Scum like you always do. I didn't even need to find you. I knew you'd end up here eventually. Don't think anyone will believe anything you say. You're all scum, dregs of society. If I had my way, I'd let you all loose on an island to fuck or kill yourselves to death. Now wouldn't that be fun to watch. She thought you were going to kill her that night. She was begging me to kill her by the end, to save her from you. She died happy, the slut. You think she was innocent? She had a life you didn't even know about."

"Fuck you."

Dizzy, something other than the hard rain hits my skull.

Crack.

"That's for my cat."

Thud.

"That's for the fire."

Crack.

"That's for your sister."

Whack.

"That's just because I can."

The world turns black.

Beaten to an inch of my life, I'm told I lay in a coma for ten days with nearly every bone in my body broken, including my skull. The hospital staff were not even sure I'd make it and dutifully called my parents to let them know. Neither of the bastards even phoned to see if I was alive.

Five months later, after a miracle I'm not even conscious of, I walk out of the hospital with only one thing on my mind.

Revenge.

Pulling myself back to my cell, my fellow inmates look at me, eyes wide, shaking their heads, pointing like they've seen a ghost. I'm told by one of them later they never thought I'd come out alive let alone able to walk. They'd heard I was minutes from death, and that the screw had made sure Rod had never uttered a single word again before he'd transferred to another unit. Rod never regained consciousness.

Hearing J is gone is like a bullet to my heart. The fucking coward. The prick. I'll fucking kill him. I'll fucking find him and rip him apart with anything I can. I'll get revenge if it's the last thing I do.

Telling everyone J, not Rod, is responsible for killing my sister is near impossible. No one listens or believes me, convinced the trauma to my head has caused me to imagine things, but I know they know more than they're letting on. Even the most dangerous prisoners ignore me, not prepared to risk J finding out they've tried to help. They know he'll kill them if he ever suspects they've gone against him.

Abandoned, my last hope is the Governor, but he just laughs, rejecting my pleas, telling me I'm just another dumb convict who lies, cheats, and deserves everything I get.

No one believes me. No one helps, or even goes to have a look to see if I'm right about where she's buried. What if she is still there, all alone? How will I ever find out?

Hating J, dreaming of his deformed face and hearing the thud of my skull as it cracks, I see his murderous hands around my sister's throat squeezing the life out of her. I see his eyes at the vigil not believing how close I was to being able to kill him. The last words he spoke haunt me.

"She had a life you didn't even know about."

What had the fucker meant? He'd said some of the girls she'd worked with were there, at the vigil with him. The sluts, whores? Were they the people he meant? Maxine wasn't a whore.

Had she hidden it from me?

How did she know them?

She wouldn't have kept that from me, not my darling sister. Was that fucker just trying to mess with my head, make me believe things that weren't real? The only time she'd been allowed anywhere was to her friends, and even then, she'd had to be back before twelve. I'd always met her from the car, dropped her off at her friends to make sure she'd got there safely. I'd even waited in the car a bit longer a few times just to see if she was up to no good, but she never was. Every Thursday it was the same. I'd take her to her best friend's house for a few hours and then she'd come home. That's all she'd ever done. What was the fucking screw talking about? What?

Adding another year to my sentence for attempted manslaughter, I'm only sorry I got the wrong guy. Every minute of every day, all I think about is killing the person responsible for ending my life. I feel so guilty for not looking after Maxine, for not being there when she'd needed me the most. I will never let myself love anyone ever again.

My mother decides to visit. I don't know why. She knows I hate her. If I hadn't been teaching her a lesson the night Maxine vanished, then I wouldn't be here, in this shithole. Maxine would still be alive. It's her fault for everything. Why doesn't she just leave me alone? I have no family anymore. She and my good-for-nothing father are already dead to me.

Refusing to see her again and again, eventually she gets the message and stays away.

Three months later, it's visiting day. I'm not expecting anyone, thinking my mother has not given up, preparing to confront her. Entering the visiting room, locking eyes with the one person I never expected to see, he looks different.

"What the fuck do you want?"

"Ain't you happy to see your Daddy?"

Sneering, looking down into eyes I hate to admit are the same as mine, they seem weaker. Instead of a Rottweiler fixed on its prey, two old bloodshot eyes flick everywhere but my face. The broadness I remember is gone, instead a shrunken version of his former self fights to breathe, like he might drop dead any minute. It could be me thirty years into the future with fewer teeth and flesh. I'm frightened. Much thinner than the last time I saw him, his cheeks are sunken, and the skin on his face and body sags, like the muscles have dissolved and all that is left is skin and bone. He still wears his stupid cap which is a little too big for his head. I want to rip it off his head but resist because I want to hear what he has to say. Giving him my best death glare, I sit, waiting for him to speak.

"I ain't gonna beat around the bush. Hfff. We both know your useless piece of shit mother is the reason Maxine got killed. Even though I didn't want the girl when she came, I seen how much you loved her and protected her, which is why I left her alone. Hfff, cough. When she died, I seen how much it affected you. I want that good for nothing bitch to suffer, to pay for what she done. Cough, Hfff. I ain't got much time left, no longer than six months. I ain't got the strength to deal with her now she's looking after me. She don't know I'm h-h-here."

The skin beneath his eyes shows off the noticeable drop in weight, the dark, deep hollows underneath making him look like the walking dead. From the smell of him, the drunken dead, too. I can taste the JD on his breath, and smell the weed on his clothes. The monster from my memories is gone, replaced by an old, toothless, frail, pathetic, wheezing, fool. Pausing for breath, an unfamiliar noise rattling from his ribs, like a wind chime, makes speaking more difficult. Finally, after a long pause, his lips start to move and the words come out in a whisper. Pulling my head forward so I can hear him properly, I flick my head to the right so his mouth is close enough for me to hear. The guards watch everything.

"I want you to promise to finish the job off. Hfff. Make her pay, make her suffer for all the things she's done wrong. Hfff. I hate her as much as you do. Hfff."

Coughing, beating on his chest to stop the convulsions, one of the guards walks over with a plastic cup of water, nodding to me. Nodding back, pushing the water towards my father, I hope he chokes on it.

"I know you hate me, boy, but I know you hate her more. I seen the way you look at her. I seen her come back from here week after week, Hfff, crying cause you don't want to see her. Hfff. You know what an evil bitch she is, what a lying piece of scum you have for a mother. Hfff. She took you away all those years ago without even telling me, and then turned up with another kid. Doesn't make sense. Hfff. Still, I let the girl stay knowing she weren't mine. She couldn't be mine. I hadn't gone near the bitch for months. Months! Hfff, cough. I did that for you... boy, not for your mother. Hfff. I left the girl alone for you. Now you do something for me. Finish your mother off. I gotta know before I go, you'll take care of h-h-her."

Listening to his words, it takes all I have not to jump over the table and rip his head off. What he's asking is something I'd already planned on doing once I was released. In fact, I'd planned to kill them both. Hearing he now only has months to live is like a knife to my chest. I will never know the feeling of sending him to his grave, and for that I will never forgive him. I will never forgive him for never having the chance to pay him back. Clenching both fists into a ball, banging the table hard, I look up towards the ceiling.

Another point to you, God. I didn't believe for one second that you, Lord Almighty, loved me as much as my mother told me over the years. Having my sister killed wasn't enough? You chose to leave me alone with both of these bastards, one of them practically on his deathbed. You wouldn't have allowed Maxine to die the way she did, and you wouldn't have given me and my sister two of the most selfish parents to grace the Earth. Fuck off, God. Fuck off!

Accepting I will only get to feel half the satisfaction of killing one pathetic parent, the frail creature who sits before me now is surely living in his own hell, and for that, I feel some sort of comfort.

"Rot in hell, mother fucker."

Looking straight into his eyes for the last time, smirking, spitting into his face, I stand up, nod to the guard, and walk back to my cell without looking back.

I will never see my father again.

Chapter Twelve
Maxine

"The clouds wept when my heart sang a song of sorrow."

— Sonya Watson

Am I dead? I don't feel anything. I'm not sure if I'm watching from outside my body which is somehow still pulsing, very slowly, with life.

How?

I felt like a pin cushion, eventually not feeling anything except a little tug of my skin as his blade entered me and found different parts of my body that hadn't been punctured. I waited for his crazy deformed face to stop grinning like a madman, covered with my blood, which is slowly draining from my body.

Am I really alive, or just imagining it?

I can see the trees through the leaves, hear noises, so I must be alive.

It's so cold.

Freezing.

My blood feels like it's hardening.

I must be dying.

Has God decided it's my time to go? Or am I going to live? I'm confused.

When I ran from my house I wasn't expecting to die. I was expecting someone to help, take me somewhere safe. I thought that freedom was just around the corner from living with two psychopaths so alike; I was sure one of them would kill me first. Neither of them did.

My body has somehow kept me alive. It wants me to live. But why? Why did God lead me into the path of another psychopath eviller than the two I ran from? I'm still trying to understand it all. Hadn't I already suffered enough?

My mother?

What's happened to her?

Is her body lying somewhere getting cold, too? Two of us, harmed by two different sets of hands on the same night. How will they explain that? Two people from the same family slain in different ways on the same night at the same time.

The same monster, just two different people.

The devil is everywhere.

I've often thought my brother's lust for cruelty would extend to me, and I didn't want to take the chance, so I finally ran. I ran to save my life.

When I stopped the car coming towards me, I didn't check to see who it was. I saw his uniform, so I thought I was safe. Isn't that what they taught you at school? Trust anyone in a uniform?

I can still see him above me. Those evil crystal-blue eyes staring into mine, enjoying every minute of my pain.

Deformed.

Ugly.

Mad.

His scarred lips repeating over and over how I was his? I would never have been his.

The knife.

When he'd started stabbing me, I'd prayed for God to take me. I lost count after the blade punctured my flesh eight, nine times.

The pain.

I thought I was already dead, but after a while I didn't even feel the blade. I'd felt like a rag doll, soft and squishy on the insides, my tissues and flesh not reacting at all.

I knew who he was, had recognised him from the club.

Those eyes were hard to forget.

Too close together, they'd fixated on my body many times, giving me the creeps, staring, watching, lusting as I'd danced. I always knew what he was thinking, his face was good at giving everything away. Even though it was deformed, the eyes never lied. He wasn't allowed to touch, only watch. I'd often wondered if he was married, had kids? Those eyes were the eyes of someone not completely sane. I knew my instincts were right. Why had he been the one to turn the corner? I hadn't even thought, I'd just jumped in his car.

Every week Jayden had thought I was visiting my friend's house. He'd made it so hard for me to do anything. I was like a possession to him, afraid to do anything he wouldn't like. It wasn't like that when we were growing up. He changed. He changed after that first punch to my mother's face.

I'd made sure to take the early shift at the strip club so I could get back to the house by twelve. I didn't want him knowing I was hooked on drugs. I was only dancing to fund my fix. I couldn't use his or my father's dealer. It had been a perfect setup - till now. I was going to stop; run away with the money I'd saved. I was going to get myself out of this nightmare and get clean. I'd only tried drugs once, finding some in Jayden's room one day when he was out. That one time had got me hooked. It was a good escape for me. I needed something to get me through living in hell.

One week later

I now know something quite unique happened to me that night. My heart went into a state of shock keeping me alive with only one beat a minute. I discovered bradycardia was a rare condition which only a few people around the world had. Why was I lucky? Some unknown force had obviously been watching over me that night and decided I couldn't end my life in such a violent way, especially as my life had been nothing but cruel and savage up till then. If I could go back, I would've chosen to die. Living with the memory is way worse.

The nightmares of him above me, casually smoking a cigarette over my body, his face smirking, scattering me with leaves to make sure no one will find me, are all I see. I still smell the cigarette, see him looking into my eyes, smiling, his waxy lips hovering over mine, nearly touching.

Pig.

When he'd ripped off my necklace and inspected it before putting it in his pocket, I'd died again. That was my necklace. My treasure. I don't know why I still wore it. Jayden had bought it for me when I was sixteen, and I suppose I wanted to believe there was some good still left inside him. I kept praying he'd turn back into the brother I knew, but he didn't. I stopped loving him a long time ago. I should've taken off my necklace. I should've kept it safe.

When the maniac's fingers were on my wrist making sure I was dead, I'd willed my body to pulse so he could finish me off, but it betrayed me and all I'd smelt was the burning of my skin as he'd stubbed his cigarette out on my flesh. He'd put the stub in his pocket and casually walked up the hill to leave me to rot. I never thought anyone could be eviller than my father.

I can't remember how long I lay in those leaves. My body was so cold, in shock from losing so much blood, but somehow or another, it refused to give up. I remember hearing the rustling of the wind in the trees low and deep, like they were keeping me company, letting me know I was still alive. The noises of the animals had freaked me out at first, but when the hedgehogs, mice, rats, insects, spiders stopped to say hello before going on their way, I'd calmed down because I knew I wasn't alone. I hardly felt any of them, but I heard them. So many of them, some coming to sniff my body before deciding I wasn't what they wanted.

Traffic above was scarce, hearing the odd car or truck passing by far away in the distance. Still, I knew I was alive. I lay there for hours and hours in the dark and cold until my body was able to move again, one finger and toe at a time. Until suddenly, I was able to breathe normally again. That first intake of breath had been so fierce, the pain that came seconds after was the worst I'd ever felt in my life. The sting of the blade everywhere.

Shock, pain, stinging, cold, dark.

One way or another, my body gathered strength, and I managed to drag myself up the same hill he'd walked me down. On my hands and knees, it took so long, collapsing many times to regain some strength. I didn't think I'd make it, praying someone would find me, wrap me up, make me warm. The wind was like a freezing cloak, making noises like windchimes through the punctures, constricting my movements with its harshness. Finally, I made it to the top and started pulling myself unsteadily along the boundary. My body so weak, I thought I might fall down the hill again. I don't know what time it was, but it was still dark. It could've been morning; it could've been night. All I knew was that it was pitch black when the car finally stopped. Dragging myself into its path, frightened it was the same psychopath coming to finish me off, I had to take that chance. The poor man nearly ran me over, having to swerve to miss me. Thank God there were no other cars coming. Falling, I waited, praying he wasn't another killer.

His beautiful, kind, brown eyes stared down at mine in shock, unable to take in what he was seeing. I must've looked like an extra from a horror movie, covered in blood, hair sticking together in matts, leaves all over me, my skin grey, near death. He laid me down in his back seat and covered me with blankets from the boot of his car, wrapping bits of material around my wounds to stop the flow of blood.

How hadn't I died?

"I'll fucking kill the monster who's done this. Shhh. I've got you, don't worry. Shhh."

Exhausted, I'd begged for water, my throat was so dry. Gulping the liquid, my throat felt like sandpaper, rough and gravelly.

Cough. Shiver. Shake. Scream. Alive.

"P-l-e-a-s-e... m-a-k-e... m-e... s-a-f-e, p-l-e-a-s-e?"

"I have to take you to the hospital, lady. You've lost too much blood. You need to be seen."

"N-O! P-l-e-a-s-e. S-a-f-e."

He'd finally agreed to take me back to his house. How I'd managed to get him to do it is still something I can't believe. If I'd found me wandering in the dark, near death, with blood all over me, I would've taken me straight to hospital, but my powers of persuasion, even in the state I was in, were enough for him to keep to his word, and he took me back to his.

He could've been another psycho for all I knew.

I hadn't cared. All I'd wanted was to be safe, warm, out of pain. He'd tended to my wounds, stitching me up with cotton, dousing the wounds, needle and cotton in alcohol, anything to make them clean. He'd stitched with such precision, I thought he might have been a doctor. I'd asked for a rag, anything to help with the screaming, the pain so unbearable I'd passed out near the end. He'd given me some tablets to help me sleep, and I'd eventually woken up a few days later covered in bandages. I'll never forget the pain. Ever.

Watching the news a few days later, police reports confirmed a body had been found, and that the dead woman was wearing a necklace?

Had the evil bastard killed again? Was that poor woman wearing my necklace? *My M?*

I didn't have the energy to go to the police. All they'd want to ask is why I hadn't gone to them the night it happened. They'd ask too many questions. They already knew my brother, so they'd connect the two and he'd be targeted thinking he'd done it. I had to protect my brother who was, undoubtedly, an uncontrollable brute. But I still loved him.

No-one except my saviour could know I was still alive. Not until I had a plan would I dare leave. The animal who did this had to be punished before he killed again.

I had to try and find him.

With the help of my saviour, who, I believe was sent to me by God, I slowly regain my strength. By some miracle, my body replenishes the blood lost and I become strong again. Allowed to stay with him, he listens to my story without once judging me, growing to love and value him, trust him. He restores my faith in mankind.

I owe him my life.

Chapter Thirteen
Jayden

"No more tears now; I will think about revenge."

— *Mary Queen of Scots*

Six months later, released on good behaviour, I step through the gates to freedom and only see one person.

Plumper, the weight around her face and hips makes me wonder if she's sent someone else. Her eyes confirm it's her, though. I'd recognise those fearful eyes anywhere.

Appearing much healthier than I want her to, there's not a bruise in sight. I'll change that. Her hair, greyer, is in plaits, and her skin, less pale and wrinkled, looks like it's been pumped full of water. She's never looked better. Outwardly she may look better, but inwardly she's still the same. The way she stares at me is like she's seen a ghost. Stepping carefully towards me, walking with a limp, her legs are frail and unsteady as she comes close enough to peer up into my face; her blue hooded eyes seek mine for just a second before quickly looking away.

"You look just like your father. Let's get you home."

There are no long hugs or emotional reunion tears. In fact, there are no obvious signs of love between us at all. I hate her, and am sure as hell the feeling is mutual.

Stretching out my arm, not needing to say a word, my mother freely hands over the keys to the car, sliding in the back, complying without hesitation. I've missed the freedom of being able to drive anywhere I want, whenever I want. Adjusting the seat and mirror, turning on the ignition and tuning the radio to my favourite hard rock station, I can't believe my luck at the song playing.

"Perfect, we'll listen to this shall we, Mother dearest?"

Staring through my car mirror at sad eyes that haven't acknowledged what I've said, I turn around, making her look at me, pouting my lips and asking in my best baby voice.

"Aren't you glad to have your little boy home?"

Raising my hand for fun, seeing her flinch, I laugh, lighting a cigarette, turning the volume up on the radio and rolling down the window before slamming the accelerator so fast, she has no time to prepare herself. Falling on the seat with a thud, I don't give a fuck about her or her safety, listening as she scrambles to put on her seatbelt.

'*Smack My Bitch Up*' blares from my speakers as two guards watch from the gate shaking their heads. Like I care. All I care about is getting the fuck away. Flicking them the bird, blowing them a kiss, I can't resist burning rubber before racing off to my new life.

"Adios, mother fuckers."

Getting straight to work contacting everyone I know on the inside who might be able to help locate the screw, they all bring a big fat zero.

Every drug dealer I know contacts every informant they know, and no one can find any information about him. Even ex-cons bring zilch. It's like the bastard has disappeared into thin air. Not giving up,

I've even tried visiting my old house growing up, but neither I, nor my useless mother, can remember the street or number of the house that burned down.

Only able to unlock certain memories from my childhood, it's like my brain is protecting me from the pain it knows I'll endure if it allows me to see.

I need to remember.

I need the memories unlocked to know what happened. If I can remember, at least it will give me something to work from. I have to keep looking. Someone has to know something.

Disappointed, angry at getting nowhere fast, the stress of not finding anything starts my reliance on drugs again. The screw has to be out there somewhere. And Maxine? Her body still hasn't been found, so she could still be alive. I need to know, need to find the woods where he left her and find her one way or another.

My bitch mother isn't helping. Being around her again only angers me. My alter ego, which I'm finding hard to control, wants to kill her. Fed up with her and her submissiveness, I need another outlet for my anger. She is no challenge, too easy for me to control, and no fun. I need more.

Home for two weeks, the beatings resume, waiting around the corner of my mother's bedroom one night, listening as she finishes in the bathroom. Watching her make her way back to her room, I sneak in, grabbing her off guard as she brushes her hair.

Throwing the brush to the floor, my fists take on a mind of their own, punching, grabbing, scratching, and squeezing her body and hair, happy to be master again. Each finger tingling, my skin is covered in goosebumps as my fists find her face, stomach, back and neck, beating her to an inch of her life with savagery even I forgot I possessed. The smell of fresh blood only adds to my ecstasy, not stopping until my beast inside is satiated.

Bleeding on her bed, cowering, whimpering, covering her head with her hands, I stand over her like a bull breathing steam out of its nose; all I see is red, stomping my right foot hard on the floor.

I should just finish her off.

I can't.

Not yet.

Breathing, waiting for the anger inside me to subside, I bend down and grab her hair to make sure she's looking right into my face, snarling at her.

"You better watch your back, you snivelling bitch. You thought you were safe? Dream on. You're mine to play with now that Father dearest has gone. Mine!"

Raising my hand to see her flinch just for fun, she doesn't disappoint.

I hate her.

"Ha, I wouldn't even piss on you if you were on fire. Clean yourself up. I can't even look at you. You look like shit."

Spitting in her face, throwing her back on the bed with force, I walk a few steps to the kitchen seeing my reflection in the mirror on the way. Inspecting the blood covering my face, I smear it over my cheeks like a tribal warrior after a kill.

I'm the King of this house now.

Hearing her snivelling in the bedroom tempts me to go finish the job, but, instead I find her favourite, fluffy, floral tea towel and clean the blood off my hands, grabbing a bottle of JD from the cabinet before slamming the back door on my way out. Glass rattling like the end of a snake, I hope the bitch hears it.

Feeling the burn of the JD as it travels down my throat, it's like nectar, swigging some more as I make my way to the only place I know I'll find peace. Inspecting my knuckles, they are bloody, sore, and grazed, and some of the wounds are still bleeding, wiping them on my jeans to stop the flow. The beating my mother took was ferocious being the first one after so long. She deserved it for just breathing the same air as me.

Risking pouring some alcohol over my knuckles, they feel like fire, adding to my pain.

"Nothing that a good joint won't fix."

Fuck!

Realising I've left my stash back at the house, I know if I go back I'll finish the bitch off. I'll have to make do with the old stash I buried for emergencies, suddenly taken off guard as the memories of digging the hole come flooding back. Maxine had followed me that day, watching me from behind a tree, and thinking I hadn't seen her, I'd carried on as usual, looking her way a few times to see her head duck into the trees. I never let on that I knew she was there.

Wiping my eyes, overcome with emotion, I quicken my pace, skipping up the hill, using my lighter to scan the area and find the spot where I buried my box of drugs so long ago. Digging, my hands throb like they have a pulse, my knuckles and bones screaming as my blood mixes with the hard earth. Using a sharp stone to help, I dig deeper, the earth getting colder on my skin, relieving some of the pain. Wiping my forehead, sweat dribbles down the side of my face, frantic to find my box, waiting to feel the familiar shape of the iron box as a rock falls into the hole landing on something metal; my hand finally feels what it seeks.

Tap, tap, tap.

My entire arm now submerged in the ground, I use my other hand and arm to pull myself up, bringing the box and rock to the surface. Did I really dig this deep? Brushing off the dirt, sitting on the damp earth floor, I open it, seeing what's inside.

"Sweet."

Trying to get comfortable, my back feels the hard bark of the tree, cold and rough, repositioning myself as I unravel the old tin foil, placing the aged weed under my nose, inhaling deeply, surprised it still smells. Rifling through the box for papers, amazed they are still intact, I gently slip two out of the packet, spitting on one and glueing it to the other. The tin box, as cold as ice on my lap, acts as a table, placing the papers on top, sprinkling the weed evenly on them. Making sure to stuff as much as I can onto the papers, I pick them up and roll them through my fingers, licking the glue of the paper, wincing at the taste as my expert hands finish rolling the fat joint. I have to admit, I'm quite excited to see if the weed still tastes the part, lighting it, listening as the dry grass crackles and the flame burns through the paper.

Sucking as hard as I can, the roughness of the old grass sends my throat and chest into spasms, making my lungs work hard, coughing and pounding my fist in between my breast bone where it takes a few seconds for it to stop contracting, and a few swigs of JD before I feel I can light up again. This time, sucking a little less hard, the leaves on my tongue taste like heaven, laying back, dragging on the joint, letting the smoke exit my nostrils like a dragon. Laughing, imagining Maxine is sat right beside me passing the joint back and forth, I remember how she used to love watching the smoke come out of my nose, and especially the smoke rings I made with my mouth. Opening my mouth wide, releasing a perfect O, the smoke sails into the air until it disappears. Imagining Maxine is here, mesmerised, laughing and giggling at how I'm able to do it so perfectly, I can feel her, sitting beside me now, trying her best to make a smoke ring as perfect as mine.

"I can't do it. Why can't I do it, you dick."

Only she was allowed to call me that. Anyone else would've got the shit kicked out of them.

A sudden gust of wind takes me off guard, swearing I can hear her voice singing from the trees, calling me to her.

Where is she?

Owls and other creatures around me join in the chorus, while the wind wraps around my shoulders, hugging me, like Maxine's pulling me close to her. Shivering, feeling her presence, rolling the lighter around my fingers, I remember back to when she gave it to me.

"It reminds me of us. I even got one for me for when I start smoking. Look? There were only two in the shop, so it was lucky I got them, eh? I even engraved them. See?"

Holding up the lighter, I'm just able to see the faint letters on the back. JW. She'd refused to have different surnames, so had engraved them both with W for Warner, her surname. Forever my favourite present from her, I'd received it for my fifteenth birthday. Why she'd bought one for herself when she was only nine still makes me laugh, using hers when she'd eventually started sneaking cigarettes from me at the age of fourteen. I'd tried to stop her, but she was stubborn and didn't listen. Stubborn was her middle name. I'd give anything to have her stubborn back.

Through the moon's light, I see the intricate designs of the metal. Two smiling skulls – one male, one female – stare at me with a pair of wings behind both their heads which are entwined together. She'd said we'd be partners in crime forever, that nothing would ever part us. She'd saved up money from selling bottles to the local corner shop, which had taken her months. Had told me she'd seen them in the shop and had cut a deal with the owner asking if she could pay them off. How she'd convinced the shop owner to let her do that is still something I marvel at. She could've been something incredible if she'd been given the chance, if she'd not been taken away. She may have only been nine, but even then, she'd had the sass of someone much older. We'd been so close once, had loved each other more than anything in the world.

That was before it all went wrong, and I joined forces with my father.

She changed towards me. I saw her questioning looks and fearful eyes. She started spending more time at 'friends' houses, not wanting to be home, not wanting to be near me.

That had killed me.

Flicking the lighter on and off, watching the flame flickering unsteadily in the moonlight, the wind extinguishes it over and over, wishing so much she was here with me now. I would tell her not to be afraid. I would tell her I would never have hurt her, touched her like that. Ever. If I find her, I will tell her how much I love her.

Clutching my hand around the lighter, closing my eyes, I feel her around me, feel her warmth and love. I know in my heart she'd forgive me, the only person I'd ever felt loved by.

Leaning against the tree, drinking, and smoking for most of the night, my thoughts only focus on her, missing her, wanting her back. The same questions run over and over in my mind, reliving what would've been her last moments on this earth.

Why was she the one to have run into that psycho's path that night?

How must she have suffered? The last face she'd seen was his. Why? Why did that fucker have to find her?

Looking to the sky, pleading to the heavens, my voice barely audible; a single tear trails down my cheek.

"Why couldn't you have kept her alive and taken my good-for-nothing bitch of a mother instead. Why?"

Everything blurry, my hazy eyes watch the sun suddenly come out of hiding, rising in the sky casting beautiful hues of blue and yellow onto the grass and woodland below. Meanwhile suburbia wakes up as lights that look like fireflies' flicker on and off. My mother sleeps in one of those wooden houses as my sister may, or may not, be laying in the ground somewhere. She may be dead because of her. I need to make things right. I need to make things right for Maxine, for me.

Staggering back to the house, stumbling through the same back door I used to exit hours before, I listen for clues to where my mother might be.

Is she still even here?

After the beating I gave her, did she run, die? Hearing the toilet flush, a door opens from another room and I stomp to her bedroom, picking up a heavy paperweight next to the telephone with my left hand on the way.

She is breathing and Maxine isn't, and for that she needs to suffer.

Giving her no time to react, I'm above her, lifting my left hand, whacking her over the head. She is unconscious before she even hits the pillow. It's her fault my sister is gone. It's her fault. Hitting her repeatedly, possessed by hate, I need her to pay for everything. I need her to pay for giving birth to me, for not protecting me, for taking me away, for causing me to kill, and most of all, for not protecting Maxine. I need her to pay for it all, for conceiving me, for never giving me a choice.

"Do you think I would've picked you for a mother?"

Whack. Whack. Whack!

Covered in her blood again, dropping the paperweight on the bed, it is done. It is finally done.

Unrecognisable, all her facial features are mashed into one big red mess, bone and teeth missing, and half of her nose hangs from her face. Barely conscious, I listen to her last few breaths, not giving her time to die, dragging her body to the bathroom. Laying her in the bath, what is left of her face stares up at me, mouth open wide. Bending down to her ear, I whisper.

"You go to hell, you piece of shit. Both of you, rot in hell. It's your fault Maxine is dead. Both you and Father dearest's fault."

Leaving her gasping for breath, running to get the saw from under my bed, I grab rubbish bags from the kitchen cupboard on my way, bending over the bath, hearing her whispering. Placing my head as close to her mouth as I can, the blood and distortion of her face makes it difficult to decipher the words.

"What last words does Mother dearest want to say to her little boy?"

I can't make out what she's saying.

"Louder."

Listening, all I hear is her rattling chest.

"Maxine... not... your... sister."

Is that a smile I see?

She takes her last breath.

"You fucking bitch. What the fuck do you mean? What the fuck do you mean?"

Grabbing her shoulders, trying to shake life back into her body, it proves fruitless. She is gone, unable to give me any answers. Wild with rage, throwing her lifeless body back in the bath, even in death she has won.

The bitch has won.

Grabbing her hair with my right hand, my left-hand places the saw on her neck.

Covered in her blood, I throw her head in the bag closest to me, dragging her headless body from the bath, leaving a trail of blood through the hallway to her bed. Lifting it, using every muscle I have, I shuffle her body to the centre of the bed, covering her corpse with blankets, the sheets starting to bleed, spreading through the fabric like dye, sure I see the outline of a bleeding heart.

Are the drugs playing with my mind?

Two of her teeth stuck to the pillow smile at me, and one on the floor, right under my feet, points to my shoe. Bending down to pick it up, inspecting the yellow-stained fang between my thumb and forefinger, I can't help myself.

"Smile no more, Mother dearest."

Placing the fang in my jean pocket, I pluck the other two teeth on the bed between my fingers and quickly run back to the bathroom, retrieving the bag with the head, throwing them in with it. Blood everywhere, the house is stained red from her death, looking at myself through a mirror; seeing blood on my face, hair, hands, clothes.

Striding to the bathroom, trying to remove my clothes, they refuse to budge, twisting, turning my body to manoeuvre my limbs out of them. I want nothing of her left on me. Using my shirt to clean blood off myself and the bathroom floor, nothing can be done about the deep-red stains on the carpet from the bathroom to my mother's bedroom, having to squirt bleach over them, hoping it will do something at least to disguise the smell.

Dumping my soiled clothes on the bed with the corpse, I retrieve the fang from my jean pocket and quickly run back to the bathroom, setting the tooth next to the soap before cleaning the bath with the shower and jumping in. Watching the blood wash down the drain, I don't stop until the water is clear, making sure I can no longer smell the bitch on me. I won't feel completely free of her until every part of her is gone.

Scrubbing myself raw, skin burning like I'm in hell, fifteen minutes later, satisfied she is no longer lingering on me, I change into fresh clothes and shoes, spraying myself with enough aftershave to sink a ship. Placing the fang back in my pocket, I quickly look around the house for anything of value, ransacking her room, avoiding the places on the carpet with bleach. Digging deep in the wardrobe, something catches my foot, swearing to myself as I drag an old box I've never seen before out to the light.

"What's this?"

Locked.

"You fucking bitch. What do we have here?"

Head on fire, running to the tool box under the sink in the kitchen, I find a hammer, running back to the wardrobe, angrily smashing the lock until it finally breaks. Flinging the box open, rummaging through it, I find old articles of an abandoned child. An abandoned child? The date, July 18th is familiar. Why? I can't make out the year.

A baby girl?

The mother was found in a train station toilet about to give birth, and later abandoned the baby in hospital. There's a photo of a nurse holding a baby. July 18th? It rings a bell. July 18th. July 18th.

Maxine's birthday!

Memories, images from my childhood come flooding back. I'm in a toilet, at a train station. But where? A woman? I remember a woman on the floor. Is it her? Gazing deeply at the photo of the nurse in the picture, she is unfamiliar. I remember another face. A younger face. Confused why my mother has hidden this, who is the woman? Who is the baby? It can't be Maxine. She wasn't abandoned. Who is the baby in this article? Does my mother have something to do with it? Why has she locked all this away in a box? Finding an envelope, opening it, inside is a lock of hair, smelling it. Faint apple shampoo. Is it my mother's? A letter addressed to Maxine is sealed. Why is there a letter to Maxine? My mother's last words to me pound against my head. *Maxine not your sister.* Will this tell me? I want to read it but what if what's inside will break my heart again? I can't, not yet. Looking towards the headless corpse under the blanket, I'm a bull red with rage.

"You fucking bitch. What the fuck have you done now? You're fucking lucky you're dead or I'd kill you all over again. I fucking hate you. I hate you, and I hate him. Why is Maxine gone? Why isn't she here, now? Just me and her? It's your fault. *Your fault.*"

Collapsing on the wardrobe floor, my gut feels it coming. From deep inside my stomach, through my chest, into my throat, it sticks, wanting release. Trapped for so long inside me, I can't stop it from growing, from escaping. I can't stop it, quickly sitting up and ripping a t-shirt from its hanger and stuffing whatever I can into my mouth before thumping the floor, the walls, the side of the door with both fists, roaring, bawling, howling, until whatever is inside me is gone. Like a caged animal, sitting, staring into space, I pull my arms around my knees tight into my chest, rocking from side to side; a single tear sidestepping its way down my cheek to the t-shirt, absorbing my pain. Spitting the shirt from my mouth, I can't breathe. The corpse, the screw, my sister, the box, the letter. It's too much. Resting my chin on top of my knees, tucking my head between my legs, the tears flow, finally allowed release.

Images of my childhood, my parents, my pathetic existence rerun over and over in my head, but it is the images of my sister, the only person in the world I ever loved, and who ever loved me back, which are the ones I cry for the most.

The loneliness has never been so near.

Shivering, the cold air wraps itself around me, feeling its pinch as it finds every part of my exposed skin, but my hands don't want it, rubbing it away, not wanting its comfort anywhere near me. Remembering a time I welcomed the coldness, the boy is still there, inside me crying, rocking back and forth in the cold dark wardrobe, hiding from my father. Back then, the cold protected me from what was imminent. Now it just protects me from myself. The fear still exists deep within me, locked away in a tiny compartment of my brain, trapped with no escape.

I want to be free.

My father and mother are dead, so why is it so difficult? Is it guilt, fear I've ended up worse than him? Every time I think of the night Maxine died, I know if she hadn't been running from me to get help, she'd still be here. She'd still be alive. The lump in my throat won't budge. Sweating, grabbing at my neck to try to shift it, why can't I breathe? Scratching my neck, all I hear are the words that haunt me every hour of every day.

"You'll be next, you fucking crazy bitch. You hear? I'll fucking kill you."

Maxine's running from me, the fear in her eyes identical to mine when I was running away from my father. She feared me the same way I'd feared him; and for that I can never forgive myself. Ever.

Would Maxine forgive me?

Would she still love me, her brother, and his monster, still grieving for their absent childhood?

The boy inside wants to feel, not be judged, mocked, pointed the finger at or beaten. I want to feel anything other than hate. Turning towards the bed, all I've felt for so long is hate, but now that both parents are gone, can my child finally be free? Slumping my arms to the floor, both child and adult in me finally unite in our grief with no one to soothe or help us but ourselves. My hands, soaked with my tears, can still smell the blood, still smell my mother on my skin.

Am I betraying Maxine?

Looking towards the bed, seeing the sheets drowning with my mother's blood, she's finally been destroyed by my hands. Knuckles still throbbing from hitting the walls and wood, I look from them to the bed, relieved she is gone.

I will never feel guilt for what I've done.

I will never miss her.

Examining my hands, questioning how I summoned the strength to finish her off, I hear my father's voice around me.

"Because she never protected you or your sister. Because she never loved you enough to want to see you safe, boy! She was a selfish bitch who only thought of herself, so don't go crying and becoming a pussy on me, now."

Clenching both hands into a fist, beating my head, my chest, my legs, I can't stop the words spewing from deep within me.

"It's because you never loved me. It's because you both never loved me, loved us. You mother fucker."

Thumping my head repeatedly against the wall, wanting the thoughts gone, I need my father's voice gone. Turning my hands over, clenching them into fists, I stare from the bed back to them.

They killed her.

They bashed her, sawed off her head, gauged out her eye, and dragged her body to the bed, but it was my child's brain and heart who'd controlled what they'd done. It was my child who'd told me to kill her and this time, I'd listened.

The beast had won.

My lost childhood, my lost sister, my lost life.

My sister?

She was supposed to be here forever. We'd planned to do so much, and now everything was gone.

"Boys don't cry, you pussy. Take your beating like a man."

"I love you more than God loves you, darling. I'll make sure he doesn't touch you."

"I never wanted you. Never. I told her never to have any kids, you little fucker. The day you were born was the worst day of my life. The worst."

"Stop! You're going to kill her. Stop, Jayden!"

"You'll be next, you fucking crazy bitch."

"Maxine, not your sister."

My mother's last words had hurt the most.

It's a lie.

What had that bitch meant? I'd never once asked any questions, and wasn't interested in what she'd had to say because I'd hated her and my fuckwit father for so long. I'd hated them so much, and now they were both gone and there were no answers or reasons for why they'd found it so hard to love? The questions would never be answered.

My father would be so proud I've turned into a monster even worse than him.

'*Well done, son,*' he'd say.

Finally, after killing the woman we both hated, I would be worthy of being called his son.

Wiping my eyes, standing, walking over to the bed, which is now completely saturated in blood, my spit lands close to my mother's lifeless hand. Leaving the room, grabbing another bottle of JD from the cabinet, and swirling a mouthful around my mouth, I walk to my room to roll a joint.

It is 8:00am.

Lying on my bed, puffing, satisfied that what I've done is right for Maxine, I run back to my mother's room and grab the box, taking it to the kitchen table, sitting down. Inside, there are thousands of dollars bundled up into neat little rolls which the bitch must've been stashing for years. Hand pausing in mid-air, staring, not wanting to touch my father's favourite cap, should I pick it up? Resting it on top of my head, the smell of the bastard is still on it.

Why did she keep it?

Should I burn it with the bitch? Maxine would've killed me. For some reason, she loved the thing.

I'll wear it for her and not because I want to remember the prick.

"Thank you, Father dearest."

Retrieving the letter addressed to Maxine, turning it over and over in my hand, should I read it? Whatever's inside might push me over the edge; I don't know if I can handle it. I've already been pushed over the edge finding out she wasn't my sister. Placing it back in the box, finding photos of myself and Maxine hidden underneath, we are unrecognisable, happy, arms entwined. The children smiling at me look like they don't have a care in the world; there is even one of us with our mother looking so content, so peaceful. Ripping the photo in half, putting the half with Maxine and myself back in the box, I throw the other half to the ground, stomping on it, a footprint over my mother's face hides her from me as I make my way out the back door to the garage.

Trying to locate the cans of gasoline I know my father kept, I'm furious at how much crap there is, throwing box after box at the wall, covering myself in dust and dirt. Hundreds of little legs crawl up both my arms, my eyes struggling to see in the darkened space, flinging them and the dirt from my eyes as I continue to wade through the hordes of junk in the dark, what I seek are right at the back, behind the lawn mower. Three full cans of petrol look to be unopened. Stubbing out my lit joint, the last thing I want is to cause an explosion in here.

Muscles hurting, lifting them one by one to the house, I take the first can into my mother's bedroom, dousing her headless corpse, and everything on her bed, with its entire contents. The fumes attack my throat, grabbing the first thing I can find, covering my nose and mouth with it. Struggling to breathe, coughing like a ninety-year-old on their way out, I splash as much as I can over every surface of the house, snatching up the bag with my mother's head, placing the three empty cans inside, transferring them all outside the back door. My heart, beating ten to the dozen, guides me back inside to turn on the gas oven and hob, making sure all the windows are shut.

Walking to the woods, my shoulders and arms wrestle to carry so many things, worried the bag containing the head is leaking, having to pick up my pace, finally arriving at the spot I want. Now my killing has extended to people, there's one more person I want to destroy.

Maxine's killer. I'll find him if it's the last thing on this Earth I do.

. . .

Half an hour later, satisfied the hole is deep enough, I drop the head and petrol cans in, carefully piling the earth back in with bits of grass and bark from the trees. Finally, placing the same stone on top to mark where I've dug, I grab my bottle of Jack Daniel's and gulp as much as I can, dancing on the makeshift grave. Welcoming my mother to hell, I'm sure her and Father dearest will have the happiest of reunions. Ha! Those two bastards belong together.

Scouring the ground, picking up dry twigs, clumsily dropping them numerous times, struggling to focus on the small opening of the JD bottle I have to put them through, I need to get this done. I need this to be over. Steadying myself, hearing birds and the gentle wind as I carefully place the small bits of wood inside the bottle, I hear Maxine in the wind, helping me, guiding my hands, guiding me quietly back to the house, watching it for the last time with me before I kiss the bottle and look up to the sky. Talking to her one last time, I don't care if she wasn't my blood sister, she'll always be my beautiful Maxine, my best friend, my sister.

"I'm doing this for us, sis. I'm doing this to make things right between us."

Sure I can feel her hand on my shoulder, I light the sticks, quickly running to the back door, opening it, throwing the lit bottle inside, and running back to the woods as fast as I can. Waiting for the explosion, head down, hands over my ears, my heart and head are thumping in time, waiting, waiting, waiting.

Nothing.

"You motherfucker."

Boom.

An explosion to wake the dead, the house bursts into flames before my eyes, seeing windows, doors, and parts of the roof fly into the air; a chunk of iron landing close to where I'm hiding.

Boom.

A second explosion I'm not expecting takes me off guard, as more debris floats my way, a photo of my sister landing near enough at my feet. Picking it up, brushing my fingers over her face and hugging the photo to my heart, a great weight lifts from me as a warmth I can't explain pulses through my body. It's almost like she is letting me know she forgives me. Kissing her face, tucking the photo inside my jacket, fishing for another pre-rolled joint, I stand and watch people scramble like ants from all directions to witness the destruction. Within minutes familiar sounds of fire engines and police cars are heard, but they don't have a hope in hell of taming the inferno now being helped by the wind.

I'm sure Maxine is helping blow it nearer.

The house, far enough away from other houses, and the direction of the wind, has assured the flames have not put anyone else at risk of dying. Puffing on my joint, sitting against a tree, watching until the house is nothing but soot and ash, people witness the angry flames' refusal to be extinguished, the firefighters eventually winning the battle.

Twelve hours later, as the sun begins its descent, bending forward to retrieve my belongings off the damp floor of the wood, I walk over to the patch where my mother's head is buried, stamping on the earth, making sure it is flat. I imagine my mother's looking straight up at me with her one eye, retrieving her other eye from my pocket, staring into it, and turning it so she can see what's left of her precious home. Finally, I can close this chapter of my life for good.

"Burn in Hell, bitch."

Chapter Fourteen

The house, incinerated to the ground, is left to the authorities who eventually blame the explosion, and my mother's death, on a faulty gas oven, and an oxygen cylinder left from when my father had needed it to breathe. It must've been the reason why the explosion was so big. My good for nothing father came good in the end, not even noticing it when I was dousing the house.

The cops believe me when questioned, and able to act out of my pants with grief, I nearly fool myself in the process. Friends who owe me favours give me alibis not daring to ask why, and as I am the last living family member, I presume everything will be left to me.

That is, if there were anything.

There is nothing.

Not even an insurance policy.

The house, council property, will be rebuilt, but I won't be moving in.

The only thing I ask to take. A rose bush at the end of the garden that grows all year round and refuses to die, even in the winter.

Maxine loved it, and I don't have the heart to see it destroyed, so it comes with me to a room I find to rent in a shared house. The only place I can put it is in the corner near the window.

Hooking myself up with a good dealer, I settle into my new, stress-free life, even managing to find a few bar jobs, but they don't last long.

Watching a guy reviewing chippies and beer has been the highlight so far. I learned a lot from Charlz Reviews, but not even he was enough for me to stay in the dump of a bar. At least I was able to ask questions to the punters, see if they knew the screw, and I even met a few gorgeous girls, one in particular, a blonde who I never ended up hooking up with. Shame. I'm becoming a bit bored with the monotony of it all.

I'm tired of work. The women aren't even a challenge; I'm questioning whether my decision to move to the city was a good one. I need more excitement, a distraction from the constant thoughts of Maxine which still haunt me.

One Thursday night, after meeting my dealer, I decide to walk through town back to my place instead of the usual cab, stumbling across a club I haven't seen before.

Asking the huge Islander on the door if there's any eye candy, he gives me the filthiest look, quickly looking at his name tag as he clicks me in. Raising an eyebrow at him, I tell Joni to cheer up, walking the twenty odd stairs up to the entrance of the club.

Waiting in line, I happily take a free chip for a free drink off the owner, a tall, suave, good-looking guy in his fifties with a kiss curl and devilish grin who, to my surprise, immediately recognises me. Telling me he's an old friend of my father's, Ricki hires me on the spot when I ask about work, not even asking for references.

"Any son of Jimmy's is welcome here."

Sipping my drink, looking him over, I'm not sure whether I trust Ricki. It's his eyes. They are smiling but I don't trust they are happy. Don't ask me why. Moving my eyes, scrutinising every man in the joint. He doesn't need to know I'm still searching for any clues on the screw. Nobody knows anything, it's like the bastard has just disappeared into thin air, and there's nothing at all that I can do.

There has to be something? Something that I and everyone is missing. That, or the fucker is more powerful than I thought.

I will kill him when I find him. Maxine deserves for him to die. Wherever she is, she deserves to know that retribution has been served on her behalf.

Tuesday night, twenty-four hours before my new job starts, I sit absentmindedly in the strip club rubbing my right arm, brushing my fingers across Maxine's tattoo as I wait for my dealer. Scanning the dingy room, watching stripper after stripper shed their clothes, I scrutinise every man entering and leaving, wondering if the screw will turn up here tonight? This can't be the sort of place Maxine supposedly worked.

Arm itching more than usual, I watch, waiting, agitated, leg twitching quickly in time to the crappy music as my whole body tingles with the anticipation of my next fix. What will Brett, my dealer, surprise me with tonight? Coke, Puff, Opium, Hash, Pills? Whatever it is, I hope it's strong because I need something to take my mind off my sister. Lucky for me one of my friend's recommended Brett. His stuff is by far the best shit I've ever had.

The women stripping on stage aren't really doing it for me. They're not even close to the women I watch onscreen most nights. The women in this seedy joint always look whacked out of their brains. Their vacant eyes and thin bodies stumble about on stage like they're drunk and just want to get on with it. How could they degrade themselves like this? Winking at me, the girl on stage now cups her non-existent breasts and blows me a kiss. I wish Brett would just hurry the fuck up.

Rocking backwards and forwards, watching the scrawny blonde slowly dance, I don't know who the fuck she thinks she's trying to tease? Her robotic moves only torment my bladder which is screaming to be emptied. Creeping to the toilet, stopping as soft music starts, the one light on the dingy stage lights up as another stripper appears. Sitting back down before people see me, a super thin, too thin for me, woman appears with long red hair that brushes against her pale skin. Unconvincingly seducing her audience, her bony hands fumble to unclip her bra, releasing two flat mounds. I'm guessing she's in her late thirties and a druggie, her saggy skin not hiding the bruises on her arms from the needles. Stumbling awkwardly around the stage, looking like the living dead, there's nothing behind her dull eyes, seeing she is as high as a kite. I suppose she's using anything to get her through. I know the feeling well.

One man up the front seems to be enjoying the show a little more than others, letting his right hand do the talking underneath his large, thick, black coat. Very fucking original. Fucking sad pervert. Every time I step foot in this place it's the same, but I can't seem to stay away. I don't know what it is. I'm just drawn to the place. It's the perfect place to do a deal, the owner of the club fully aware of what goes on. A little part of me identifies with the girls in here, sad and drugged up, moving like programmed robots. God knows how many times a day they have to do this. Seedy, the place is dirty as hell and smells like shit, but, to me it's like home. Degrading, desperate and high.

Jumping out of my skin, a tap on my shoulder signals Brett is here.

"Away with the fairies, mate? Everything you ordered is in its usual place."

Handing him the cash, ordering two more drinks, we watch the show continue. Recognising the next girl on stage, I can't pinpoint where from. Have I fucked her? Did she go to the same school? Where do I know her from? Excusing myself, walking to the loo and peeing into the heavily stained bowl, I open the cistern, which is still slightly open, retrieving my stash, happy with what he's left.

"Nice, pills today."

Shaking the bag, opening it up and quickly popping a couple of them in my mouth, I hide the bag down my crotch, rearranging my dick, still thinking of the woman on stage and how I know her.

Maxine's vigil!

She was there with at least three other women all claiming to have worked with Maxine. Surely not? Surely Maxine didn't work in this joint? She wouldn't have done anything as degrading as this. Would she? Rushing out, the woman's not on stage. Room spinning, where is she? Another woman I think I recognise dances on stage. Stumbling to the front, waving my arms at her to get her attention.

"Who the fuck are you? How the fuck did you know my sister?"

Jumping up onto the stage, a security guard grabs me from behind wrestling me to the ground, watching Brett run out.

"I'll fucking kill you. I'll fucking kill you, you whore. *How did you know my sister?*"

Dragged out of the club by my arm, I'm told I'm barred, never allowed to return. The hefty security guy watches, waiting for me to leave as the bouncer on duty nods to a massive muscular man entering. Tattoo suddenly itching, I can't see his face. His huge hat is concealing it, oversized like his big black blazer. He side glances me with eyes I don't like.

"Another fucking pervert seeking cheap thrills?"

Ignoring me, the huge guy nods to the bouncer as he enters, and I'm left standing, looking at the dingy dark doors, not believing Maxine had anything to do with this place, these women, these filthy perverts.

Pushed on my way with a force that tells me to do as I'm told, my hands are up before the security guard can say go, gesturing I'm leaving. Laughing at me, the bouncer turns away. I want to kill him. I want to kill them both.

This night is turning into a fucking disaster. My mind, all over the place, can't think straight as all my thoughts fight each other. I've been to this joint however many times not once seeing anyone I recognised. Had I seen them and not realised? Are my eyes only just beginning to open and the fog of Maxine's death is now lifting? I have to return, wait in hiding until the women leave. They must tell me what they know. I'll make it my mission to come back and watch every man who enters and leaves.

Maxine's slayer is imprinted on my brain forever; he could be in there now. This could be the place that holds the clues to where I can find him, find my sister.

Dragging my feet home, at least I have something to work on.

I finally have a start.

The bar work is easy, and if I'm honest, it keeps me occupied and gives me plenty of time to think of ways of returning to the strip joint. I still won't believe Maxine had anything to do with the place, thinking it must've been a trick of the mind, or the pills? I'll go back and see if the women I thought I recognised were actually real. Every night off will be spent watching until I have some answers.

Ricki, my new boss, loves telling me stories about my father who was well known around town. He apparently had a whole life I knew nothing about.

"Your dad loved everyone; he had no preference as long as they had a pulse. Ha! They loved him. You look just like him."

Nudging my arm with his elbow, nodding to the door, winking, and walking to the entrance of the club to welcome two young girls, is this where my father came the nights he stayed out? Why and how did he come to the city?

Scanning the room, I can't help but notice the women who turn up, every night. They are all the same. Skimpy dresses, lots of makeup, piss easy to woo, and piss easy to control. The filthier the better for me. From what I see, they enjoy being treated like shit, happy to serve men and their needs for next to nothing in return. Was this why my father came? They're all like my mother, except for one.

Watching Ricki welcoming her, I've seen her before in a bar I'd previously worked at. Catching her eye, it's like she doesn't remember me, or, if she does, she's not letting on. Hoping I'd see her again, she is gorgeous, a little over-confident for my liking, but I welcome the challenge. Every man in the place seems to want her, which adds to her allure. I want the recognition of 'bagging' her, and I want every man to know I've had her, including Ricki who's told me what he'd like to do to her. He has no chance. She looks at him like he's a dirty old man. She obviously knows what he wants but plays the game to get what she wants. Smart girl. Giving me eye contact, she may as well already be in my bed, but playing hard to get, she seems to enjoy leading me on just as much as I enjoy seducing her. Superior to any other woman, there is definitely something about her that I'm drawn to, and not as easy to woo as the rest, it takes me at least two attempts before she gives in, openly laughing at my lame pick-up line.

"Yeah ok, I'd love to go for a spot of red wine, you freak."

When I finally have her in my bed, the sex is more explosive than I could ever have imagined, which has only reignited my need to find the one girl who I can use, own.

Later, over a few spliffs, she opens up about her life, telling me more than I want to hear. I don't really want to get to know her or her sad story. She's just another pampered princess, one of plenty I've seen and already had. High maintenance and trouble, all I want is a fuck, nothing more.

Telling me about a friend she's moved to the city to be near, my ears prick up as she freely gives up information about her friend's childhood problems with her mother, which makes me curious to see if our stories are similar in any way. Telling me she is her closest and longest friend, the way she speaks about her doesn't convince me she even likes her. I get the feeling she's trying to put me off, that she's ever so slightly threatened by this girl called 'Jesse.' I'm interested. I'm definitely more than interested, curious to meet her, see for myself if what she is saying is true.

Stopping her at a story about rats, that's more than enough information, and anyway, she looks far too provocative under the dimmed lights with her hair falling slightly over one of her perfect breasts. Nipple playing peek-a-boo, I nuzzle up to her pretending to be one of the furry rodents she speaks of, sniffing around her beautiful body until I get to her perfect bud and suck on it, biting it between my teeth. Purring like a cat as I lick all the way down her body, I eventually settle between her legs, licking her slowly as she lays back and lets me explore every part of her with my hands, fingers, and tongue. Bringing her to climax again and again, she tastes like a peach, lapping up her juices like a hungry dog, stroking my fingers up and down her body, even inserting one of them inside her butt, which makes her gasp. It's so easy for me to do. Her hazel eyes seem familiar. I can't quite put my finger on it. There is pain, loss, insecurity, definitely not the same person she shows her adoring public. I sense there is lots of trouble where she is concerned, and I guess she masks the pain through her confidence like a lot of other girls. If she wasn't so gorgeous, I might consider her, but as beautiful as she is, she isn't the girl I seek. I want a girl who doesn't seek attention, one who will do anything who is desperate to be loved.

I want her friend.

Chapter Fifteen

Two weeks later, finally fixing my eyes on Jesse, watching as she covers her ears with her hands, she's not happy about the noise, repositioning herself awkwardly beside her gorgeous friend who I've already forgotten the name of. The unease is obvious by the way she rocks back and forth on the balls of her feet. Eyes darting around the room like a fly on speed, men behind begin to encircle the gorgeous one like hyenas, waiting for any chance to pounce, competing against each other for her attention. If I hadn't already had her in my bed, I'd swear she looks a little bored with the attention. My trained eye says there's more to her than meets the eye. Jesse gives each and every man daggers, killing them with her eyes, warning them to back off. Quite territorial, this isn't going to be as straightforward as I thought.

A song comes on, Jesse nudging her friend to dance who isn't having any of it. I can't say I recognise the song, either. Obviously used to the rigmarole of it all, the look on Jesse's face shows nothing but boredom as her friend basks in all the attention from the adoring men surrounding her, including Ricki, who fusses and giggles like an old fool, touching her in places a man his age shouldn't. His stick-insect girlfriend doesn't look happy, and neither does Jesse who busies herself, watching, looking at something on the floor completely absorbed with what she's doing. The difference between the two is like chalk and cheese. The beautiful blonde is tall, slim, and curvy, while Jesse is plain, brunette, short, over-curvy and clumsy. The blonde knows she's gorgeous. Jesse, though. She's used to the non-attention, used to being the sidekick, the nobody.

Fantasising about finding someone like her for too long, Greg the geek DJ must be picking up on my energy, suddenly hearing *Milli Vanilli* singing '*Don't forget my number*.' My perseverance has finally paid off, longing for a distraction, someone to take my mind off my sister. The timing couldn't be more perfect.

Retro Wednesday, Jesse's body language speaks volumes, watching her arms fidget with her clothes while her clumsy feet step side to side pretending to enjoy herself. She's not fooling anyone, especially me. The eye contact with anyone except her friend is awkward, sometimes defiant, killing people with her eyes, quickly looking away and backing down if she's challenged. All bark no bite. I'm guessing she's here for one reason, and that is to serve the one who struts about in her low-cut leotard like she is under a spotlight marking her as the only woman in the room. She may as well be; all the women in the world let alone a small club, don't stand a chance. Everything I've been told about Jesse, though, is true.

Zero confidence, ungraceful, fidgety, her gestures pretty much let me know straight away how she feels, especially around her friend. The worst dress sense I've ever seen on a woman, she pulls at her black crop top which is a little too snug for her frame. Struggling to cover her exposed midriff, it brings to light how uncomfortable and klutzy she feels, the clothes alone sending a clear message to me, and everyone around, that she does not want or seek attention. I'm one hundred percent sure the top she's worn wasn't chosen by her. The boots, however? *Dr Marten*'s would not have been my first choice. I'll change that. Taking in every mannerism, every expression, she gazes at the blonde awaiting her command. I wonder if she knows how much her 'so-called' best friend detests her? Puts her down. Uses her.

Boom.

The DJ's microphone suddenly sends feedback throughout the club, causing people, especially the ones close to the speakers, to grimace while holding both hands over their ears. One man doesn't react, not even batting an eyelid. Understanding why a few seconds later, I watch him signing to his friend, who is obviously telling him what has just happened. While the DJ apologises and sorts the music welcoming the crowds in with one of his personal favourites, Ant Music's opening drumstick riff rumbles throughout the club. The deaf guy, right by the speaker, actually manages to keep in time to the beat so engrossed by him and his moves, I hardly notice the customers who have started lining up at the bar, pissed off that I have to start preparing cocktails, shots, and beers. Serving them at the same time looking for Jesse, she's thankfully right above the deaf guy, holding the rails, also moving to the music. Beside her friend like a loyal dog desperate for attention, she could have a leash around her neck being pulled along, and still, no one would notice her. She is used to being invisible, that I can tell.

Preparing three Tequila Sunrises for three identically dressed women who all look like they've stepped straight off the set of Dallas, I have to look through their huge, backcombed hair at the deaf guy who is now dancing like he can hear everything. It's awesome. Suddenly a massive shoulder pad obstructs my view, smiling, stepping to the side as a woman starts giggling, staring, and pointing at other people's outfits, one squealing so high, I have to stop what I'm doing to stick both fingers in my ears. Eardrums vibrating, shaking my head backwards and forwards like they could explode, the guilty woman's hands and face apologise before she does.

"Sorry, love. Just saw someone I know."

Paying for her drinks, mouthing sorry to me without speaking, she slowly walks towards her friend while I bend my neck, inserting a finger in my ear like I've got a load of water in it. Quickly scanning the room for the blonde, I see Jesse right next to her, practically glued to her hip. How am I going to make eye contact?

Suggesting clearing the tables of glasses, I'm told to stay at the bar, hoping she comes my way soon. I'm becoming impatient to meet her getting the picture it's going to be near enough impossible to tear her away from her friend.

How will I do it?

I need her to look at me, just once.

She'll be putty in my hands when she does.

All she has to do is look my way.

Fed up with girls who are easy, I've been looking for this one for far too long to let her slip through my fingers, now. The void my mother left when I rid the world of her has brought to light the need for me to find someone else to dominate, control, use, my inner beast slowly regaining control, reminding me often how good it felt.

Scrutinising Jesse's body, she stands beside her friend at their table. Her thick thighs, accentuated by the tight skirt she's wearing, desperately clings to her body like an uncomfortable second skin. Carrying a bit too much flesh for me, I usually prefer women a little smaller. I'll get her looking the way I want in no time.

Watching her and her friend's interaction, Jesse's uncomfortable with the attention they're getting, looking around nervously as the lights of the club bounce off her face, highlighting her facial features. Pretty in a plain sort of way, the heavy make-up around her eyes doesn't suit her delicate face. I'd prefer her to wear no makeup at all, except when we're in the bedroom. I'll make sure that changes, too. Comparing the two girls, wondering how they're even friends, I'm thankful my girl is nothing like the other one. She'd be far too hard to control, mould into what I want. Rolling my tongue over my lips, rubbing my hands together, I'm tingling with excitement that she will soon be mine.

Tattoo suddenly itching, just like that, my thoughts wander back to my sister. Scanning the room, I can't help but notice a lot of the women in the club remind me of her. Their shape, colouring, age, are all very similar to hers, clasping eyes on one who reminds me of her more than others, the UV lights make it look like she is covered in blotches. Suddenly called to the dancefloor by Greg, he starts playing 'Come on Eileen,' as she bows to everyone, suddenly getting what her costume's about. Laughing to myself, I imagine that is something Maxine would've done for a laugh, wishing so much the woman was her.

"Take a photo, why don't you? It lasts longer!"

Snapping back to what I'm doing, apologising to the woman waiting at the bar for a drink, my heart bleeds a little more.

Maxine's murderer is still out there, and I'm still none the wiser at finding him. Many nights my eyelids have fought to close, the last image being the one of the pig responsible for taking her life. His face is imprinted on my brain, dreaming of the different ways I'll kill him when I eventually find him. Will I find him, though? It's not looking good; all the potential leads I'm getting ending right back to square one. I haven't been allowed back to the strip joint, and I haven't seen any of the girls I recognised ever again. It's like they've suddenly disappeared, too.

Checking out every man coming into the club, scrutinising their faces and builds, I'm a programmed robot. What would I do if the pig walked in right now? Right at this minute? Would my inner beast unleash of its own accord? Kill him on the spot? Or would it stalk him like a lion following its prey, hiding in the shadows ready to pounce and kill?

I know exactly what it would do.

Banging my left fist on the bar at the same time the DJ changes the song, a few women jump at the sudden noise. Glaring at them, opening the dishwasher, the steam hits my face, distorting my vision for a tiny second. Flinching at the hotness of the glasses, placing them on shelves, letting my eyes linger on the crowds of people dancing and chatting, this job has given me plenty of opportunities to meet women and freedom to scrutinise every man who frequents the joint.

Becoming friends with some of the clientele, I've been able to ask questions in conversations, storing whatever I feel is helpful in the little part of my brain I've saved for my sister's slayer. I will find him if it's the last thing I do.

In just a few weeks, I've already met three ex-cons, two dealers and one pimp, easily identifying which girls are being pimped out. They stand out like sore thumbs. Wearing teeny tiny dresses that look like they've been painted on, they show off every curve to perfection; I especially love seeing the outline of their nipples through the sheer fabric. It reminds me of a scene in a film I've watched a thousand times. Humming *'Young Lust'* to myself, rearranging my balls, my eyes trace long bare legs to the highest heels I've ever seen. Observing the women as they talk to their pimp, the lights bounce off their faces showing lashings of makeup, reminding me of the girls I watch on screen most nights when I'm alone. Indisputably high on cocaine, they slide up to men full of energy who have no idea their very excited, euphoric behaviour has got nothing to do with them. Undeniably stupid, the men lap it up thinking all their Christmases have come at once. I've seen it a million times before. One of the hookers looks my way. Draped over a stocky, middle-aged man's shoulder, her beautiful oval face grimaces at me, obviously not happy with her pimp's choice for the night. Pitch-black, spiky, punk hair stands to attention with the help of super strong glue as her translucent skin glows blue, yellow, and pink under lights that flicker above with different colours. Her little black dress struggles to hold in her huge breasts which look like two magnificent orbs under the club lights. One thick heavily black-lined green eye winks at me, and ruby-red lips smile showing off teeth so straight and white, you'd swear she could be the face of any dentist practice. Licking her lips with her tongue, eyebrows asking me a question, the poor man she is with has no idea what is happening behind him as she grinds into his groin with fake ecstasy. Winking, swigging some coke around my mouth like mouthwash, I use my tongue to clean in between my teeth, thinking back to the night I met her...

Two weeks earlier

It's the end of the night and my third shift at the club is now finished. Quickly wiping down the bar with a cloth and placing the last glass on the shelf from the dishwasher, I wonder, will she and her magnificent breasts be waiting for me? God, I hope so. Saying my goodbyes, rushing to meet her, running down the stairs two at a time towards the exit, Joni, the huge Fijian doorman, glares unfriendly from the cloakroom straight at me. Why the guy hates me is a mystery. I'd never laid eyes on him before landing the job. Giving him my blackest look, saluting him on my way out, I don't bother saying anything other than "adios," the inner beast wanting more than anything to give him a reason to hate me.

Opening the door out onto the street, the early morning air whacks me straight in the face as a few drunks still linger about shouting at each other aggressively. Moving them on, wanting nothing to delay me getting to her, I'm tired, the past few nights shifts taking its toll on my body clock. At least I have something to look forward to.

Where is she? I told her to meet me outside.

Strolling past a tall exotic-looking prostitute, whistling to her, arching an eyebrow in recognition, I know if she didn't look so much like a bloke, I might be tempted to let her blow me off. I've always been curious whether a blowjob from a man would be better than any women. Who knows? One night I might give it a go. Suddenly seeing her waiting on the corner, standing under a street light, smoking a cigarette, she is a vision of beauty. Spiky, punk, black hair, magnificent breasts, and legs all the way up to her neck, she leans against the street lamp in her little red dress blowing smoke out of her mouth, which floats up to the light, intertwining like two dancers in a slow embrace. Skin like a plucked goose, she shivers involuntarily in the morning air, straight away offering her my jacket, draping it around her shapely shoulders before she can say no. Rubbing my hands to make them warm, I know what will warm us up. Retrieving a smoke from inside the jacket I've just given her, sniffing the length of it while giving her my most seductive look, her eyes smile back at me.

"You're going to like this. Nothing but female head."

"How did you know I like female head?"

Winking at me, I notice a small black spot on the top of her lip, wondering if it's real or painted on. Lighting the end, the skulls on my Zippo light up in the moon's glow adding to the magic of the moment, and smiling, pleased with how smooth the grass feels on my throat, I pass it to her, watching her greedily suck on the end wishing it was me she was sucking. Holding her breath, she releases the smoke from her mouth as her raspy voice comments on my lighter.

"That's very cool, where did you get it?"

Not in the mood to talk about Maxine tonight, I ignore the question, instead asking her about her night, which she is more than happy to answer. Smoking another joint as we walk the rest of the way to mine, she talks but I don't hear her, stopping to scrape something off my shoe. Slightly ahead of me, I notice my jacket doesn't cover much of her legs, watching as she suddenly readjusts her G-string underneath her dress, scratching, looking back at me embarrassed. She shouldn't be. The sexual chemistry is stronger with her than anyone else I've met before. I can't pinpoint why.

I'd noticed her as soon as she'd walked into the club. I knew straight away she was a hooker, but that hadn't put me off. In fact, it had only made me more determined to have her knowing I sure as hell was never going to have to pay. The pimp's look had warned me off, but I'd ignored the wimp. His silver suit and hundreds of medallions hanging around his tiny neck and chest had only spurred me on, wanting to show her how a real man treats a girl.

Arriving at my place, telling me her feet hurt from walking in her high heels, she takes them off holding them in her right hand, walking up the stairs in her bare feet to let the fluffy carpet soothe them. The joints we had now affecting our balance, we nearly fall over the last step, passing some hobo in a stupid Kermit the frog top outside another room, asking if he's alright, finally stumbling through my door and crashing into the wall. Not giving her any time to breathe, I push her hard up against the wall, turning on the light, looking into her eyes with lust as my lips, centimetres from hers, feel her breath inhaling and exhaling fast, her eyes fearful, exciting me more than they should.

Ordering her to my bed, I dim the lights telling her to stand in the middle of the room with her shoes back on, which she grimaces at but still does while I flick on the radio to hear Marvin's smooth voice. Sneaking up behind her, seductively peeling off her dress with my teeth, I nuzzle her neck, her tiny ears, her strong but small arms, her cute little butt and finally, divine legs, until she stands in nothing but a microscopic red G-string and heels. Scanning her body, my eyes are automatically drawn to her breasts of which I've never seen anything like before. Not even the girls in my videos have breasts as perfect as hers. Full, round, and pert, they seductively lure me in, my lips and tongue finding her budlike nipples which harden at my touch. Biting one of them hard, she gasps, taken by surprise and, commanding her to undress me, she hastily pulls off my shirt, quickly unzipping my trousers, pulling them down. Grabbing me between the legs and looking me straight in the eye, her raspy sexy voice asks.

"What do you want me to do, baby?"

Laying her on my bed, opening her legs wide, the glistening between them tells me she is more than ready, snapping off her G-string, ordering her to play with herself. Arching her eyebrow towards me, stroking herself with her fingers and licking her lips, she doesn't take her eyes off me, rubbing myself in perfect rhythm to her, crawling up the bed until I'm just above her mouth.

"Suck me."

Licking her lips, her mouth is warm and moist as I enter, opening her legs, feeling the wetness between them. I can't help myself. Bending down, licking and biting, I lap up her juices with my tongue and mouth as she sucks and moans, turning her so she is on all fours before me. Those breasts are bringing me close to climax. She is everything I thought she'd be and more, grabbing her hair with both hands, moving her head back and forth until I'm near. Suddenly withdrawing, pulling her head up so she is looking at me.

"Now it's your turn. Lay down and open your legs."

Doing as she's told, I lick her like an animal feasting on its prey, my mouth and tongue exploring, caressing her freshly shaved skin. Writhing under me, her fingertips play with her nipples and breasts as I lick, watching her play while my tongue and hands explore her body. Suddenly there is movement from down below, stopping what I'm doing, seeing four tiny white worms squirming around her butt as she moans, totally unaware what is happening below her. Our eyes meeting, she looks down, straight into mine like she knows. Should I tell her? Pretending to stroke her, gently removing the worms with my thumb, I quickly squash them between my fingers, resuming what I'm doing. Bringing her to climax with my tongue, wiping my mouth, I work my way up her body to her breasts, pulling her up towards me, ordering her to stand. Quickly swigging my leftover drink, which is still sitting on my bedside table from last night, I gargle, ordering her to turn around and bend forward until her arms rest on the bed in front. Grinning over her shoulder at me, I order to stop.

"Don't fucking look at me. Face forward."

Moving her head with my free hand, positioning myself right behind her as I quickly fasten my condom, I don't give her time to wait, ramming inside her with such force, it takes her only a second to orgasm again. I'm not finished. Grabbing her hair with my left hand, pulling in and out, I reach for my remote and switch on my video rewinding to where the two beauties on screen caress and undress each other. Kissing, rubbing, sucking each other, I'm close to climax myself, seeing her breasts through the television moving in time with the girls on screen.

"You fucking bitch."

Exploding inside her, she gasps as I pull her up to me, grabbing her right breast, throwing her on the bed as she lays breathing, covered in sweat and our juices. Throwing my condom across the room, collapsing on the bed next to her, I close my eyes, senses alert, listening to the noises around me.

Tingling, sweaty, the two women on screen continue to moan in ecstasy as a siren outside passes on its way to who knows where. A couple next door scream at each other as something hard suddenly hits the wall; the sound of crashing glass signalling something has been thrown against it. *Dire Straits*, my favourite band, comes on the radio, wiping sweat from my forehead with my hand, tilting my head towards her while I light a joint. Clutching her breast with both hands, her eyes are slits, eyeing the joint with lust.

"You filthy, dirty, slut."

Rubbing her breast, facing me, she looks straight at me with arched eyebrows.

"Fuck you, you barbarian."

The girls on screen continue to writhe in fake ecstasy as we pass a joint backwards and forwards, watching.

"You know that stuff isn't real, don't you? They're probably not even into girls. Men are such morons."

Smiling, raising both eyebrows in question, twenty minutes later, I'm escorting her to the door, giving her a hoodie to cover herself with.

"Keep it to remember this night. So, what's your name?"

Waiting for her to respond, the homeless guy in the Kermit the Frog vest stares, smiling at the both of us as she throws the hoodie back at me and walks slowly to the stairs. Nodding to him like she knows him, she pulls her dress down and turns, smiling at me, winking, her raspy voice echoes through the house.

"I'm still hot, thanks. It's Angie. See you around."

... Angie. She was by far the best fuck I've had, but I wouldn't be going back there any time soon.

Swishing my drink around my mouth, cleaning my teeth with my tongue and finger, watching as she makes her move on the middle-aged man, he has no idea what he's in for. Using my fingernail as a toothpick, I will never forget my close encounter with her, a first and last for me.

'She Drives Me Crazy,' starts to play, and I have to laugh at the irony, watching her walk out the door with her escort, whose hand is wrapped tightly around her little waist. Turning and winking at me, blowing a kiss, she's still as gorgeous as ever.

"Filthy bitch."

Unloading the dishwasher, eyeing up a lot of the ladies as I do, I'm not surprised to recognise at least six of them, having successfully wooed them into my bed, including the blonde, who I see is still surrounded by her entourage of sad men. The women were all good, especially Angie and the blonde, but they were way too eager to please me and give in to whatever I wanted. From what I'd witnessed so far, nearly all the women in the joint were on their way to Alonesville, the desperation oozing out of them like a dog craving attention. The initial attraction had soon disappeared once I'd laid them. The blonde, though? I had wondered about her. Of all the women I'd had, she'd surprised me the most. She could have her pick of anyone, so why is she still alone? It's obvious with all the other women, but her? She's different from the rest, I just can't put my finger on why? Rearranging my balls again, searching for Jesse, I spot her.

"Alone no more, my pretty."

Still walking with her friend, waving at the DJ, who blows her a kiss, I'm suddenly jealous. I'll knock that on the head. The geek won't stand a chance when I've got her. Locking eyes with him, there's something about him I don't like, already deciding weeks ago we were not going to be friends. The stupid sequinned jacket he'd been wearing had been enough for me to know. Seeing my girl wave, smile at him like she cares. That will definitely stop. The geek won't dare look her way once I'm in control.

Following her with my eyes as she walks towards the bar, she stops at the other end, head down, waiting to order her drinks.

Willing her to look my way, her head lifts, and for a fraction of a second, she sees me, quickly looking away with cheeks that look like they've suddenly been kissed by the sun. Watching her make her way back to her friend with their drinks, she has to wade through the crowd of men, which has grown, busying herself in the background, tending to all of her friend's needs. This is a dream come true for me, keeping a close eye on her as she scans the joint oblivious of my interest towards her. Her friend suddenly slaps her hard across the face, screaming at her, mentally willing Jesse's eyes to seek mine.

"See me, see me, see me."

Pow.

As though she's heard me, her eyes suddenly dart towards mine, grabbing my chance, smiling, and winking at her, seeing confusion and panic as she blushes and looks over her shoulder to see if I'm looking at anyone else. Pleading, wanting her to stay with me, I need her to look back at me.

"Come on, come on!"

Bam.

With a flick of my head, I invite her over, not taking my eyes off her as she nervously interrupts her friend to tell her she's leaving. Shouting into her face, her friend is obviously not happy to be distracted from what she's doing. Cowering, Jesse slowly makes her way through the men, head down until she finally arrives at the bar, where I eagerly await.

Sashaying to her, asking her name with my most seductive smile, I quickly ask what she wants to drink, seeing she's unable to look me in the eye. I need her to know it's her I want and not any other woman, especially her friend. She's so desperate to be loved, so awkward, unconfident, unused to attention. I want her.

Rubbing her left wrist, there's a faint outline of some letters. M. a. X. It can't be. Shivering, seeking my tattoo, scratching my arm, her eyes suddenly dart to it, looking down to her wrist in shock. This must be Maxine's way of telling me she approves. Of course. Busying myself with making her drinks, my eyes flick backwards and forward to her wrist, which I can't stop seeing. Placing the drinks on the bar counter, covering her hand with mine to stop her from rubbing, she looks around at her friend, taking her chin in my hand and lifting her head so I can look into her eyes. She's already mine.

"Don't look away, then I won't see those beautiful eyes. What's your name?"

Cheeks on fire, she tells me her name is Jesse, but I don't let on that I already know.

Successfully hooked in, I tell her my name but just to call me J, her blushing again, unable to keep eye contact. Placing a napkin in her hand with my number, she will call me, of that I'm pretty confident.

"See you around," she says.

She'll see me more than she knows.

Grabbing her drinks, in the blink of an eye she is gone.

Following her, watching her make her way in and out of lines of people, nearly knocking into a woman who suddenly steps back into her path, drunk and wearing a huge pair of glittery glasses. Her bright-pink curly wig jiggling about, a bright-yellow feather boa strapped around her shoulders nearly falls as she laughs, dancing in front of Jesse, who's smiling nervously, trying to step away as she tries to not spill any of her drinks. Suddenly stopping and looking my way, she smiles because she's seen the little heart I cut into her drink. I knew she'd like that. The blonde isn't happy, watching, waiting for her to arrive. Hands on her hips, standing over her, screaming into her face, a finger pointing straight at me, she's not happy with the exchange that has just taken place, ripping the napkin from Jesse's hand, reading it. My eagle eyes continue to focus on the exchange as I serve another customer, the blonde's face contorting into all kinds of shapes. She is far from pretty when she screams. Spitting, the droplets spray everyone around her, and men start to disperse, looking at each other, nodding in agreement, slipping into the background before she quickly picks up her coat and storms out of the club. People all around them watch, some with hands to their faces laughing, pointing, mocking them both and my poor baby just stands with the drinks in her hand, confused, alone, pathetic. Rubbing my hands together, I'm delighted. The fun I'm going to have with these two. Wait. Someone is waving.

Out of nowhere, a tall, good-looking man with dimples smiles at her. Who is he? Looking up at him, gushing, Jesse is putty in his hands. They know each other? This is not good, not good at all. Flicking my head to the door, the blonde is still there, watching them, too. Without warning, dagger-like eyes dart to mine, slicing through me like sharpened machetes. Over the noise I can just lip read what she mouths to me before storming out.

"You bastard."

Who are you, my pampered princess? Who the fuck are you?

Part Two

Chapter Sixteen
Zoe

"Boys think girls are like books. If the cover doesn't catch their eye they won't bother to read what's inside."

— Marilyn Monroe

I was blessed with extraordinary beauty. I don't know why? I knew from as early as four years old how different I was. For some reason people turned to jelly when they spoke to me, something that didn't happen to other girls. As I grew, I listened to my 'so-called' friends and their mothers make excuse after excuse to stop being around me.

"Sorry, Katie has dance class."
"Stacie can't come over today. I'm cutting her hair."
"Michaela would love to come play, but she has to go see her grandma."
"Tina has to finish her project, otherwise she'd love to come over."

And so on and so on. I didn't notice the loneliness so much when

I was little, my parents usually distracting me with fun things being that I was an only child. It wasn't until I finally started school that I realised just how different I was. Mothers didn't invite me to play with their daughters, possibly afraid I'd show their daughter's up, or, I guess, it made themselves feel better if they made stuff up that wasn't true. It didn't take long for me to see their judging eyes mimic what my alleged friends felt. I knew the truth. I was only ten years old.

As I matured, men, in particular, didn't have a problem with how I looked. I was able to use my looks to get everything I wanted. I bloody deserved it after having their eyes leer at me for what seemed like forever. I knew I was different and liked the feeling of superiority over other girls; even extending to my mother, who, I knew tolerated me, but who also treated me differently around people. I think she secretly loved having a daughter nobody could compete with. She, however, didn't love having a daughter she felt in competition with. I knew how she felt. I saw it in her eyes whenever she brushed my long, thick, wavy blonde hair, complaining the ends looked like rat's tails. She'd say my hazel, almond shaped eyes were too dark, and my face would be better if it wasn't a perfect oval. She said it would show off my bone structure more if it was a different shape, like hers.

She was so transparent.

She told me my eyelashes were too thick, and that the genetic mutation I was born with wasn't lucky at all. Unlike most people with one set of eyelashes, I was born with two which made my lashes appear as if they'd been coated in lashings of mascara. I'd always thought that was quite a lucky mutation to have.

My straight white teeth looked too false, as did my full round lips, and my personal favourite, "*a few freckles would make you a bit more interesting to look at, don't you think? Nobody really wants olive skin, Zoe. Pale skin is so much more alluring.*"

She picked on everything, even my height, which she knew I was particularly sensitive about.

"*It might be difficult for you to find a man taller than you. At least if you were petite, then you could wear high heels. Such a shame, darling, you'll have to wear flat shoes forever."*

Everything was the absolute opposite of her, and she hated it. She said I was too perfect and that everyone should have at least one outward flaw. I couldn't figure out why I was so different from both my parents.

My mother told me I lured everything in my path to me like Medusa, only nobody turned to stone. When I'd looked Medusa up in the school library I'd thought the comparison disgusting, cruel, but then cruel was my mother's middle name. No one knew how vicious she was behind closed doors, except me and my dad. She showed just how much of a bitch she was on my sixteenth birthday when she announced I was adopted.

I've never forgiven her.

I knew I was born beautiful, but understanding why still baffled me. Nobody was just born that way? Look at Marilyn Monroe, Elizabeth Taylor, Grace Kelly, Brooke Shields? They'd all paid for the way they looked. I especially empathised with Brooke, being shoved in front of the camera at a young age by a pushy mother. There had to be something I was missing, a reason I was one of the chosen. In the meantime, I'd decided beauty wasn't all it was cracked up to be. Everyone focused on what I looked like and no one, not even my mother, really cared what lay beneath.

We'd be walking to an appointment or just shopping, and she'd spot a photographer on the street and make us walk just close enough so she could shove me in front of them. She'd conveniently make it look like an accident. I'd apologise, they'd look at me and straight away ask to take some photographs, and then she'd end up with their cards for modelling work, blah, blah, blah. I didn't want to be a model. My dream was to become a vet, but she soon put a stop to that.

"Why do you want to waste so much time studying when you could so easily make money in front of a camera? You know it loves

you. The world loves you and your face, Zoe. Such easy money to make. Don't waste your time thinking anyone wants your brains."

So, I gave up on my dream and listened to her. I knew she was right. No one really gave a crap what I wanted to do except Jesse, my best friend, but she didn't really count. I focused on what would make me the big bucks, hid my real self from the world and gave everyone what they wanted. A pretty girl with no brains. No one wanted inner beauty, especially mine. The more beautiful you were on the outside, the more you got, plain and simple.

From my experience, men and boys didn't queue up round the block to find girls with inner beauty. They quickly ran past the perfectly ordinary ones and almost always made a beeline for the beautiful girls they could show off to other men and boys. They wanted their trophies, the girls on their arms to say, 'look what I scored.' They wanted the girls who'd have them eating out of their hands and acting like fools just to be near. Girls like me. If you were beautiful, you certainly had the world at your fingertips, but, as I read and so often saw, it came at a price. If, for one second, you stopped looking perfect, or God help you, started making decisions or having opinions of your own, then there were a hundred other girls queuing up around the block willing to step in to take your place. I, fortunately, was unlike other girls and knew it. I was exceptionally beautiful, up there with Elizabeth Taylor who shared my eyelash mutation, and Brooke, who shared a forceful mother, and that gave me the upper hand. Males couldn't get enough of me.

Even my own father took pleasure in showing me off to his friends who, more often than not, surprised me when they'd compliment me on my clothes choice or jewellery. His friends weren't predatory, more fun than anything, but every so often the odd one would look at me with devouring eyes I didn't trust. I found older men's attention especially creepy because I always knew what they were thinking. It made me feel like meat on a plate, an object of desire to people who shouldn't have looked at me with anything other than protective, paternal, pure eyes. Even the wives of the men didn't want me near them, jealous of the attention taken away from them. They knew they didn't stand a chance. Their husbands were so far away from what I really wanted. If only they knew. If only anyone knew.

I was constantly lonely. It got worse when my best friend Jesse, disappeared. She was the only person who'd ever treated me next to normal. I knew I was horrible to her over the years, and I'd often wondered whether this was part of the reason why she suddenly left. A freak I'd protected from bullies who would've hunted her down in and outside of school, our friendship had definitely been tested at least a hundred times over, even coming close to calling it a day with her. But, for some reason I decided to keep her around. She was the only person who ever showed me any kind of normal, any kind of love. I had to pay her back.

When she disappeared, I had panic attack after panic attack. I couldn't explain why. I had everything I could've possibly wanted in life, so why I gave so much thought to her leaving made me feel pathetic. When she suddenly left it felt like something was missing, like a part of myself was gone. I gave up finding anyone who would love me the same way. The other girls at school weren't the same. I'd never find anyone else like Jesse. She hadn't cared one little bit about my looks, had loved me for nothing but myself.

I thought there was no chance anyone would ever feel that way towards me again, especially as I was getting prettier. My introduction to the world hadn't helped. My bitch mother had rather enjoyed telling me, remembering the look on her face when I'd fallen to the floor, hyperventilating after finding out my real mother had abandoned me at hospital.

It sent me down a spiral I still couldn't get off...

Chapter Seventeen

"A birth mother always puts the needs of her child above the wants of her heart."

— Skye Hardwick

Gail. Zoe's birth mother—age sixteen

Pregnant, I settled that life was already complicated enough without becoming a mother. The fact I'd decided to have the baby was a miracle. I'd always known I wasn't going to keep it after the birth, I just hadn't got around to finding anyone who might want it. Living on the streets hadn't helped, and the prick who'd got me up the duff had run for the hills when I'd told him. I really thought he'd stick around. I really thought he loved me.

The contractions that started in the cubicle of the train station toilet were more painful than anything I could've imagined. The nagging pains were more like a dull period, and I didn't for one second think I was actually having the baby. The pain became more and more intense, and the next thing I knew, I was wet, and there was a gooey liquid in my pants. When I saw blood, I panicked. The pain was unbearable. I felt something hard, down there, coming out of me, like I was being ripped apart. If it weren't for the Angel Lady, my baby would've been left, wrapped up in a coat on the floor for someone to find, and the other unexpected one? She might not have even made it. Instead, the lovely Angel Lady somehow managed to keep me calm and helped me during the birth, even cleaning up the mess and waiting for people to help so I could be taken to the hospital to have the second one. She left with my first baby before I realised what I'd asked her to do. A decision I'd regret till the day I died.

Forty minutes later, confused, and exhausted after an exceptionally fast labour, my second baby came unexpectedly into the world. Pushing the placenta out was easier than the first. At least I knew it was coming. I'd never heard of anything like that happening before. I was told I was lucky the second baby was even born alive, and that five minutes longer, it may have been a different story. A tiny 4lb, no-one but me, the Angel Lady and her evil looking son, knew about the first baby.

I wonder how much the first one had weighed. Was she bigger, stronger than the baby I stared at now?

Perfect in every way, her first few days in the incubator assured her a fighting chance of survival. It also allowed me to hold her for a few minutes every day. I was so thankful she was safe. She looked like her father, the dark eyes already starting to develop. She was so utterly beautiful. Her tiny eyelashes were so thick and curly, anyone would've sworn she'd been born with mascara on. Every time I fed her, her perfect oval face smiled up at me and her tiny fingers held tightly on to mine. How was I going to let her go, too?

Four days after she was born, standing over her in the neonatal ward, tightly wrapped up in her pink blanket, I readjusted the tubes coming out of her nose and arms to make sure she was comfortable; gave her one last long kiss, and slipped out of the hospital for a smoke break, disappearing into nowhere.

My heart broke for a second time.

Abandoned, the media tried in vain to reunite mother and daughter, but it was no use. I couldn't come forward, and as far as I know, no one passed on any information about where I might be found. My baby, who they named Zoe after the midwife's mother, was now just another statistic for the state to deal with. I loved her so much, but knew I couldn't look after her the way she needed. The only thing I left her was a note.

Please take good care of her. A x

Affixed to the note was a silver crucifix. If you looked through the tiny centre, you could see the Lord's Prayer...

Chapter Eighteen
Louise

"O, beware, my lord, of
jealousy! It is the green-eyed
monster which doth mock
the meat it feeds on."

— William Shakespeare

Paraparaumu, a place close to the beach and a highly sought-after area to live just outside Porirua, North Island, New Zealand, was beautiful, picturesque, and blessed with the most magnificent views across the bay from the hills. At the top of one of those hills lived a couple who'd always dreamed of having a child of their own. Little did they know their dream was going to come true, and it was going to change their lives forever...

September 10th 1976

After three attempted IVF treatments failed, we are done with trying. Our hearts just can't bear another loss, and if we're honest, our marriage is close to coming to an end because of it. Accepting we'll never have any offspring of our own, we set about registering with the best adoption agency money can buy. Only on the books for six months, we are asked to be parents to the abandoned child on the news. Us? It has to be a dream.

But it isn't a dream. Attending meeting after meeting, we are finally allowed to bring her home after passing all the checks, deciding to keep the name they've given her because it was one of the names on a list we'd written years before if we'd ever had a girl of our own.

Two months old, welcoming Zoe into our home with loving arms, we dote on her from day one; every available space is adorned with photos of our beautiful girl.

As she grows, it becomes evident we've adopted a child unlike any other.

Stopped by random people whenever we go out, we quickly become aware that the child we've adopted is a force to be reckoned with.

"What an utterly glorious little girl you have there, she should be a model with those looks."
"Look at those eyes and face?"
"If I had a child as beautiful as her, I wouldn't take my eyes off her."
"Wow, lucky things. That girl will be famous one day."
"Where does she get her looks from?"

That was the hardest to hear.

Hating to admit she looks nothing like either of us, her blonde hair and dark hazel eyes are the complete opposite to mine and my husband, Alan's, brown hair, and blue eyes. Both of us, a little on the tubby side, look nothing like Zoe, whose legs keep growing all the way up to her neck. On and on and on it goes until I can no longer bear any more.

Realising the attention Zoe receives is unlike any other little girls her age, I implore Alan to help, but he seems oblivious to it, transfixed, almost bewitched by her too, which, in time makes me feel resentful of the attention she receives. I'm used to being the centre of his world, his number one. Bitter at not only being demoted to number two, I also have to share his love, now. He used to call me beautiful, but that stopped almost the minute Zoe came into our lives. My heart ever so slowly starts to harden towards the child I always thought I wanted.

Avoiding people, deciding to keep her at home for the first five years, I admit, I am jealous of her. No-one knows what it's like to parent a child so unearthly. Other people's children are so plain in comparison, and as each day leads on to the next, I begin to feel as plain as all the rest.

Unaware, or so I think, of all the attention she receives, Zoe still manages to thrive in Paraparaumu's unspoiled expanses of grassland and beaches. They become her playground and she has what others would describe an idyllic life, especially as the start of it had been so hectic. The first five years are the best we have, and although I would hide her from the world forever, Alan puts his foot down insisting she goes to school to learn to socialise with other children.

Hours are spent worrying how I'm going to tell her; sure I can teach her all she needs to know, but both Alan and I know there is one thing I can't do. I can't give her a playmate. After discussing adopting another child, we agree Zoe is more than we can handle, and decide against it. She needs to be with things other than insects, fish, and birds, enrolling her in a primary school twenty minutes by car from our home.

Quaint, Manor School is perfect for her, and as she is only one of twenty children in her class, we're sure it won't overwhelm her too much. If I'm honest, I'm quite excited for what lays ahead, not only for her, but for me, too. I'm sick of how Alan pours all his attention on her. I was here before her so why should I feel inferior to a child that isn't even mine by blood? I'm glad to see the back of her for a few hours, and it gives me much needed space to focus on myself and my relationship that is on a downward spiral. It's Zoe's fault. Before her, Alan and I were perfect.

Only at school for five minutes, one day the teacher takes me aside at the end of the day explaining that making friends is proving difficult for Zoe. I make it clear she isn't used to socialising with other children, or sharing attention, or toys. I hate to admit, but I know exactly how her peers feel. From what I hear, the girls think she is spoiled and selfish, and the boys, even at the tender age of five, already feel intimidated by her beauty. Teachers on the other hand love her and are easily wrapped around her little finger. She has the power to do that to most adults, even me for a time. Very soon she becomes every teachers' pet which only adds to the other children's disdain.

It's the beginning of the end for me. Once she starts school, our relationship is never the same.

Chapter Nineteen
Zoe

"The hardest thing about "everything happens for a reason" is waiting for the reason to come along."

— Unknown

I hated my mother for sending me to school. My father, even though he was the one to push it, knew how I felt back then. But his reasons for sending me, I think, were more from the heart than my mother's. She couldn't bloody wait to throw me into the lion's den. She hated the attention I got, but I didn't really start to notice how bitter she was until I started middle school. Before that, I was just a little girl having fun with other kids my age.

The way I see it, is, when you're growing up everyone is equal. Your parents take you off to pre-school playgroups or the park to play with other children, and there is no competition, there are no threats. You just get on and play. I didn't have any of that in my early years so, all of a sudden, I had to get used to sharing, being sympathetic to others' feelings, and making friends. I was different, not just by the way I looked, but by the way teachers and parents treated me. I can't remember any of the girls at school really liking me, except one. She made school bearable, even though she was crazy. I knew from the very first day I started how easy it would be to make her do what I wanted. Singled out often for being socially awkward, I followed suit with my classmates and targeted her frequently. One Wednesday morning, something changed...

Wednesday August 12 1981

Ambushing her in the reading corner, I and some of the other children take turns slapping her hard across the face, others poking her with their paint brushes while the teacher is otherwise engaged dealing with Gregory, the troublemaker of the class causing merry hell outside. He hates it when we gang up on her and never wants to join in. He's just as much an outcast, but for some reason we leave him alone. The girl is a much easier target.

"Leave me alone."

"Cry-baby, cry-baby, Ronstink, Ronstink."

Watching her cry, we circle her, backing her into a corner like a fox waiting to be slaughtered by a pack of dogs. We may as well pull her apart physically. It might be easier for her to bear. The mental torture she sustains is far worse. When you're young you either decide to go with the crowd, or you don't. She, unfortunately, hasn't had the choice of either. I don't think she likes the attention; attention likes her. She oozes someone who is so desperately unloved, that you either feel sorry for her, or you join the crowd and bully her.

Surrounded, trying in vain to stop the jeering and poking, her arms flinch every time a paint brush touches her. Her cheeks, after all the slapping, look like they've been burnt.

I don't know what it is, but something inside me snaps. All of a sudden, I am ridden with tremendous guilt because I know what I'm doing is bad. Dropping my paintbrush, ordering the others to leave her alone and go away, everyone does as they are told. They know I have the power to make the class turn on them if they don't.

Alone with her, comforting her, telling her I'm sorry, she smiles and stops crying, extending her hand to mine. I still don't know why I do what I do next.

Whack.

Without warning, I hit her hard across the face; she backs away, eyes wide, tears flowing down her face. I'm immediately pulling her back close to me, laying a protective arm around her shoulder and rocking her back and forth.

"Shhh, don't cry, my baby. I'll look after you."

Holding her face in my hands, she smiles again as I wipe her tears and stroke her red cheeks.

Smack.

This time she pounces and I back away in fear. Something instinctively tells me not to risk any more. There's a darkness behind her eyes I don't like. Suddenly I'm very scared for my safety, trying to reassure her it won't happen again, noticing several scars on her arms and legs, like she's been whipped or burnt. She keeps rubbing her left wrist, which I can see has letters on it. Grabbing it, holding it tight, the letters M. a. X look to have been etched or scratched onto her skin with something sharp; for a split second my eyes question hers, sure she knows what I'm thinking because she yanks it away. What do the letters mean? I don't have time to ask because something little and black jumps off her head onto my arm, squashing it between my fingers, staring hard at her hair. I think I'm seeing things, leaning in close, seeing little white globs of glue stuck to her hair, and more tiny black bugs are laying on her neck where she's scratching uncontrollably, like a cat that has fleas. A cat with fleas probably smells better. Retreating, hand firmly under my nose, I go and inform the teacher, ashamed of my behaviour, unsure why I've been so cruel. Overcome with a sense of protection towards her, I vow never to physically hurt her again...

. . .

Taking her under my wing, the girl, Jesse, is spared any more teasing from myself or the other classmates, turning our attention on the other troublemaker of the class. She is so grateful to me for stopping her torment. She doesn't get off Scot-free though. I make damn sure she does as she's told, and as our friendship flourishes, I'm able to encourage her to do things I know she shouldn't. Like stealing from shops and classmates' bags when they aren't looking. I tell her to make fun of teachers, especially the ugly ones. No-one is left guessing who's in charge.

I have to admit, I love the control. I love using her like a puppet knowing I have the power to manipulate her any which way I can. She'd do anything to stay friends with me, by now the most popular girl in school.

Our friendship continues into middle school, and then secondary school. My control over Jesse increases so much so, I can now tell her to do almost anything I wish, and boy does she jump. One English teacher, Mrs Glennis, is targeted more than others.

Not much to look at, I guess her parents looked at her at birth and slapped her. I know I would've if it was me.

Unblessed with the most unappealing features I've ever seen on anyone, I've never seen a nose like it. Fat and round, like a pigs, the tiny slits for nostrils point up towards the sky which makes her unusually large front teeth pull upwards, which in turn, makes her look like a cross between a gopher and a pig. Her slanted, small, brown eyes permanently squint, drooping down towards a thin mouth bent at the corners that makes her look forever sad. Big, thick, unshaped eyebrows and short eyelashes do nothing but enhance the infortunes of her features. You couldn't think it gets worse, but it does. Her round face, covered in pock marks, still has scars visible through her badly applied makeup which assures she is always at the top of the list for teasing wherever she works. As if her luck wasn't already bad enough, her wavy, out of control, dark, straw-like hair and thick body from the waist down, make her a bully's dream. Tiny breasts don't help her out-of-proportion five-foot two-inch frame any better, as do her cankles, which are quite impressive for someone only in their early thirties. Not overweight, her thick calves give the impression she is. No self-esteem at all, you can tell just by the way she dresses how she feels. It confirms to the world just what the world thinks.

Every day an oversized jumper, quite often adorned with stray hairs from herself and her cats, give off the impression that she is dirty and unkempt; her skirts repeatedly showing remnants of whatever she's eaten the night before, sometimes wearing the same one to school the whole week. Ugly, dirty, brown sheepskin boots, which she never deviates from until summer, and that is only because the temperature goes above twenty-five degrees, never come off her feet. When it becomes too hot, only then will she even contemplate wearing other shoes, fearful the comments about her cankles, which she hates more than her nose, become too much. It doesn't help that she chooses the ugliest shoes she can find. Red Jesus sandals, as wide as a river, show off feet that are fat, hairy, and ugly. She has absolutely nothing going for her, and the girls, especially the pretty ones like me, target her every given chance we get.

When Mrs Glennis walks past our classroom, Jesse barks at her like a dog howling to the moon, or if she feels especially cruel, snorts like a pig snuffling for food; a particular favourite of the class. All I have to do is nod my head to her and she commences the bullying while others laugh and join in on the fun desperate for my attention. Mrs Glennis walks past, head down, used to the torment.

Sometimes I even feel sorry for her.

Ms Kaley, my favourite teacher, is in contrast the complete opposite to Mrs Glennis. Anyone would think we're being taught by a rock n roll star. Her slick, black, leather jacket and all sorts of trendy garments, quite often made by herself, forever inspire us to channel our inner creativity. Long, black, wavy hair, usually tied in a ponytail high on her head, accentuates her gorgeous bone structure and unusually piercing blue eyes which never deviate from the black pencil drawn around them. Shaped, arched eyebrows, angular nose with green nose stud and full red lips have us all believing she is fifteen years younger than she actually is. The most remarkable thing, however, is her penchant for wearing a different pair of earrings every day. Competing with each other every day, guessing which colour or length they will be from one day to the next, none of us ever gets it right.

Head of Sewing, Ms Kaley is the only teacher who makes school sufferable. Her bright gentle way and calming approach to teaching make the effort of getting up in the morning worthwhile. That, and the fact she is quite the rebel, always telling us stories of her youth and what she got up to, she is more like a mentor than a teacher. She is someone my classmates and I look up to and aspire to be like. Gutsy, talented, assertive, and gorgeous, I admire everything about her, even when she's telling me off, which is rare. I can't find it in my heart to mock her for anything she does. We make all sorts of different garments in her class, and as it happens, this term we're making our own Rara skirts because we loved the eighties fashion. Challenging, fun and fair, Ms Kaley is the only teacher protected from mine and the others jeering. It seems everyone has a soft spot for her, even Mrs Glennis, who, I see, spends many afternoons in her room, probably asking for advice on how to deal with all of us. My intuition proves right when Ms Kaley takes me aside one day in class and kindly asks me to tell the others to stop teasing, explaining the hurt it is causing Mrs Glennis is too great. She knows I'm able to manipulate my fellow students into doing whatever I want, so dutifully instructing all teasing to stop, I only do it because Ms Kaley has asked. If Ms Kaley ever leaves though, all teasing will most definitely commence but, in the meantime, Mrs Glennis will be left alone. There is such a turnaround in our behaviour towards her that instead of teasing her, we try our best to find ways to improve the way she looks, stopping to give her fashion tips which she laps up like a puppy. I end up leaving school as her friend, something I could never have imagined.

The power I have over people, especially Jesse, grows. Able to mould and shape her more than others because no one, except me, wants to be her friend, the control over her increases to the point where I dominate her on every level. There is some sort of connection between us, a bond I can't explain, which bugs me. I don't know what it is about the freak that keeps me interested? All the other girls hate her and ask me so many times why I hang around with such a loser. I'm always protective of her because I understand a lot about her life that they don't, and I sort of feel sorry for what she has to endure daily. My own protective, overbearing parents love me to the moon and back and are pains in my butt more often than not, but even they are nothing compared to Jesse's mother, who, I'm certain, has been resurrected straight from hell itself. I only met her once, but that was more than enough to last for a lifetime...

Friday April 13th 1991—Age 15

Out of the blue, one Friday after school, we're walking towards the bus stop when Jesse stops, takes me by the hand, looks straight into my eyes and bounces from side to side, like she has something stuck in her shoe. Looking around to check if anyone is watching, she grasps both my hands, her lips trembling like she's going to cry; I'm worried what the hell she is going to say thinking I've done something wrong. Holding my breath, waiting for her to speak, her concerned eyes speak before she does.

"D-d-d-do you want to come over to my house for a bit today?"

Not believing what I've just heard, I'm unable to speak, quickly unclasping my now sweaty hands from hers.

"*What?* You actually want me to come over? You've never asked me before. Why today? Is there something special going on?"

The hundreds of times I've asked to visit before. She'd always told me that hell would freeze over before she let that happen. Jumping at the chance to finally be going, I accept without hesitation, curious to see whether the hellhole she's described living in is real or if she's making it up.

It's a decision I very soon come to regret.

Thirty minutes later, after an uncomfortable bus journey crammed like sardines in a can, I've had enough of listening to three old women talking about their stubborn bodily functions. Pressing the buzzer, waiting for the bus to stop, I glare at them, stepping off into some welcome fresh air, breathing in hard, fanning myself as the sweat drips off my brows. My hand, feeling cool on my forehead, wipes the sweat off, quickly removing my heavy woollen school blazer, pissed off I didn't take it off sooner. God knows why we have to wear it, even in the summer. Jesse does the same, folding it over her arm and, following her lead, I trudge towards her house. Spying her fidgeting with her hair and strap of her school bag, I'm guessing she's nervous, or her enthusiasm for the visit has started to wane. I'm sure she's going to change her mind. I am not going to let that happen, quickly talking about the old women on the bus in the hope it will distract her from her thoughts. The excruciating small talk about nothing is torture; questioning Jesse's verbal diarrhoea more than once, still not entirely sure what she's even talking about. I admit, my own nerves are starting to get the better of me too, upping the pace so I can't change my mind either.

The beautiful tree-lined street she lives down is gorgeous, full of evergreens and Pohutukawa's, the complete opposite of where I'd imagined she'd live. Boys pass us in school uniforms emblazoned with St Andrew's College, whistling at me from all directions while Jesse walks with her head down, uninterested in any of the attention. She's never once told me she lives across the road from a boy's school; I'm feeling a little more than shitty with her for not telling me. I can guess why she hasn't. She knows I'd want to come to hers more often, and she'd be right. Thirty seconds later, abruptly stopped from watching cute boys, my heart remembers why I'm nervous.

Standing outside a light-pink brick bungalow, looking at a tattered wooden fence's arthritic limbs screaming for relief, the wood is bent and curved which gives it no protection whatsoever from the outside world, or the forest of weeds which fight each other for space. Wrapping around the deformed panels, strangling them with their twines, the thorns try to warn me not to enter, but I don't take any notice.

I'm nervous and nauseous at the same time.

Questioning whether I really want to go into the weather-worn house, it's covered in different shades of green moss growing up the sides, like grass, patchy in places where it's especially damp. A long, green, thin patch, resembling a finger, points at me, swearing I see it curling right in front of my eyes, luring me in like it wants to hypnotise me. The outside has already terrified me enough. How am I going to go in? Turning to Jesse, her look of dread is something I, for once, agree with.

"When did you move here again?"

Smiling nervously, she answers me quietly.

"We had to move here about five years ago when my mother couldn't walk up the stairs anymore."

Nodding, scared stiff of what I've let myself in for, my head flicks, telling her to go, following her, noticing all the other perfectly groomed gardens on either side of her house. They make Jesse's house look unkempt and dangerous, contemplating whether I should run while I have the chance. Before I can answer myself, out of the forest comes the most beautiful silver cat, squeaking with a high-pitched meow. Frantic and happy to see us, it starts hissing at me like I'm some kind of demon and I forget about the house for a second, bending down to give it a pat. Snarling and hissing, thinking this can't be the cat I've heard so much about, maybe it's trying to warn me not to go in?

"Samantha. Hello, baby. Have you missed me?"

Picking her up and hugging her close, Jesse kisses her cheek and rubs noses with her, the meowing deafening as they greet each other. Holding her as she walks up the path to the door, Jesse places Samantha on the ground, shooing her off while she fumbles for her keys in her now hairy blazer pocket which is still draped over her arm. Keys in hand, rattling, her eyes stare fixed at my face as she shakes, inserting the key.

"I don't know what I was thinking. You can leave now if you want."

Half of me wants to run for the hills, the other half is desperate to go in, head and heart fighting, locking wide eyes with hers, not blinking while she waits for an answer. Throat dry, tongue stuck to the roof of my mouth, I'm hoping my face isn't betraying how I feel, squeezing out a half-hearted high-pitched squeak I don't recognise, sure Jesse knows I'm bluffing. She doesn't say a word.

"Don't be silly. Of course I don't want to leave."

"Don't say I didn't warn you."

Chapter Twenty

The smell hits me first. A cross between urine, cigarettes, peanuts, vinegar, and damp, it sort've reminds me of what an old person's home might smell like, but a thousand times stronger. It's not exactly inviting me in. In fact it's doing the exact opposite. Maybe it's trying to warn me off, like the outside just did, but I'm not interested. I have to see this hellhole for myself.

The mould growing outside the house has spread inside, crawling up the walls to the ceiling, the black fuzz caving in around me suffocatingly. Shivering, the goosepimples take turns showing off as I cough involuntarily; my hand staying underneath my nose as I look around blindly until my eyes adjust to the darkness. Old-fashioned, musty, and dark, pictures of Our Lady and Jesus stare at me from all angles, covered in dust. Thin yellow nicotine tears fall from each of their eyes and hands making them look more creepy than godly.

Escorting me into the lounge, Jesse points to a chair.

"Sit down, make yourself comfy. I've just got a few things to do."

Left on my own, I don't feel comfy at all. My senses are telling me to run, but I can't. Eyes feasting on my surroundings, I see furniture I'm sure is meant for the garden resting along two walls, the sun-damaged fabric covered in yellow sunflowers clashing badly with the gold crushed-velvet curtains half drawn across windows, opaque with black smudge. Sliding a finger across the glass, half tempted to write 'clean me' in capital letters on the filthy pane, I decide against it, worried the walls might have eyes. I feel so awkward, so scared, and don't know why? It's like I've been suddenly teleported back to the seventies, everything dust ridden over years of misuse. Catching Jesse through the filthy glass, she's outside and looks to be emptying a bucket into the bushes underneath another window. What on earth is she emptying?

Dodging behind the curtain, quickly turning, scared she's seen me, my eyes are drawn to a huge, rectangular, gold mirror sitting above the fireplace. Walking up to it, it looks out of place, standing on tippy toes to see myself through the filthy glass. Who the hell puts a mirror so high up on a wall that you can't see yourself through it?

Feeling for my chewing gum in my shirt pocket, I automatically place the packet between my front and bottom teeth, manoeuvring two pieces of spearmint spheres onto my tongue, all the while looking around, chewing, welcoming the minty freshness into my mouth. Where is Jesse, and why is she taking so long? Tapping my right foot to imaginary music, an ancient television and video recorder with dozens of tapes underneath without labels, or names, are piled on top of each other like Jenga bricks ready to fall. What's the point in having videos without labels? The wallpaper, yellow with white stripes and yellow garish flowers, also drips with dark-yellow tears.

Hearing voices in the next room, wondering what's going on, I think I hear Jesse speaking to her mother? Fanning myself with my hand, scared stiff of meeting her, I question whether I should just go?

"C'mon, Jesse. Before I change my bloody mind."

Feeling like I'm standing in a room full of people all staring at me, they're pointing with their hands all over me. I don't like it. Something, maybe an intuition, wants me to go. It's beginning to feel creepy, lowering my head to breathe, making myself concentrate on anything other than what I'm thinking. Staring at even more flowers, this time they are multi-coloured, like I'm standing in a field, only the field is drowning in oil, black and gooey underneath my feet.

"Good God."

It's like nothing I've ever seen before.

"What about God?"

Snapping my head up, nearly peeing myself, Jesse's mother stands in a see-through nightie with three rats of different colours sitting on her shoulders.

"What about God? Are you taking the Lord's name in vain in my house?"

Terrified; black icy eyes stare at me, waiting for an answer.

Mute, it takes my brain seconds to connect to my mouth, focusing on the rats and her mother's huge body. Jesse's grimacing at me from her mother's side.

"No. I-I-I was just saying what lovely pictures of God you have?"

Eyes wide, not blinking, my knees and legs are shaking like jelly, waiting in fear to see what her response will be. Even the rats have stopped, staring at me like they are in cahoots with her. What kind of freak show am I in?

Stepping towards me with eyes that stare right through me, her creepy clown grin is terrifying thinking she's going to hurt me as I raise my hand, instinctively flinching, like I'm going to be hit. Stopping right in front of me, stroking her pets one by one, all I do is stare.

"This is Fidget, Roly, and Ben. My babies. Do you want to hold one?"

Taking one off her shoulder, holding it out to me, I don't know what to do. Jesse stands next to her, not helping in any way. She knows how much I hate rats and mice. I hate her so much at the moment.

Closing my eyes, hoping I'm just having a bad dream, reopening them, my nightmare is still very real as eyes as black as the rats on her shoulders remain staring, waiting for me to take the creature from her hand. Stuck to the floor like I have super glue on the bottom of my shoes, the silence is deafening as our three sets of eyes darts backwards and forwards to each other; mine settling on the rat in her mother's hand, which she puts back on her shoulders and lets nibble her neck.

"N-n-n-no thanks. I'm alright."

Looking to Jesse, pleading for her to intervene, she just stands with the same awkward smile on her face as her mother's.

"Come to my bedroom, meet the others."

Meet the others? Panic. What does she mean? Jesse's eyes are widened in horror and I know straight away that whatever her mother has just said is something she isn't expecting. Ungluing my feet from the carpet, legs that feel like lead follow, trying to look anywhere but through her mother's nightie to the blobs of flesh that lead the way to the dark, unwelcoming room ahead.

Stinking worse than anything I've ever smelt in my life, the urine smell is so strong, it's making my eyes water and burn, like they're on fire. Arm over my nose, blinking a thousand times, not believing what I'm seeing, the room is full of clutter and dust, like something from a horror film as cobwebs hang from the ceiling over more pictures of Jesus and Mary who stare down at me crying. Jesse doesn't seem to be as affected, not even holding her nose. Are we in the same room?

Bumping into something under the bed, bending to rub my foot, her mother stands beside the rat's cage introducing me to the other fourteen one by one, I don't take any of the names in, head spinning, wanting to run as far and as fast as I can. Jesse's no help looking just as scared. Holding my breath, staring from her eyes to the same bucket I saw her emptying outside, I mouth the first thing that comes to mind.

"Help me."

Her mother sees me.

"What did you say to my daughter?"

The smell, the rats, the see-through nightie, bucket, her mother's eyes, the walls with eyes. It's all too much. The room caves in around me, feeling faint with fear, backing out of the room, unable to breathe, plucking an excuse from the air, promising Jesse I'll call her as soon as

I get home. Stumbling to the front door, grabbing my bag off the floor, I run; the last thing I hear is her mother's voice.

"You little bitch. You'll pay for embarrassing me like that."

Turning, running back to the front door, looking through the glass, Jesse's mother starts beating her with something I think looks like a hairbrush.

"Jesse."

Banging hard on the door, sure my face is glued to the filthy glass, all I hear is the thud of the brush as it comes into contact with Jesse's skull. Screaming, I can't get back inside, watching her be dragged into her mother's bedroom by her hair.

"Jesse. Jesse. I'm so sorry."

Running to the bus stop, not looking at anything but the ground, the need to get away is fierce, not even noticing my own tears until I've stopped. Should I go back? Puffing, out of breath, shaking like jelly, steadying myself, my legs might give way any second. Never in a million years did I ever think Jesse's life was this bad, thinking back to times I thought she was just making stories up for attention. Stepping onto the bus, relieved to be away from hell, a little part of me feels guilty for leaving her behind. Running home, ringing her as soon as I get in, there is no answer. There is no answer the whole weekend.

Chapter Twenty-One

Monday morning when Jesse doesn't come to school, I really start to worry. I can't ask my parents to drive me around to her house because they don't even know she exists. When she returns to school the following week, I cry with relief. She is so quiet, withdrawn. I try asking what happened, apologising more times than I can count for my early exit from her house, but it's like talking to a brick wall. My words bounce off her body like she has a protective shield around herself which no one, not even I, can penetrate.

... Convincing myself from that day on that whatever happens to her at home really has nothing to do with me, Jesse's mother is Jesse's problem, not mine. I'm not going to burden myself with anyone else's problems because I still have two very big ones of my own at home to deal with. My overbearing parents are suffocating, stifling, sad. Jesse's my escape; doesn't she know that? She has no idea how much I need her. She's like a favourite toy, and I'm not ready to let her go. If I'm honest, I'm a little possessive of her. I've done so much for her in her life, she owes it to me to stay loyal, be mine, even if that means distancing her from everyone, including my parents.

Jesse's nothing without me and she knows it.

A bittersweet love, I don't really want her too close to me, but I don't want her too far away from me, either. I'm confused. Sometimes I even feel a little threatened by her. She has certain qualities I know others will be drawn to; I don't want them to take her away from me. Jesse's mine.

At times, her eyes remind me of her insane mothers, and that scares me. Nobody else knows about that side of her. Nobody knows her like I do. If and when I get bored with her and let her go, I really don't want to find out what she'll do. I'll keep her close until I'm ready to let her go, not the other way around.

A year passes pretty much a repeat of the last, until the day of my sixteenth birthday. This is the day my life changes forever, and not in a good way.

Chapter Twenty-Two

Thursday July 18th 1992—Age sixteen

Deciding to bunk the last lesson and go to the park to talk about how we'll celebrate my birthday, Jesse and I buy a couple packets of chippies on the way, entering the park and finding a space on the warm freshly cut grass to eat them. It's spiky and uncomfortable to sit on from just being cut, but the smell more than makes up for how it feels, picking a few buttercups that have survived the mowing and placing one under each other's chins to see how yellow it is. I'm not really interested in finding out whether Jesse likes butter or not, there are other things on my mind that I've spent quite a few nights wondering how to tell her. Staring into her eyes, she's staring back, looking confused, her head tilting slightly waiting for me to speak.

"I'm going to change my name. I hate Zoe. It's soooooo boring. Look at Madonna? Her name is cool, not boring like mine. I just haven't figured out what I want to call myself yet. My mother will spit the dummy, but I don't give a shit. I didn't choose my name, so I reckon I've got the right to do what I want. Dad probably won't care. What do you think?"

Shaking her head from side to side, Jesse's squinting her eyes towards the sun like I've just talked to her in Chinese. Impatient for her to answer, I arch my eyebrows raising both hands in question.

"Where's this come from, Zoe? Your name is fine. Why do you want to change it? You're such a fucking weirdo."

Pulling at the buttercups with a little too much aggression, there is definitely something else Jesse wants to say.

"I know exactly what I'm going to do. I'm going to leave my psycho mother and never ever go back. I'll never have to see her or her disgusting pervy friend again. No one will control me. I mean it. Not even you, Zoe."

Not sure if she's serious, the intensity in her eyes is unnerving, like she wants to challenge me. I'm not used to it, and I'm not sure I like this ballsy side to her. Staring back at her twice as hard to make my point, I crumple up her chippie packet and throw it at her head.

"No way. You'll end up with a loser who makes you do all sorts of strange things in the bedroom. You'll never leave me; you need me too much. Everyone knows it, except you."

Her eyes change, staring like she can see straight through me. Unnerved for a second time, I don't like it when she's like this. It's as though she's another person. Careful with what I say next, I watch her face to see if she changes.

"I'm going to be a success, Jesse. I'll own my own house; have friends I want when I want, I'll buy my own designer clothes, hang out with lots of famous people, like Princess Diana, just because of who I am. I'll show my mother. She thinks that I'll be nothing but a pretty face. My new name will be my trademark. You just wait."

Jesse's cheeky smile tells me she's about to say something outrageous.

"Maybe me and you could go into business? We could pretend to be sisters. Wouldn't that be cool?"

Placing buttercups under each other's chins again, it's something

I never want to be a possibility, but I don't spoil the fun, happy that her mood has changed. Just thinking of being related to her send's shivers down my spine, but she doesn't need to know, quickly saying words I know she'll love to hear.

"You never know, we might've been sisters in a past life?"

Laughing, slapping her with more oomph than I ought to, I'm inwardly dying at my words. Not in a gazillion years do I want us to be related - ever, quickly shutting the conversation down, praying the Universe has paid no attention to what I've just said. Placing another buttercup under her chin, I change the subject.

"We're definitely not related. You don't even like butter. There's no yellow under your chin at all, you freak."

Grabbing the buttercup from my hand, scrunching both hers and mine in her hand, throwing them away, laughing, I know she secretly wishes we were somehow connected. My guilty look tells her all.

"Oh shit, I'd better get home. My parents want to take me out for dinner."

Not looking forward to it, they, like Jesse and everyone else in my life, are way too easy to control. I need a challenge, something other than my boring life. I figure there simply has to be someone out there who will give my life some meaning? There has to be someone who will look past the way I look.

Worlds miles apart, sitting on the grass, we promise to be each other's friend forever and pinkie promise that nothing will ever come between us. I know my words are far from true, only saying them because I know one day I'll eventually let Jesse go. She doesn't need to know.

Digging inside her bag, handing me a tiny parcel, she tells me to open it.

Turning it over in my hand, ripping at the paper, I see she's made me a mixtape with my name scribbled across the top in her handwriting.

"All your favourite songs are on it."

Promising to listen to it when I get home, I have no intention of doing anything of the sort, walking to the bus stop, waiting less than five minutes for our buses to come. Jesse's comes first, hugging her before she hops on and waves at me.

"Ring me later if you get bored."

Thirty seconds later, waving from the back window, little do I know that will be the last time I see her for two years.

Even before I have the key in the door, my panicky mother has opened it.

"Thank God you're safe. I was so worried."

I hate that my parents, especially my overbearing mother is so clingy. I wish they'd give me some space. I wouldn't be so rebellious, so desperate to get away if they did. I don't know why my mother pretends to care so much. I think seeing me safe is more for her benefit than mine. It only means she can continue tormenting me for something else I haven't done for another day.

Flinging her off, telling her I'll quickly change, the softness of the white shag-pile carpet in between my toes is heaven walking to my room. My parents decorated the whole house in it, even a rug in the kitchen. I'd hated it to begin with because it reminded me of the old porn movies I secretly watched at my friends' houses. Nearly every film seemed to have couples shagging on carpets that were the same. Even my parents' friends commented.

"Ooh, Alan, and Louise, you dirty devils. I can see you both in front of the fire, just don't let poor Zoe see you."

That had made me feel sick.

Walking the two flights of stairs to my huge room, my massive four-poster bed in the middle is perfectly made, my walk-in wardrobe with my own en-suite, is gleaming from being cleaned. I know how lucky I am, instantly thinking of Jesse and the filth she is returning to. Just thinking of her mother sends shivers down my spine. How does she live with her every day?

Ejecting *Swingout Sister* from my tape deck, inserting my new mixtape and listening as I undress and change into clothes for my night ahead, *Duran Duran*, *Madonna*, *Queen*, *Spandau Ballet*, and *Adam and the Ants* keep me company, deciding I'll have to ring Jesse later to tell her how much I love it.

"Ooh, *Simple Minds*. Yes."

Sliding my finger across my lips with gloss, the song comes to an end, pouting my lips, blowing myself a kiss, singing along to my favourite part at the end. I know exactly why Jesse has added the song. It's my favourite film from the eighties and I've had a huge crush on John, the bad boy for as long as I can remember. Who hasn't? I love all of The Breakfast Club, especially Claire, the pretty rich girl I identify with so much. That's something both Jesse and I have in common. We love the eighties. The fashion, music, attitude. We've talked so many times about wishing we were born that much earlier so we could've been teenagers in that decade. It's nowhere near as much fun today.

Switching the light off, nearly jumping out of my skin, Jesse's high-pitched voice suddenly squeals.

"Don't you ever forget about me, or else."

"Whatever, freak."

My mother screams from downstairs.

"Zoe, hurry up or we'll be late."

Chapter Twenty-Three

Dropping the biggest grenade of my life tonight, I'm numb, dead inside, sure my mother knew just how much it would hurt. Even though I hate her, I never thought for one second I wasn't hers.

I've always felt a disconnect with her, but I thought that was because she was a jealous bitch. Now I know why. The whole night has been a disaster. My father, angrier than I've ever seen him, actually showed some gumption and stood up to my mother tonight. It's certainly assured this is the beginning of the end for them.

Dialling Jesse's number for the twentieth time, I need to tell her my news, but all I get is the answer machine, trying again another half an hour later with still no luck. Why isn't she picking up? It's not late?

Ready to explode, going to bed with so many questions still rolling around my head, I'll call her tomorrow when she gets home from school because I sure as hell won't be going in for the rest of the week. I can't. I'll tell her why when I speak to her.

Calling her every hour after school the next day she doesn't pick up, or the day after that, or the day after that, out of my mind with worry. Where is she?

Arriving at school on Monday she's not there, not hearing anything from her at all, fearing the worst, remembering back to the last time she wasn't at school. Has her mother hurt her more than usual?

Waiting at the school gates day after day proves fruitless. It makes me late for class, which in turn gets me into a lot of trouble with the teachers. Where is Jesse?

Phoning her house as soon as I get in every day, every hour she doesn't pick up, my anxiety worsens. The phone rings off, not even going to answerphone. Intuitively I know something really bad has happened. I can feel it in my gut, ending up taking matters into my own hands and deciding to come clean with my parents about her. Even though they don't know her, I have to know what's going on. Plucking up every ounce of courage I have, asking my mother to drive me to her house, I have to know if what I'm feeling is real.

Droning on about nothing beside me, I don't hear my mother, unable to concentrate on anything other than finding out what has happened to Jesse. Driving down her street the blossoms have gone, making my memory flood with images of the day I met her mother, which in turn sends my anxiety off the scale. Head foggy, all my thoughts intercept wanting answers to questions I don't have. Absent-mindedly twirling my hair around my finger, it's a deep shade of purple and numb, staring blankly out the window seeing nothing but rats, clutter, and dark eyes boring into mine. I'm not prepared to confront those eyes again. Feeling as dark as the clouds above, do they know something I don't? Turning black almost as soon as we've parked up, it's like the clouds are forewarning me that something bad is going to happen.

Wiping my hands down my skirt, I can't look at my mother who's staring back at me like I'm a helpless child. She's not here for me. In fact, I think she probably wants to witness teaching me yet another lesson. Her eyes are cold, empty, not wanting to ease any of my pain one little bit. We've not talked about the adoption at all since my birthday. It's like she wants to pretend it never happened. Staring at me like a stranger, her eyes tell me to hurry up, impatient with my hesitancy. Her and my dad are chalk and cheese. I should've asked him to be here and not the cold-hearted snake sitting beside me. If something happens, or I find out something about Jesse that's bad, then she won't be able to handle it. She'll tell me I'm panicking over nothing which I know I'm not. Something isn't right.

Nervous, I won't dare let my mother see how I'm feeling, pretending to be fine.

"Come on. We haven't got all day. I told you I've got a nail appointment in an hour."

Glaring at her, pointing to the house, she's already looking out the window at something else.

"Wait here, I'll hopefully only be five minutes."

Fighting with the latch of the gate for what seems like minutes, eventually I win, entering the forest which has grown to half my height. Wading through it, the path is covered in weeds, scratching my concrete legs all the way up the path to the front door. The cat? If she doesn't appear then there is definitely something to worry about. Jesse loves the smelly puss more than anything in the world.

"Please let her be home. Please let the cat come to greet me."

Two, three minutes later, there's no sign of the cat. Honking the car at the exact same time I knock on the door, I jump out of my skin, nearly peeing myself, turning, telling my mother to stop with my hand. My stomach is in knots.

"Please open the door, Jesse. Please be there. Please don't let your mother open the door. Please?"

Tapping on the fragile glass again, someone walks to the door, but it isn't Jesse, or her mother. Looking through the glass, squinting at me through rectangular spheres that make his eyes look miniscule, he opens the door and I stand face to face with his little goatee beard, instantly disliking him and his majorly creepy stare. His eyes, beastly, beady, and brown, leer at me like I'm food, sure that if he could, he would devour me. I already hate him. Who is he? Have I got the wrong house?

Trying to remember, thinking of anything Jesse might've said that could give me a clue, I look back to my mother for reassurance hoping my nervousness doesn't show, but she's gesturing with her hands to hurry up, me giving her the fingers back to signal two minutes. What I'm really doing though is telling her to get stuffed. Most mothers would've come with their child to the door, but not mine.

Where is Jesse? I can't be left on my own with my mother. I need her more than ever. Turning to the creepy looking man, I don't know how, but I manage to get the words I want to say out of my mouth.

"I'm looking for Jesse. Is she in?"

His voice, nasally and high-pitched, is not what I expected.

"Well, well, well what do we have here, eh? Jesse actually has friends. And pretty ones to boot. Come inside my beauty, and I'll tell you where she is."

I don't like him. Sensing danger, his eyes are devouring me, and his smirk isn't friendly at all. It's predatory, perverse, poisonous.

"N-n-n-no thanks. My mother is waiting for me in the car."

Pointing to my mother, she's seen me and waves at him, smiling, making him quickly change his tune.

"Jesse doesn't live here anymore. She ran away weeks ago. Haven't seen her since. Good riddance if you ask me."

I know who he is.

"You're that old perv, aren't you? Aren't you? Have you done something to her? I'll fucking call the police if you have, you dirty old bastard."

Pushing me from the front step to the long grass before I even know what is happening, I trip and fall, hurting my knee. His face, above mine, contorts into shapes that make him look like the predator he is. Looking straight at me, mouth curled, snarling, he spits, pointing his finger at me.

"What's she told you? *What's she told you?* If you want to see her again, I'd quickly change your tone. If I were you, my beauty, I'd forget this conversation ever took place. You get my drift?"

Jesse's mother shouts from her room. I have to get away.

"Who the fuck is that at the door? Tell whoever it is to fuck off and go away. Jesse doesn't live here anymore, you hear? Now piss off."

Finally my mother gets out of the car pretending to care.

"What are you doing to my daughter? Zoe! Come back to the car."

Lifting myself quickly from the ground, not even noticing the long line of blood crawling its way down my leg to my shoe, I limp to the gate where my mother waits. Turning, screaming at him while he laughs from the porch, I hate him. I hate him and his stupid grin.

"What the fuck have you done?"

Dragging me back to the car while I'm still screaming at him, my mother looks embarrassed, more worried about keeping face than looking after me. She even apologises to him.

"I'm sorry for disturbing you. We're leaving now."

"Piss off, and don't ever come back. She's gone, Zoe. Hee haw."

How can she have done that to me? She saw how he treated me? She doesn't care where Jesse is. I hate my mother. Hate her.

"She's gone, don't you get it? Jesse's gone. What the hell did you say sorry to him for? He's hurt her, done something to her. What am I going to do? How am I going to find her? She doesn't even know where I live. She doesn't know."

There is no concern in my mother's voice or on her face.

"Who doesn't know where you live? Your friend? Bloody hell, Zoe. Stop being so dramatic and get in the car. I've got a nail appointment to go to. I said sorry because you were being rude to him. I didn't like the look of him anyway, so you won't be coming back here, ever. I'm not going to bother about a girl I don't even know. She's your friend yet you've never introduced her to us. This is probably another one of your games, and I'm not interested. You hear? You won't be coming back here. Ever."

Chapter Twenty-Four

I blame myself for never mentioning Jesse to either of my parents. I'm so stupid, so mean. Why did I expect either of them to help someone they didn't even know? After what my bitch mother did to me on my sixteenth birthday, she owed me. She owed me big time.

I should've introduced Jesse to them. I should've given Jesse a safe place to go.

Weeks pass thinking of ways of finding her, even visiting the local Police Station telling them everything I know. Without any proof, and the fact she is over sixteen, they tell me there is nothing they can do, that I just have to wait and see if she contacts me. They don't care. The only thing they cared about was eyeing me up like a piece of prime meat, one officer even licking his lips and telling me to come back when I was a bit more 'useful.' I'm so sick of people, especially leery old men.

Every effort to find Jesse going nowhere, I'm not ready to let her go.

. . .

Weeks turn into months, which turn into years. If she's alive I hope she's at least found a safe place to live; that her life is better? I've listened to the tape she made me at least a thousand times, sure I've worn out the only thing I have left of her. Depressed, lonely, sad, I hear her voice for the one thousandth and one time.

"Don't you ever forget about me. *Or else.*"

Two years to the day Jesse went missing, it's my eighteenth birthday, which should be happy, but it's not, and even though I should be celebrating, inside I feel anything but. No one, not even my parents know the true extent of my anxiety around losing her. My own guilt at not keeping her safe, is what I struggle with the most. If I'd introduced her to my parents, she'd still be here, with me. But she's not, and all the guilt in the world isn't going to bring her back.

Doing the same boring things with the same boring people every day, I ignore what my gut is feeling, knowing if I don't, I might do something stupid.

Walking down the same thirteen zigzags after school, moaning to my same boring friends about my boring night ahead with my boring parents, they all listen, looking on as interested as watching paint dry.

"I'll have to listen to my parents' dumb speeches again. I wish they'd just piss off and let me do what I bloody want."

Rolling their eyes at me, something feels off. Instead of agreeing with me, they start sticking up for my parents, telling me not to be such a drama queen. What the hell? Turning eighteen isn't as much fun as I thought it'd be.

Turning left onto the pavement, a girl across the road catches my eye. Leaning against a pole oblivious to me stopping in mid-walk, I bend down, holding my heart as it suddenly somersaults in my chest. Ground and sky reversing, I have to breathe in and out fast, finally able to look up to see if I'm hallucinating. Head shaking, staring hard ahead, it can't be. Jesse? Could it really be her?

One of my friends feels my forehead, concerned I'm ill.

"What's wrong, Zoe? You look like you're gonna be sick. What's wrong? Have you got your period or something?"

Staring ahead at the ghost from my past, little black dots float in front of my eyes.

Chapter Twenty-Five

Slap.

Lizzy, my short, ginger-haired, freckly friend, strikes my face hard, making me come to as someone stands over me wearing black leggings, a black, oversized, long-sleeved top with writing I can't see clearly, and something glistening from around her neck sparkling in the sun. Smiling under big round sunglasses, helping me up, I catch a glimpse of her thick black socks pulled over black Dr Martens boots; headphones connected to a Walkman on her waist dangle around her neck and falls onto my hair, quickly shoving them off.

A little plumper than I last remember, her hair is slightly longer, now a stunning shade of black with red around the ends. Waiting for some sort of signal, a look, a gesture, anything that will confirm whether I'm right or just clutching at straws, she takes off her sunglasses and stares right at me, smiling.

"Jesse? Is it really you?"

Shoving my friends off, without looking too pathetic, I grab a strand of my hair, and start twirling it frantically around my finger until it turns a deep shade of purple. My heart, beating like a drum, is excited to see her, giving her the once over, pretending to glare.

Reading her t-shirt, bursting into laughter, I'm unable to hold it in any longer, pulling her in close for the longest hug. I simply can't believe she's here.

"Where the fuck have you been? I didn't know where to look. I even went to your house and that fucking perv answered the door. I told him to fuck off. I didn't know what had happened to you, Jesse."

Crying, hugging each other tight, my hair has caught the necklace around her neck and tangled around it. Up close, enough to feel her breath on my cheek, I wait for her to untangle my hair, staring in disbelief, hoping I haven't woken from another dream. Waiting while she tucks the necklace inside her top, I hear her voice for the first time in two years realising just how much I've missed it.

"I'm sorry, Zoe. I didn't mean to make you faint. Are you ok? I had to leave in a hurry, I'll tell you all about it later. I've missed you so much. I'm sorry. Forgive me, please?"

Embracing each other again, jumping up and down, people start to wonder what's going on, especially my friends, who are waiting behind me. Lizzie's fat freckled face shouts.

"Jesse? Is that you? *OMG*, you've changed so much."

Seeing Jesse acknowledge the girls, something inside me snaps. I don't want anyone spoiling our reunion. I want her to myself.

"Fuck off and leave us alone."

"Zoe. You can't tell us what to do. I can speak to whoever I want."

"No, you can't. Not today anyway."

Shooing them away with my hands, needing some space from them, they eventually get the message.

"Just fuck off. *Now*."

They know not to mess with me when I'm in a mood like this. Eyes like thunder, both hands on my hips daring them to defy me, their sad faces move away, which I ignore, turning back to Jesse, whose eyes aren't as soft as five minutes before.

"That was mean, Zoe. You didn't need to be like that. They were only being nice."

Ignoring her words, touching her face, hair, and body again to make sure I'm not dreaming, I take her hands in mine speaking in my sweetest voice.

"I didn't want them spoiling our moment, Jesse. I haven't seen you in... forever! Is it bad to want you all to myself?"

Eyes softening again, shrugging her shoulders, I can't help myself, hugging her close, watching our bodies cast long shadows on the pavement as the unexpected sun beats down on our heads. Not making the reunion as comfortable as it could be, I suggest we go somewhere private to talk, skipping excitedly towards our favourite park, arm in arm, passing familiar shops and stopping in unison in front of one of them.

Automatically knowing what each other is thinking, we sidestep pedestrians and run into the same corner shop we've always bought our favourite chippies from. The same man we've always bought them from is there, but today I'm not interested in getting them for free, rushing out of the shop before he has any time to try his luck.

Making our way to the park, walking through the familiar entrance, and strolling down the pavement to a spot which is shaded and far enough away from people to be out of earshot, the freshly cut grass welcomes us, smelling the winter air. Today, it's not cold at all, sitting on an old coat I've found in my school bag. I never thought the sound of the chippie packet opening would be a sound I'd ever miss. It's still a little surreal, both of us sitting, eating our chippies like we've never been apart.

Retelling her story, going back to the day she was flung out by her lunatic mother, Jesse only gives me a tiny account of what happened, saying it would bore me too much to hear it all. Forgetting I'm eating, too engrossed in her mini story, I tell her I'd love to hear it all one day if she ever feels like telling me?

I'd love to know how she survived on her own. How it was on the streets. I know in my heart if it had been me I wouldn't have coped for one day, let alone two years.

Not going into too much detail, which I'm a little sad about, when she starts talking about Gail, a homeless woman who took her under her wing, it gets even more interesting. The way Jesse's eyes suddenly glaze over and the slump of her body tells me it hurts her to talk about Gail, which I'm guessing is why she's keeping it short. I think she's just too sad to tell me it all?

"Without Gail, I don't know what I would've done. I probably would've died. You don't know how rough it is on the streets until you're in it."

Telling me Gail was her saviour in more ways than one, Jesse's face is animated as she explains Gail was responsible for saving Samantha from being run over. I know how much that would've hurt. God, if anything had ever happened to Samantha. It's not worth even thinking about. Gail, I hear, took both Jesse and Samantha in those first few weeks on the streets and even helped Jesse land her job at The Orchard, a 'massage parlour' in the city.

"Losing Gail was the single worst thing I've ever experienced."

"You work in a massage parlour? Get the fuck out of town."

Stroking Jesse's face, tucking a lock of hair behind her left ear, wiping away a single tear escaping from each eye, they are pained and far away, her hand absentmindedly pulling at the grass beneath all the way to the roots, the little patch underneath her now just dirt. Laying my hand on top of hers, encouraging her to stop, I try to lighten the mood.

"Even worse than not seeing me for two years?"

Raising my eyebrow in question, hoping a little humour might cheer her and the conversation up, I'm not good with people opening up and even worse with dealing with emotions. I don't think she's heard what I've said, shaking her head like she's come out of a trance, asking me to repeat what I've said.

"I said, was losing Gail more painful than not seeing me for two years."

Her eyes boring through me like acid, she definitely doesn't like what I've said. I've upset her.

"Does it always have to come back to you? I thought two years apart might've changed you just a little bit. Of course I missed you,

Zoe, but it's a different kind of missing. Gail was my family in more ways than one. Without her, I think I would've died."

I've pissed her off. It's the last thing I want her to be feeling, sensing there is more to this Gail than she is telling me. I won't push it. She will open up when she's ready.

Eating our chippies in silence for a bit, looking around, watching children in the park running, jumping, and squealing as they whizz down the long slide and swing backwards and forwards on the swings, a dog barking suddenly comes up behind us. Black and white with short curly hair, its cold nose sniffs our chippie packets as the owner, a handsome man with dark eyes, dark hair, little beard, and skinny body smiles apologetically, dragging it away. Ignoring me, looking at Jesse with squinted eyes, he's smiling flirtatiously at her.

"You look like Saffron from Republica."

His eyes are nowhere near me.

Pulling Jesse towards me, she's blushing and flirting back with him, turning our backs to him, asking her to continue her story. From behind we hear his voice again, both of us looking back.

"Bye, Saffron girl. Hopefully, I'll see you around."

Winking, pointing in Jesse's direction, running off after his dog, I want him gone, yelling at him.

"Control your dog. Stupid man. Who the hell does he think he is? And who the hell is Saffron?"

Laughing, shaking her head at me, she pats my shoulder.

"You haven't changed one bit, Zoe."

"Whatever, I don't give a toss who Saffron is, now continue with your story."

Listening, seeing how much she's changed, I'm not entirely sure if I'm not a little jealous of her and her independence.

Sharon, her boss at The Orchard, was very upset about Gail's passing. Apparently they were best friends for a very long time.

After Gail died, Sharon moved Jesse into one of her rooms in the back of her massive house, and even extended it to letting her have the whole of the downstairs a few months later, which Jesse's now furnished and decorated. It's really worked out for her.

"This is the best birthday present I could've ever wished for. You don't know how happy I am to see you. I thought you were dead. I didn't think I'd hear from you ever again. I haven't told you yet, but on my sixteenth birthday, the day you went missing, my bitch mother told me I was adopted."

"What the fuck?"

"I know. I wanted to tell you that night. It was so awful. Anyway, my parents owe me, the bastards. I can come to the city too and live near you. We'll have so much fun. I can't live in this deadbeat place for a minute longer. All I have to do is make up a plan to get to Wellington, one that they'll believe. Don't worry, give me your number and I'll check in every week with you. I'm not losing you again."

The Wintery sun, beginning to descend, signals it's time for us to leave. My parents, especially my mother, will probably be freaking out. Grabbing my bag up off the ground, accidentally brushing my finger against something sharp in the grass, the pain makes me cry.

"Ouch!"

My middle finger, throbbing like it has a heartbeat of its own, winces, sucking the blood with my mouth, inspecting the tiny puncture to my finger, seeing a microscopic stone has pierced the skin right on the tip. Shaking my hand fiercely, Jesse takes hold of it looking into my eyes, smiling.

"Don't freak out."

Picking up another stone, she slices her middle finger and quickly grabs my own bleeding finger, touching the two open wounds together.

"What the hell are you doing?"

Trying to pull her finger away, she won't let me.

"We're now not only best friends, but blood sisters, too, never to be separated again. Now we're bonded for life."

"You bloody weirdo. Why would I want to exchange blood with you? Get off."

Wiping my finger on my school skirt, looking at her in a way that warns her she's gone too far, I don't want anything to spoil our reunion, quickly changing the subject and telling her to walk me to the bus stop.

Arm in arm, sucking my wounded finger, waiting for the number seventy-five, we're barely at the bus stop twenty seconds before a full bus turns the corner and stops right in front of us. Waiting till everyone is off, I hug her, pulling her necklace from inside her top.

"What a pretty necklace. Where did you get it?"

Without any time for her to answer, I hop on the bus quickly pointing to her top, laughing.

"FYI, you'll never be as popular as me. Freak."

Blowing a kiss, not caring how much attention I'm drawing to myself, this has been one of the best days of my life and nothing, including the attention from the full bus will spoil it. Waving out the window until Jesse is only a dot, I already miss her.

Chapter Twenty-Six

Planning an escape, my parents believe it making up some cock and bull story about leaving school and trying my luck in the modelling world. They agree, especially my mother, without batting an eyelid, drawing the line at letting me find my own apartment. In the blink of an eye, they've organised a little flat for me to rent in the city saying a friend they know happens to be looking for a tenant. I can't believe how easy it's all been.

Booking a photographer to shoot my portfolio, my parents are sure I can't possibly fail, feeling my insides bursting for joy. I don't have any intention of modelling, but they don't need to know. Once I arrive in the city, I'll be able to do as I please. I'll miss my father for sure, but my mother, she can go to hell for all I care. I'll have people eating out of my hands in no time and I'll introduce my alter ego to the world, which reminds me I need to choose a name. I have to choose one that is as far removed from boring Zoe Freeman as I can get.

Beyond excited, I can't wait to leave my old life behind. Reuniting with Jesse has been like finding the missing piece to a jigsaw that's long been lost. No one at school has ever filled the void left behind by her, and if I'm honest, my life has definitely dulled over the last two years. Now that I can see some brightness coming back to it, I want to chase it more than ever.

Listening to my parents one night deep in discussion about my future, they have no idea I'm eavesdropping from the next room. Ear practically glued to the door; my mother's overly happy tone has me worried there might be an imposter in the house. I don't like her much these days, having caught her more than once looking at me in a way that didn't exactly exude love. Her green-eyed monster has reared its ugly head plenty of times over the years showing me her true colours clear as day. I wish my father could see her for what she is. I know that when and if I ever have a child, my mother has definitely taught me how never to treat it. Her words will stick with me forever.

'Don't think you'll get everything you want by just being beautiful. Men want more than a pretty face, Zoe. You've got to have brains too, my love.'

'You know that colour doesn't look good on you. Makes you look fat.'

I remember when she told me men didn't want brains. I remember when she told me my beauty would get me everything I ever wanted.

I'd desperately wanted to be a vet; she'd done nothing but discourage me from a profession that 'wouldn't fully appreciate my beauty.' I was never interested in being just beautiful. I was too young to really know the impact of it. She'd encouraged me to only focus on being pretty, because that's what she thought would get me everything I wanted.

I guess she was lying all those years ago.

I was young, believed what she was telling me was the truth. I now know she wanted me to fail, even then. What mother would discourage their child from reaching for the stars? What mother would discourage their child from believing they could be so much more than an object for people to look at?

My mother.

Listening through the hollow door to the conversation behind it, I can only guess from her happy voice that she's ecstatic at me leaving. I've never felt overly connected to her, the way a mother and daughter should. Most of the other girls at school, apart from Jesse, had mothers who'd openly shown their love for them. You'd clearly seen from the way they'd interacted just how much they'd adored each other. I always knew that the connection I had with my mother wasn't the same. I'd always felt something was missing. Just the act of hugging over the last few years had become quite strained, and it'd constantly left me thinking I'd done something wrong to upset her. It seemed the older and more attractive I'd become, the more distant our relationship had. I'd always put it down to jealousy and her not coping with the attention that came with it.

When I found out I was adopted, it confirmed why the disconnection with her was so strong. I remember sitting in shock while the whole restaurant had sung Happy Birthday to me, numb, watching her openly enjoying my pain. I've never really forgiven her. My father hugged me so close to him that night, apologising over and over, saying how sorry he was. He told me that if it had been up to him, he would've told me at home, in private rather than in front of all the people at the restaurant. He said that my mother obviously thought it would be better that way. Of course she did.

I don't know why he always makes excuses for her.

Everything had made such perfect sense that night.

Not having Jesse to lean on killed me. Losing her and finding out about my adoption on the same day destroyed me. I just got on with it, crying in my room most nights, miserable and alone. The only person who really helped was my father, who, I've always felt genuinely loved by regardless of how I look. Out of the two parents, I've always felt it was he who wanted me more.

I can talk to him more freely and ask him for anything knowing he'll always give me his best advice, and more often than not, give me anything I want. That is, up until when Jesse disappeared.

"I'm sorry, darling, I wish I could magic your friend back, but not even I have the power to do such a thing. She'll come back; you just have to be patient."

He was right, but I didn't know then that I'd see her again.

Being told no had been a hard pill to swallow. Up till then everything I'd ever wanted had been granted, regardless of whether I deserved it or not. Jesse disappearing was something I felt I never deserved. One day she was there, the next day she wasn't, never having had time to prepare for her disappearance. My mother revelled in my pain, and my father tried to absorb it.

I love him more for that.

As much as I love him, he's never really challenged me or told me no. Jesse has, but only a few times. After she disappeared I thought long and hard whether she deliberately left to teach me a lesson. In my heart I knew she wouldn't hurt me like that. In my heart I knew she loved me.

Having spoken to her recently, and hearing about her experiences over the last two years, I know I was wrong to think she'd deliberately hurt me.

Unsticking my ear from the door, leaving my mother deep in conversation about what modelling agencies are best to approach, I'm tired of listening to her make decisions about my life. Very soon, when I'm finally free of her, I'll start making my own choices, my own decisions like the grown up I long to be.

Walking the few steps to my bedroom, closing the door, and sitting down on my stool, I turn the radio on, humming along to the song being played. Leaning in close to my mirror, inspecting my features through the glass, I flick my long wavy hair through my fingers, pulling it away from my oval face. Considering I have no makeup on I'm still striking to look at, smiling, posing in different ways in the mirror, seeing what angle my face looks best. My life would've been so different if I was plain, frumpy, and ordinary, like

Jesse. I've never known any different. It's not like I can just magically make myself ugly. Would I, though, be happy being plain having known what a pain being beautiful is?

I don't think I would.

My looks have helped me get everything, and they will again once I move to the city. Dozens of actresses and models have done it before, so why not me? It's not as though I was given a choice. I can't exactly hide it. Turning my head to the left, a song playing in the background pricks my ears. The words are beautiful and sad at the same time, making me stop what I'm doing, giving the radio my full attention.

A woman sings about meeting her mother again. Was she abandoned? Braiding my hair, mimicking the words of the song, thinking of my own situation, who was my birth mother? What was her story?

Wanting to know more about her, I wonder, do I look like her, even a little bit? Did she want me, spend time with me before she gave me up? Is she even alive? What will I do if I ever find her? Should I try to find her? Should I be brave enough to ask for information about her, the person who dared abandon me at four days old? There must be information I can look up from when I was born. There can't have been too many babies abandoned around that time.

Knowing nothing about my birth parents, I'm desperate to know just a little bit. Who they were, how old they were, whether I was loved? I found out so late about my adoption, it's made me question a lot about myself; I've become more curious to find them. I want answers to my questions.

Who do I look like the most?

Who am I most like in personality?

Do any of them like cold baked beans straight out of the can, or gag at meat dishes with fruit in it, like me?

I need to know why they let me go, why they didn't want me? Just knowing something would give me so much.

I don't know how the hell I'm going to start. Even worse, how am I going to broach the subject with my parents, especially my controlling mother? She won't be happy. Just thinking about the conversation I'll have to have makes my chest tighten. How in God's name am I going to manage to get them on my side for this one? Brushing my tears aside, flicking to another channel, I've heard all I want to hear of the song.

"Another time, but not tonight."

Chapter Twenty-Seven

24th September 1994—Age Eighteen

The day finally arrives to leave school, saying goodbye to my teachers, who all wish me luck, especially Mrs Glennis and Ms Kaley who ask me to come visit. School friends cry and tell me to keep in touch, which I one hundred per cent won't, and neighbours come the next day to wave me off as my parents drive me, and my belongings to the little flat above the pizza shop they have rented for me in the city.

Parking in a tiny car park at the back, we're lucky it's open discovering it's owned by the betting shop downstairs from me. Using the only thing I know will work, I flutter my eyelashes, smiling seductively at the manager who straight away allows us a couple of hours in the carpark to unpack, lugging box after box up three flights of steel stairs. Finally, placing the last box in the kitchen, I grab my chance to look around.

Tiny, it is perfect for what I need. Five rooms, including the kitchen, my bedroom looks out onto a High Road where I see hundreds of people walking, going about their business, like little ants. I think I'm going to like living here.

After Dad checks the locks on my door, satisfied I have enough, we all set about unpacking into my new space.

My mother looks so happy. It's like she's swallowed a happy pill and can't stop smiling. My father is not so happy. He loves me with all his heart and only wants what's best for me, worried that the attention I'll undoubtedly receive from people, men in particular, will be too great.

Walking down the hallway, accidentally stumbling upon a conversation my mother is having on the phone to one of her friends in another room, my ear glues to the door, listening.

"I can't wait, actually. It's been long enough I've been in Zoe's shadow, and if I'm honest, it'll be a breath of fresh air not to have her around and actually be the focus of Alan's attention again. It's been a very long time since that has happened. Eighteen bloody years to be exact. God help me for being so wicked. I know she was the child we always wanted, but I wasn't counting on her being the focus of Alan's attention for so long."

I knew it.

Confirming what I've thought for a while, it still hurts to hear it out loud. Catching my reflection in the dingy hallway mirror, why has my appearance caused so many different reactions over the years? My own mother can't even seem to look past it to the person I am beneath, the person I so desperately want her to see. Finding my birth mother is even more important to me now. Perhaps if I find her, she'll love me the way I long to be loved.

Trudging to my bedroom, leaving my mother and her hurtful words behind. Three hours later, she takes me aside before she leaves, asking to have a private word. She never just wants to talk to me about anything. Puzzled, her eyes are smiling, but not in a good way. Unzipping her handbag, she looks into it and grabs something. Holding a small white box, I know what's coming isn't good.

"I've always wondered how I'd do this. Give this to you? But all

I'm going to do is let you open it when we've left. What's inside belonged to your birth mother. She left it to you at the hospital the day she left with a note saying she wanted you to have it. I've kept it hidden away in the safe in the house for all these years, that is, up until today. It's rather beautiful, Zoe, much like you. I don't think I've ever seen anything else quite like it before. I thought long and hard about giving it to you, but it's the right thing for me to do, giving it to you today. It's important for you to have something of hers."

Handing me the box, I stand there, mouth hanging to the floor. I simply can't believe it. This is the last thing I was expecting to happen today. How can I have something tangible, an object that belonged to my birth mother in the tiny white box, now shaking in time with my breathing in my hand? Has my mother been reading my thoughts? How does she even know I've been thinking about my birth mother? Seeing the shock on my face, my mother comes close, takes my head in her hands, and looks right into my eyes.

"Now you have a bit of her with you. I do love you, Zoe. I may not show it all the time, but I do."

Leaving me staring at the box, she walks off to find my father. Why, of all days, has she chosen to give it to me today?

"Come on, Alan. Time to let the bird fly."

Walking from the kitchen with open arms he suddenly stops on the spot. Turning to my mother, he yells at her in a voice I've never heard from him before. His face is on fire.

"Why didn't you tell me you were going to give it to her? We discussed that we'd both choose when the right time would be. Why did you give it to her today? Why?"

Looking back at me with eyes as soft as cotton wool, he takes my hand, trembling.

"I'm so sorry, darling. Now is probably not the right time to be dumping this on you. Do you want to come back home for a bit?"

My mother, seething with anger behind him, grabs him by the arm, yanking him to her.

"Nonsense. She'll be perfectly ok. Don't bloody overreact, Alan. We knew this day would come. Let's go. Leave her to settle."

Still staring at the box, more hurt by my mother's actions and words today than I have ever been before, my father doesn't want to leave, but is being pushed towards the door by my mother who is smirking at him. Turning back to me, smiling, she drops the second grenade of the day.

"By the way, Zoe. You've got six months. If after that time you haven't secured a proper job, don't think you're coming back home. We're only paying for six months' rent, after that you'll have to fend for yourself. Don't think we're that stupid!"

The room flips upside down.

Running to the door with the box still in my hand, they're arguing as they walk down the stairs and into the car park. My father looks back up and sees me watching, mouthing 'sorry.' Raising my hand, wishing he was still here with me, I want his hugs and comfort to make me feel better, but he doesn't come because my mother is still yelling at him.

I hate her.

I bet she's been planning this day forever.

Watching them drive off, the freedom I was expecting to feel is now replaced with confusion and sadness; there is no exhilaration at all. How can it have been stolen from me in one tiny second? I thought nothing my mother could do could hurt me more than when she told me I was adopted. How I underestimated her.

Trembling with fear, the little box in my hand does the same. How can I open it? I've never felt so alone than I do now. Staring hard at the box, not even blinking, I contemplate opening it? Should I open up a whole new can of worms today?

Why has my mother really given this to me? To gloat, feel some sort of satisfaction knowing I'd probably sit here for hours and agonise over whether to open it or not? Probably. It was probably her plan all along. Looking at the box for what seems like hours, I'm desperate to open it, but at the same time I don't want to give my bitch of a mother the satisfaction of making my first night of freedom crap and anxious.

But should I, just take a peek, see what it is? I've wanted some sort of connection to my birth parents for so long. Could this be it? Could this be the missing piece to the puzzle.

Hand on the lid of the box, my trembling fingers start opening it, anxious to see what is inside.

"Oh, fuck! Why? Why!"

Chapter Twenty-Eight
Lola

"If I was meant to be controlled I would've come with a remote."

— Susan Epstein

I can't. I can't open it.

It's all gone so wrong. I'm supposed to be feeling elation, all I feel is dead. Why has this happened? Why has my mother done this to me, today?

I'm thrilled my father actually showed some gumption and stood up to my mother, swearing I'd seen steam coming out of his ears. But it hasn't made a blind bit of difference. His angry eyes left with her! Him and his angry eyes left me here on my own to deal with the grenade waiting to go off in my hand.

Looking at the small white box trembling like it has a heart, I can't open it. I can't – won't – give my mother the satisfaction of ruining my first night of freedom. *I won't.* I'll show the bitch once and for all who's in charge now. She thinks she can get to me, but she can't. *She can't.*

Running to my bedroom and yanking open my bedside drawer, I

throw the box inside, turning and snatching the first dress I see in the wardrobe, quickly changing into it. Feet on a mission, they guide me to the bathroom where I slap on some make-up, throwing some into a tiny silver bag hanging over the door. Briskly walking to the bedroom again, falling to the floor, looking for my heels, I drag them out from underneath the bed, quickly putting them on, giving myself a quick once over before leaving. Carefully descending the steel stairs, I know I'll chicken out and run back to the box and open it if I don't leave now. The box, as small as it is, already has me hooked and if I let it reel me in, I may as well pack everything up and go back and live with my parents. Still reeling from the shock of my mother's last words, I want to die.

"By the way, Zoe. You've got six months. If after that time you haven't secured a proper job, don't think you're coming back home."

I don't care what she says. She wouldn't fling me onto the streets. My father wouldn't let her. If I have to go back to Hell in six months, then tonight I'm going to have some fun. Tonight, I'm free.

A week later the noises of the city, especially at night, are really hard going when I'm trying to get to sleep. The sirens wake me at all hours, easily distinguishing which is an ambulance, police car or fire engine by the intensity and how much each one pierces my ears. Ambulances definitely win. They are relentless. I've never heard so many. Ever. I'm sure my mother picked this flat just for that.

Once I'm awake falling asleep again is usually impossible, so I just get up, make myself a cup of coffee and watch the world go by out of my front window. Tonight, a prostitute on the corner I've started waving to has her back to me; trying to get her attention but she doesn't see me.

I've seen her most nights standing in the cold wearing next to nothing, and tonight's no different. Looking radiant in a tiny pink sparkly dress and killer heels, she's showing off her long, dark, shapely legs. If I traded places with her, I'd be dying from the cold. If I didn't already know, I'd easily mistake her for a woman. Her blunt, black, bobbed hair doesn't look out of the ordinary, it's her manly arms and bulging Adam's apple that totally give away the gender she was born. Not that I care. She's rather gorgeous, and I sort've know why she's so popular with the men who pick her up regularly throughout the night. Dropping her off at the same corner every half an hour on the dot, she must make a fortune.

Opening my window to let in a bit of fresh air, I hear some noise below, looking down to see a grubby-looking man who has stopped. Standing right underneath my window, he's looking up at me, his croaky voice whispering.

"Hey, pretty lady. Got any spare change?"

As Kermit the Frog smiles up at me from his grubby vest, his legs hardly fill the tatty grey track-pants he has on, looking at his long scruffy blonde hair and matted beard, wondering how long it's been since he's washed. Under the light, his pale-blue eyes look wild and scary, quickly pulling my window in and watching him walk to the prostitute who gives him some money and a hug. Walking off together, it's definitely a very different life on the streets. Just thinking of when Jesse was out there with people like him makes my skin crawl. I wouldn't have lasted five minutes.

Suddenly noticing the sun casting beautiful hues of orange, pink and blue over the buildings below, have I really been awake this long? Looking at the clock, it's five am, the bakery right next to the pizza shop right on cue as the smell of fresh bread starting to cook wafts up making me feel like running down and buying some. I won't, but instead will look forward to buying a pizza later on when Jesse comes over.

Lying back on the couch, closing my eyes for five minutes, I wake up well after two in the afternoon, panicking I haven't cleaned before Jesse arrives. As this will be the first time she sees my flat, it being Wednesday, her night off, I don't want her to witness the pigsty I live in, quickly giving it a once over, satisfied it looks acceptable, even for me. I can't wait to bring her up to date on my first week's shenanigans, already decided I won't mention anything about the box my mother gave me. It'll only encourage her to pester me to open it, and I'm still not ready to do that. When I start looking for my birth mother, that's when it will be the right time. Until then, it will remain a secret.

Jumping in the shower, dressing, and watching the rest of the day drag by, I finally hear footsteps on the metal stairs outside, looking at the clock seeing she's right on time. Six o'clock on the dot.

Running to the door, my arms are already wide open for a hug, but she ignores me and walks right past and into the flat. I don't care, I'm just glad to have her here. Handing me a little plant, she looks around.

"Cool place. A bit small, but I like it. You're lucky. The modelling work must be coming in thick and fast."

Handing her a VB beer, clinking bottles, toasting to new beginnings, I'm embarrassed to tell her I'm still living off my parents' money. Somehow, I think she already knows. Ignoring my paranoia, I quickly change the subject.

"I've already ordered a meat feast, garlic bread, and a big tub of caramel ice-cream."

"Cool. I'm starving. When's it coming?"

Hearing more footsteps on the stairs outside, I rush to the door as the delivery boy carrying my food arrives. Feeling a little guilty about getting it delivered; I can't be bothered to walk down the stairs to go get it, and, I figure, if he's still getting paid, he may as well do it. Tall and skinny, his pimply face smiles goofily at me under his long, brown, greasy, frizzy hair, taking the boxes from him and handing them to Jesse, who's right beside me. Trying to pay him, he's staring at me, already knowing what's coming.

"It's alright. It's on the house. I'll still get paid for the delivery even though you're only upstairs. It's my 'welcome' treat. You're new, aren't you? The other tenant wasn't anywhere near as pretty as you."

Licking my lips the way I know works with men, I promise to make it up to him, watching him readjust his trousers. Winking at Jesse, who's rolling her eyes, we leave him and his goofy smile at the door.

"Nothing's changed much, eh? You know you're probably going to have to give him a blow job, now."

"Fuck off. I'll show him my tits. I'm sure he'll be happy with that."

Chatting as we eat, we listen to music and talk about what we're going to do now we're together again.

"I'm so happy to be free of my boring parents. I get to do what I want, when I want, every day. I'll never be completely free, though. I still have to bloody answer phone call after phone call about what agencies I've been to, but I lie every time. I let them think I'm on the road to supermodel stardom."

"I thought you were. How are you paying for everything?"

"Oh, I have savings from birthdays and Christmas's I've saved up. I'll use it until it's gone, especially if it means my mother's eagle eyes aren't watching my every move. What's this you're making me listen to?"

"Just another CD I like. Sharon—"

Listening to it, my ears prick up at a song playing, my finger stopping Jesse in mid-sentence, asking her to turn up the volume.

"It's perfect. This is the one. This is the mother-fucking one."

Tapping my head in time to the beat, I can't believe how perfect it is.

"Lola. I love it."

"What the hell do you mean? Lola?"

"It's my new name. It's perfect. I told you I'd change my name one day, didn't I?"

"What? When? Whatever, Zoe. Don't be stupid."

"Zoe no longer has any room in my life. She's fricking boring. Lola is going to make it. I can feel it."

Cranking the music up, pulling Jesse up from the couch, I make her sing along to the song, dancing, not caring if anyone can hear us from below.

Falling to the floor, laughing, puffed, laying on our backs, looking to the ceiling as our breathing starts to stabilise.

"You do know that Lola in the song is a cross dresser and in fact a man, don't you?"

"Why would I care about that? I just like the name. Bloody hell. I need to start working out. Just dancing around like that has given me the stitch. C'mon, freak, let's eat the rest of that pizza before it gets cold."

Listening to the rest of '*The Best of The Kinks*,' soon the subject of work comes up.

"What's the money like at The Orchard?"

I already know what Jesse's going to say by the way her eyes scan me.

"No. No fucking way. Don't even think about it, Zo. Those men are nasty pieces of shit. They all have wives or girlfriends. Some have boyfriends and come fuck a girl up the arse for the hell of it. A few of them even asked me if I wanted to make a 'quick buck' when I was still only sixteen. There's only a few who are ok, regulars, but the majority that go aren't what you'd call 'normal.' The things they have the girls doing. One, a judge, likes to dress up in a nappy and suck on Gwendoline's titties for hours. He's a fricking freak. At the end, she has to change his nappy. It's disgusting. You're way too classy. You'll easily get a job."

"It's Lola now. Don't call me by that bloody boring name any more. I'll work where I want, thank you. When have you ever told me what to do?"

Staring, Jesse backs down. She's never told me what to do, ever, and she sure as hell isn't going to start now. What Lola wants; Lola is going to get. Killing her with my eyes, I don't want her here anymore, escorting her abruptly to the door.

"Time you left; I think. I have to get up early tomorrow to look for work."

Slamming the door on her, listening to her thud down the stairs, I walk through my tiny flat and watch her cross the street from my window. She's right. I am too classy to work in a joint like The Orchard, but if all else fails, I need a backup plan, and if that's it, then that's where I'll end up, whether she approves of it or not.

Chapter Twenty-Nine

A month later, staring out my front window a little bit bored with my freedom: the same traffic and people whizz by all blending into each other. Sick of the sirens that keep me awake all night, an ambulance, as if reading my mind, races by on its way to another emergency.

It'll be coming to get me soon if I don't find a job.

I'd rather top myself than have to beg to go back to my parents who, my mother in particular, are pressuring me to find work.

It's proving near enough impossible to find anything, and my lack of qualifications isn't helping, having had no experience doing anything except being pretty. No employer really cares how gorgeous you are if you can't do the work. I've applied for a few normal jobs and been successful in getting interviews, but after freezing up each time any of them asked me what my strengths were, it was obvious all I could offer was my winning smile. That had been torture.

Confidence I thought I had slowly chipping away, the few thousand dollars left in the bank by my parents is only going to keep me going for so long, and then what will I bloody do? I know exactly what will happen. My mother will lecture me about being responsible and then back down on everything she said and order me home and my life will officially end. She left strict instructions that the money left in the bank was to pay for my modelling portfolio and food, expecting that I'd already had it done. The photographer my mother pre-arranged was useless. He'd asked me to pose in lingerie the second he saw me. My stupid mother had no idea he was more into glamour modelling when she booked him and was beyond horrified when I told her. She'd ordered me to look up other photographers, preferably women, but even they had pointed me down the glamour modelling route.

"With your looks, you'll be a star."
"Every boy and man will have you on their wall, sweetheart. Wink, wink."
"Let's see what you look like in just panties?"
"How old are you?"

Fed up with it all, I'd cheered myself up by using some of the money to decorate my little space, mostly nik naks from charity shops around my area. My favourite piece, a carved wooden box with intricate, almost tribal markings, has been used to store my weed, which keeps me sane. But weed, like most things, is costly, and with only a few months to show I can look after myself, my dream of living in the city is going to be shattered before it's even begun. I have to get some work soon; anything to stop me from being forced home to the last person I want to return to. My father I can cope with. My mother, though? Even though she threatened to toss me out onto the street, I know she wouldn't. My father wouldn't let her. Just the thought of being near her again sends shivers down my spine.

Ding, ding, ding. The sound of the crossing outside distracts me, gazing out to the people and traffic below. Do any of them understand how I'm feeling? Do any of them understand the personal dilemma I'm going through just a few feet up? Would any of them care if they did?

Yelling at the window, a tall, blonde, skinny woman standing at the lights opposite me looks up, catching me in mid yell, making me feel even more pathetic than I already do when she starts laughing and pointing up at me while she nudges her frumpy friend who also starts pointing and laughing.

Slumping to the couch, grimacing, asking myself the same question for the hundredth time. Should I just bloody get the portfolio done? I've had enough people tell me over the last eighteen years how good I'd be as a model. Even some of the teachers at school, including Ms Kaley, so why not? Why not take their advice?

Remembering school and how I'd taken no interest in much of it except sewing, I didn't think I'd be in this position, ever. I always thought the bank of Mummy and Daddy would keep me going, and that my looks would get me everything. I never thought having silly qualifications for anything would matter. Why didn't I pay more attention and be less lazy and make more of an effort to think about my future? There is no way I'm going to end up middle aged wiping my parents' arses.

"Arghhh."

Hot and dizzy, I won't let it get to that, fanning away the panic with my hands. Trying my best to stop the images of my parents' old saggy bums in my face, I try to distract myself by looking out the window again, counting the people walking by. That would be my bitchy mother's ultimate revenge, having to wipe her saggy arse.

Depressed, feeling like shit, I need a pick me up, an escape from my thoughts, remembering my stash of weed under the couch. Grabbing it and rolling myself a big fat joint, the taste of the sweet grass on my tongue makes my body relax and a familiar warmth spreads across my body, like a ray of sun has descended on it. Wishing I hadn't told Jesse I'd go out; all I really feel like doing is eating pizza and watching trash telly. DevO's better be worth it. I've heard so much about the place, I can't believe it's taken this long for Jesse to take me. I might even get a job there if I'm lucky. If not, then working at The Orchard it is. Jesse won't like it, but right now I'm in no position to even care how she feels.

The life I envisioned for myself very quickly fading before my eyes, there's nothing at the moment I can do but pray someone employs me soon.

Lifting myself off the couch, dragging my feet to my room and popping on the radio to help brighten up my mood, I flick through my dresses finally deciding on a sexy red number. Laying it on the bed before jumping in the shower, I wash all my worries down the drain and dry myself off, quickly walking to the empty fridge, pouring myself a gigantic glass of wine. Sipping it, dancing back to my room thinking I know all the words to the Nirvana song playing, I have to laugh at my own tone deafness. Obviously, God hasn't blessed me with everything.

Feeling a little better, I'm looking forward to seeing Jesse now, the song and wine exciting me for the night ahead. Dressed, and ready to go in only half the time I expected it would take, I inspect myself in the mirror, reckoning I'd do me.

"You fucking hot bitch."

The cold pinching me almost as soon as I exit my flat, my goose-pimply legs regret the choice of clothing, wishing the coat I'd chosen was long enough to wrap around them. With no time to go and change it, I rub my arms, folding my coat close to me, trying to retain some warmth as people give me filthy looks, especially the women hanging off men's arms whose leery eyes are wandering my way. Winking at me behind their girlfriend's backs, they think I'm interested, but little do they know that men bore me. They are so transparent. I've yet to find one who gives me any semblance of a challenge. Women, and their judging jealous eyes, need to give me a break. It's not my fault their men can't be trusted.

Upping my pace, ten minutes later, finally arriving at DevO's, the club Jesse hasn't stopped telling me about, I pace backwards and forwards ignoring two old men giving me the eye, meanwhile my bladder is pulsating, like it has a mind of its own, doing my best to squeeze it hard, hoping nothing trickles out.

Walking around the corner, Jesse saunters towards me dressed head to toe in black, oblivious to everything going on around her. Moving in time to the music she's playing on her ever-present Walkman, she looks like an extra in a horror film, wondering if she's confused whether it's Halloween?

"You're bloody late, I need to pee, and what on Earth are you wearing? You're supposed to be attracting men, not scaring the shit out of them."

"Nice to see you, too."

Giving her the finger, queuing up, my bladder is threatening to empty itself involuntarily, moving from side to side to alleviate the pain.

Joni, the big Pacific Islander on the door Jesse's told me about, is gorgeous. Huge biceps and toned body, his tight black t-shirt and trousers have most of the women in the queue melting at the mouth, me included. Watching as he calmly speaks to a man at the front of the queue who's too drunk to come in, I'm impressed by how soft he is, eventually persuading the drunk man to go on his way. He's done it with such ease and no aggression, even my bladder has stopped to watch. Bending close to Jesse's ear, I whisper softly.

"Why, he's more gorgeous than you said. No wonder it's taken you this bloody long to bring me here. He'll be eating out of my hands in no time."

Unable to make eye contact with him, he's not looking at me. Everyone else is, even the girls. Why is Joni ignoring me? He must be in a bad mood. That, or he's gay.

Hang on. He's looking at Jesse. Why? She looks like an extra in a vampire movie. Moving to the front of the queue, we wait to be clicked in.

"Ladies, welcome to DevO's. Jesse, you're looking particularly lovely tonight."

He can't mean it. Is he blind?

"Hey, Joni. This is Zoe - I mean Lola, the one I told you about who's just moved to the city?"

Prodding her in the back for messing up my name, she turns, giving me a filthy look while Joni clicks us in not paying any attention to what she's said. Smiling, trying my best to make eye contact, he's having none of it, almost pushing us out the way.

"What a prick. He must be blind if he thinks you look particularly lovely."

Looking back to see if his sneaky eyes are taking a sly peek at me from behind, they are still focused on Jesse, who I'm following to the bottom of some steps.

"Are you having a laugh? In these heels? How the fuck am I going to walk all the way up? People will see right up my dress. I've only got a bloody G-string on."

Rolling my eyes, starting the ascent, I'm far from happy, taking my coat off and pulling it around my waist. I'm not usually this prudish, but I'm afraid I might pee myself.

"Eighteen, nineteen, twenty. Fucking hell, I'm going to kill you for not warning me about these."

Rolling her eyes at me, Jesse opens the door where we are welcomed by a boom from the speakers, and Ricki, the owner, who gives her a chip for a free drink at the bar. Introducing me, I feel his hand as it slips down my back and pats my bottom while he seductively looks into my eyes and places an extra chip into my palm.

"Have another one on me, pretty lady."

Wide-eyed, laughing, thanking him, Jesse's waiting, rolling her eyes again, pointing to her watch. It's only half past nine, what's her hurry? The place is half empty, so I don't know why she's made us come early. She says it's to take advantage of the free drink and free entry for ladies before ten o'clock. Bloody hell, if this is her favourite club, I'm doomed.

Waving from his booth to us, the DJ starts playing the opening riff to 'The Model' by Kraftwerk. Blowing him a kiss, Jesse explains who he is, smiling at him, pretty sure I recognise him from somewhere but I can't put my finger on it. He's definitely put the song on for me. There's nobody else here except a handful of older men hanging around the bar who nudge each other's elbows as we approach.

"I hope this is not grab a grandad night. C'mon, this is going to be way too easy. Time to get tanked."

Arriving home with the same amount of money I left with, all I had to do was flutter my eyelashes at the old guys who ended up buying every one of mine and Jesse's drinks. One guy even paid for our taxi home. All I'd had to do was give him a few minutes of French kissing and a little grope of my breasts. I'd felt charitable tonight and let his tongue lick me in other places, too. He'd cum even before I had. Thank God no one needed the disabled loo. Win, win all round in my opinion. I can't even remember what he looked like. I think he was cute. I vaguely remember passing him in the street on the way to the club, but I can't remember if he was with anyone. I'm sure there was a woman somewhere hanging around at the end of the night. More fool her. I would've told him to rack off. He was a good kisser though, and his tongue had worked wonders below. I needed that. Jesse wasn't happy and didn't want to leave me on my own, so had just chatted to Joni. The woman hanging around ended up leaving with the guy after I'd finished with him. Why are some women so stupid? I don't know why I worried so much earlier in the night. Living in the city was going to be a doddle.

Chapter Thirty

"Long before I became 'rich and famous' I just sat around drinking wine and staring at the walls."

— Charles Bukowski

A month later, staring out the same window at the same scene, I still have no job. My parents are constantly breathing down my neck about work, and I'm terrified I only have a few months left to start making some money. I can't go back to living in hell. My dad I can cope with. My mother? I'd rather live on the streets.

Sleeping with however many men in the hope any of them offers me a job, all I've managed to pick up is a dose of Chlamydia and a reputation for being a slut. Why I'm the slut is a joke. The men I sleep with are just as much sluts as me. They hook up with however many women as they please, and most of them are married, or with long term partners, saying they needed to 'add a little spice' to their dreary sex lives. I, at least, am single and am happy to admit to how many people I've slept with. My sex life is far from dreary, but it's not exactly mind-numbingly good either.

Counting the men in my head, visualising each one, I can't single out any as being drop-dead amazing in bed. Their poor wives and girlfriends. If that's how they performed for me, then God only knows what those poor women have to put up with. I'm yet to meet a man who is as adventurous in bed as myself. I'm bored with them and their inability to connect with what they're doing. It's wham-bam-thank-you-mam. They're only interested in how I look, the usual story. If one more man tells me he's 'visual' I swear, I'll bloody go nuts.

Impatient for something to happen, alone with a bottle of wine for company, I look from the window to the clock seeing the little hand is in between ten and eleven. Officially bored o'clock, I'm tired, depressed, and coming round to the fact I'll probably end up back at home wiping my parents' arses, so I may as well make the most of the time I have left and go and have some fun.

Lifting myself off the couch, clutching the wine bottle with one hand, my other hand clings to the arm of the couch, helping my legs steady themselves while they try to walk in a straight line. Thinking they are walking around corners, I have to grab the walls to stop myself falling, wondering just how much I've drunk. Managing to navigate myself to my room, the wine bottle is still in my hand, glugging some while I stare into my wardrobe with no idea what I'm going to wear or where I'm going to go.

I have to admit, I'm feeling suffocated in my little space tonight and need to get out, away from the four walls I stare at most days. By now I thought I'd have loads of friends. I thought I'd have a life too, but no one, except Jesse, really wants to get to know me.

Throwing the wine bottle against my bedroom wall, screaming, instantly regretting it as glass shards bounce everywhere, the smell diffuses through the air like air freshener. Even worse, the wine is all gone and I'm not even able to lick it off the carpet.

"You stupid bitch. Why did you go and do that?"

Laughing at myself in the mirror, I'm more than a little drunk. I look pissed, and my makeup is smudged everywhere. How have I let myself get like this?

The wine smell is everywhere, and now I can't walk on the carpet in my bare feet because of the glass. Quickly, but very carefully, manoeuvring my way out of the bedroom, the brush and pan have decided to play hide and seek and it takes me ages to find them. Why did I put them outside? My slippers, just beside the door, are cold, checking for spiders before slipping them on. I'm obviously not too drunk then.

The big bits of glass are much easier to find, not so easy are the little glistening shards, which I decide need to be sucked up with the hoover. Dragging it out of hiding, I listen for every slither until I can only hear the suction of the wool being pulled from the carpet. The last thing I want or need is a cut foot.

Back at my wardrobe, satisfied I'm out of harm's way, I browse through the huge amount of dresses I have. The only time I really get to wear any of them is when I'm out with Jesse. I'd love to date like other girls my age, but I only ever end up fucking the men I like, none of them ever seeming interested in anything other than that. So many people find me intimidating. Stuff them. Tonight I'm going the extra mile. Tonight I'm going to make myself the intimidating queen.

Deciding on a sparkly silver dress, it always brings attention, and God knows I need some tonight. Throwing my grubby dressing gown and pyjamas on the already full floor, I catch a whiff of myself, sniffing my armpits, debating whether to have a shower. Fuck it, I can't be bothered, and anyway, whoever I end up with won't give a flying fuck about how I smell. They will just have to have me au natural. Scouring the floor for clean G-strings, they make a pretty trail to my bed picking them up one by one, smelling each of them to try and find a clean pair. Why have I left the washing so long? Smelling them, keeping the cleanest one in my hand, I throw the rest back on the floor and make sure the one I have has no glass on it. Wouldn't that just be my luck? To end up in A&E with a cut fanny.

Pulling them on, carefully draping my dress over my body, I

watch through the mirror as it clings to every curve. Turning around to check my booty, bending over to see just how much ass will be on show, I'm happy with the way it looks. I'll definitely be getting attention tonight. My five-inch silver heels, which I find under more piles of crap, prove more difficult to put on, struggling to balance. My legs don't like the height from the floor to the bed, having to go back into the lounge to sit on the couch to do them up. If the wine, quite clearly still in my system, wants a fight, I'm up for it. I won't let it get the better of me. A good ten minutes, and a lot of huffing and swearing later, my shoes are secure.

Quickly checking the time, it's half eleven; if I don't get my butt into gear I won't end up leaving. My smudged make-up needs touching up after spending the afternoon relieving my boredom by giving myself a makeover. Not a very good one, I have to redo my eyeliner, foundation, and rouge, which is not a very good idea when you're half pissed. My hair, still in a side ponytail, looks like I've just stepped off an 80's music video set.

Releasing it, managing to tangle some of the hair around my nails, I end up fighting with the strands, unknotting the clumps with my fingers. Rummaging around my horde of clothes for my crimpers, I find them under a clump of clothes, turning them on, waiting for them to heat up while I tease my non-existent fringe with a comb I've found on my dressing table. Not really having a clue what I'm doing, I throw the comb away and crimp whatever I can, grabbing my hairspray, covering my entire head in mist, suddenly unable to breathe. Coughing, closing my eyes as the fumes fill the room, I don't know what it is about the smell of hairspray. I love it. It reminds me of being young and going to the hairdresser with my mum. Those were happier times for me. That was before she changed, before I changed.

Looking through the haze to my mirror, I think I look good. Something's missing, though. The sides just hang, not really doing anything. Tying them up with a scrunchie, fluffing the top into a fountain, it's ok considering how pissed I am.

Something's burning, turning to see my crimpers eating one of my G-strings on the floor, grabbing the crimpers and quickly yanking the plug from the wall, running to the kitchen like a maniac and standing them on a ceramic plate to cool down. I don't want to be responsible for any fire. My mother would love that.

High heels already killing my feet, I ignore the pain for the sake of my legs which are looking the best they've ever possibly looked. I won't let anything get in the way of me having a good time tonight, especially my feet.

Standing before my full-length mirror caressing my curves with my hands, inspecting my work to make sure I look the part, my nipples harden, standing out like spotlights on a car. Rubbing them to make them warm, I'm tempted to play with myself before I go. Men these days don't really give me what I need or want, finding my own hands do a better job. I do need a little skin on skin, though, just for one night. No one ever just wants to enjoy me for me. Will tonight be any different?

Not aroused anymore, my thoughts have put me off, stumbling to the kitchen to retrieve another bottle of wine I opened earlier in the day. Warm and sickly sweet, it makes my stomach swirl a little, only managing to finish half of it, calling a cab at the same time giving the flat a once over. Satisfied everything is switched off, I make my way, very carefully, down the stairs to the waiting cab. Tonight, I'm going to have some fun.

The driver straight away checks me out through the mirror asking where I'm from and where I'm going. I should wind him up and tell him I'm on the game, but I don't, making something up and smiling sweetly. I don't actually know where I'm going, but I quite like that I don't have a definite plan. It makes my night already seem that little bit more exciting. Asking him to drive down Vivian Street, it's not busy tonight at all which I'm surprised at. The usual girls are on the usual corners, and the seedy little bars have the usual line of seedy little people queuing up to get their cheap thrills. Apart from that, there are only a few homeless strays wandering about. I wonder if the driver thinks I'm a stripper, or high-class hooker. God knows I look like one and we are in the area where they are known to come.

Asking to stop at a random bar I fancy the look of, I'm about to get out when the scary man with Kermit the Frog on his vest starts walking my way. Looking a lot scarier up close, he's like the living dead with eyes as crazy as the ones on his vest. I'm pretty sure he's stoned or high on something by the way he holds out his hands in front of his body, like a zombie looking for food. Walking past my cab, quickly turning my face, paying the driver so he doesn't see me, I prefer seeing the scary guy from my flat where I feel safe. The driver looks at me puzzled, like he's asking himself a question, looking from me to the bar, shaking his head. I know exactly what he's thinking.

"I'm not a prostitute!"

"No. Sorry, lady, I just thought this kind of place isn't somewhere you'd come, that's all."

"What do you mean? This kind of place?"

Before he can answer, a huge doorman is at the car door opening it for me. Short, wavy blonde hair that perfectly accentuates his chiselled jaw and angular nose, makes him look European. Handsome, he holds the door open with a smile that doesn't tell me he fancies me at all. In fact, he's looking at me the same way the driver is. Is there something wrong with my makeup? My hair?

Checking my reflection in the cab window, nothing seems to look out of place, panicking, checking my boobs to see if any of them have slipped out, but they are exactly where they should be. I'm not used to reactions like this.

The huge Hulk-lookalike doorman, and his perfect black bow tie, welcome me with an unusually high voice, something I wasn't expecting. Stepping through a dark-red velvet curtain, instantly feeling like Alice in Wonderland, a secret corridor reveals itself leading me to a bar inside, the hazy smoke welcoming me in, blinking a thousand times until my eyes are focused enough to see. Quickly scouring the room with squinty eyes, spotting another woman on her own at the bar sitting on a stool, I make a beeline towards her, sitting a few stools down, just close enough to be comfortable.

Dingy and dark, the place smells of sex, worried I've chosen some drug den or underground brothel. It'd be just my luck. Busying myself with the cocktail list, deciding on one I've never had before, I smile at the cute barman to get his attention, asking for a frozen Margarita, intrigued, watching what he puts inside, regretting my decision when I see him layer the rim of the glass with salt. Pouring into my glass from a slushy machine on the side, I'm not impressed, him explaining it's already pre-made, me pretending to be happy.

Screwing up my face at the salt, he laughs, handing me a straw, gagging at the coldness of the drink which is sending my brain into spasms, feeling like I've swallowed a massive lump of ice, rubbing my throat, and waiting for the pain to subside. I need something to line my stomach, spotting some nuts on top of the bar, nibbling a few and secretly wishing they were the sexy bartenders; but he's ignoring me, engrossed in listening to some man who's just come on stage to review beers and chippies.

Seeing a poster for Open Mic night, guessing he must be one of the acts, I'm presuming this guy can't find work anywhere else. Quite amusing, he's tall and handsome in a geeky kind of way. Stocky in frame, his brown mousy hair, which is cut short, makes his eyes look too close together, but not too close that they look weird. His long, strong, square jaw shows off nice straight white teeth, and his bobble nose must have something on it because he keeps wiping it with his left hand, like he's flicking something off it. It must be some nervous twitch because there's nothing on his nose I can see. I wouldn't like to be him. The audience don't seem to be engaged at all, most of them going about their business talking over him. I think he's quite funny and very knowledgeable, but as I know nothing about beer, I can only take his word for what beer goes with what chippie. Speaking in an Italian accent, he's yelling into the microphone that it's his favourite time and our favourite time. Guzzle time doesn't look much fun, watching him skull the entire glass, almost wincing in pain.

Guzzling my own drink, now at room temperature and a little less painful on my throat, the rim of my glass is smeared with my lip gloss, quickly retrieving my mirror from my tiny handbag, inspecting my lips, and reapplying it with a slightly steadier hand than when I originally put it on.

Clutching the glass in my hands for dear life, using the straw and sipping the last of my Margarita, it's not very busy in here tonight, and there doesn't seem to be a lot of women. Most are watching the guy on the stage who's now donned a black curly wig and is dancing to Italian music as he leaves the stage. I wonder who'll top that. Clapping him off, the compere thanks 'Charlz Reviews' who I must tell Jesse about. She'll think he's hilarious.

People to the right of the stage openly deal in what looks like drugs, oblivious to anyone around them. A small, round, fat, oldish man with dark eyes threatens me to keep watching, quickly averting my face, turning towards the bar and ordering another drink from the barman whose attention is now focused on me.

"Another one for a beautiful lady?"

"Another cocktail please, but not that one. I want one that's a little sweeter on my tongue."

I look at his name tag.

"Jayden."

Smiling and recommending a Cosmopolitan, I lick my lips at him wondering if he'll be the lucky one tonight.

A few seats down, the other woman, who, I see is similarly dressed to me, turns, smirks and winks. Hand in the air, her voice is familiar, but I can't put my finger on it.

"Never trust a man with a tiny cock."

Winking at the barman, she looks me up and down.

"You're hot. Nice to see you this close up."

Extending her hand, long pink fingernails invite me to shake.

"Tiffany, darling."

Taking her hand, I know exactly who she is. Even more gorgeous close up, her big dark-brown eyes are covered in black eyeliner, and her eyelids look like they've been sprayed with a rainbow. Long false eyelashes, tiny nose, full pink lips, and the highest cheekbones I've ever seen, her smile is genuine and welcoming. The wig however, Adam's apple and big hands are the only things that would indicate she is indeed a man. Legs all the way up to her neck, they are crossed over, uncovered by a dress that looks like it's been painted on showing her pins off to perfection. It's obvious why she's so popular with the men. That, and the breasts, which are being pushed up and out to an inch of their lives, her big boobs, tiny waist, long legs, and tight little butt are the perfect caricature of what men want women to look like. The only person I've seen who comes even a tiny bit close to being as perfect as myself, I extend my hand smiling back.

"I'm Lola. You're quite hot yourself. Get a lot of business from where I watch? Not working tonight?"

"Night off. Us girls need some fun too, don't we? My mouth could do with a rest. There's only so many cocks you can suck a night. Ha."

Winking at me, laughing, clinking glasses, we chat, bonding immediately.

"I'll leave you ladies to it. I'll hopefully see you around, Lola?"

Smiling, the twinkle in his eye is hypnotic. Arching my eyebrow, licking my lips, I don't leave him guessing what I'm thinking.

"Hope so, Jayden."

Talking for what seems like hours, I find out Tiffany's real name is Rice, and that she's originally from Fiji. She's not happy about her birth name.

"That's one of the reasons I chose to be a woman. My parents must've been on drugs to call me after something people bloody eat."

One of four children, her other siblings, two brothers, Happy and Joni, and sister Carole, knew very early on that she was 'different.' Identifying as a girl for as early as she can remember, she'd loved sparkles and pretty things, especially My Little Ponies, remembering combing their different coloured hair for hours underneath her sheets at night with the support of a torch her sister had given her.

"Carole always snuck me toys she knew I'd love; but my brothers, they were not so cool. Anyway, enough of talking about me. Let's get out of here and go have some fun."

Looking at her tiny diamond watch, it's now one in the morning. Grinning at me, holding my gaze with a cheeky arched eyebrow, I wait, holding my breath in anticipation of what she's going to say next.

"Wanna go to a party? It's at one of my friend's bars. It's the fourth anniversary of being open. You can be my plus one."

"It's one am. Will it still be open?"

"Darling, of course it will still be open. This is the city remember? The party will go all night. Are you in?"

"OMG, yes. Let's go."

"Ok, but first we have to do something about that hair! Girrrl! Come to the bathroom, I'll fix it for you."

Walking a few blocks in my high heels, my feet are already dying, and I'm cold. At least my hair looks good, now beautifully teased to an inch of its life. Fighting against the bitterly cold wind, I hang onto Tiffany's arm for dear life as the early morning chill slowly creeps all the way up to my neck, pissing myself off that I've worn a tiny dress. Suggesting to Tiffany that we walk faster to warm ourselves up, it's like we're taking our lives in our hands desperately trying not to break our necks falling on the uneven pavements. My bladder is howling too, full to the brim with cocktails; I could kick myself for not emptying it before I left. I was in such a hurry to party I thought I could hold on. I don't know if I can. Contemplating whether to risk peeing in an alleyway, I'm very quickly reminded where we are.

"Open for business?"

Jumping out of my skin, nearly peeing myself, I glare at the seedy looking man with shoulder-length hair, shifty dark eyes, and a small goatee.

"You fucking bastard. I nearly pissed my pants. No! We are not open for business, now fuck off."

Apologising, he raises his hand, laughing like a hyena as he walks off sending chills down my already cold spine. Tiffany's eyes laugh at me.

"Never a dull moment on the streets, honey."

Passing a lot of people she knows; I'm astonished to see how many men are still out and about looking for thrills. It's a different world than the one I'm used to. I have to admire the girls' bravery. Tiffany rolls her eyes, laughing at my naivety.

"They're not brave, honey. They just need their next fix."

Thankfully arriving at the bar five minutes later, I'm happy to be off the streets, watching as the big burly doorman recognises Tiffany, nods, and lets us straight in.

Bam.

All my senses alert, I already know this is going to be a night to remember.

Chapter Thirty-One

"No one looks back on their life and remembers the night they got plenty of sleep."

— Marcel Pantera

Stepping into a world buzzing with an energy I've never seen before, 'Hot Flush' is draped in wall to wall Drag Queens of all shapes and sizes who talk, dance, snog, and fuck with an abandon I've only ever seen in porn films. My eyes are spoiled for choice as groups of men and women openly partake in what looks like orgies from different corners, making even me blush.

I thought I'd seen it all.

This is on another level.

It's like every Drag Queen, and everyone they know, has descended on this little bar tonight. I've never seen a place so packed full of different looking people.

Already in love with what I see, the DJ plays a song I adore, nudging Tiffany in the ribs to dance with me, but she's pointing to different people, saying something to me, not hearing a word she's saying. Singing along to 'A Little Respect,' I see another queen below moving her hands to the music, while another queen watches her intently. Intrigued, I can't keep my eyes off them, seeing another queen spot me, nudging the one who's being signed to on the shoulder, who points at me and smiles. Blowing her hand as if to give me a kiss, she signs something to me, pointing to her hearing aids behind both ears, laying two front fingers on top of her right ear to let me know she is deaf. I'm mesmerised, wanting more than anything to be able to sign back, but all I do is wave and blow her a kiss, which she seems happy with.

All at once, a great rush of energy descends on the place as the crowds, including my deaf friend, stops what they're doing and starts to part, making way like Moses himself is in the bar.

Floating through the bar, waving at everyone like she's royalty, a seven-foot-tall Amazonian Queen smiles and blows kisses to her adoring crowd, walking in the highest heels I think I've ever seen. Adding at least three inches to her already gigantic height, electric-blue strappy heels show off legs that never end, covered in black and white stripy tights; a bright orange, tiny, fluffy tutu, striped black and white, long-sleeve midriff top make sure her and her abs stand out. All that is exotic enough, but it's her bald head I can't stop looking at.

Across the top of it rests a mohawk as green as a Keel-billed Toucan, and all around it her head is emblazoned with intricate markings which I can't figure out are tattooed or painted? A long extravagant bright-blue curly beard and chunky blue eyelashes, at least five inches long, compliment her huge brown eyes to perfection. Eyelids that have been carefully painted yellow, purple, blue, and red like a rainbow, look similar to Tiffany's, quickly glancing over to her eyes, understanding why she's painted hers the same. In fact, nearly all the queens have the same eye makeup on. Why didn't I notice it when I walked in? The seven-foot-tall queen's overdone rouge and huge red lips smile down at Tiffany, embracing her in a big bear hug. I've never seen anything so alluringly bizarre in my life.

"Hello, daaarling. I thought you'd never come, where have you been, bitch?"

Introduced to 'Delirious,' it is her bar's anniversary tonight. Of course. It had to be. Embracing me like a long-lost friend, kissing me on both cheeks, I'm in love.

"Welcome, daaarling. Enjoy the night. You're gonna have the best time you've ever had in your life. Stay with Tiff though, or you'll be eaten alive. Ha, ha, ha."

Striding away to greet more people, her bright-yellow shawl glides two feet after her, surprised no one stands on it.

Looking around in utter amazement, my eyes feast on one queen in full Marilyn Monroe regalia. White halter-neck dress and huge white wig, she has extra-long black eyelashes, thick black eyeliner, rainbow eyeshadow and non-existent eyebrows pencilled on her fore-head. Sharp red rouge on her cheeks, and overdone red glossy lips, her face is older, sagging in places that give you a clue to how old she really is. The breasts, obviously false, defy gravity and are the only youthful thing about her. Nowhere near as beautiful as Marilyn, she stands in a corner rubbing her huge exposed false tits, licking her lips at a young man, who sits with his back to the wall in obvious terror. Grabbing one of his hands, she urges him to touch her, meanwhile, a woman, who is probably his girlfriend, sits open-mouthed, glaring at her, waiting for her boyfriend to respond.

"Good luck with that, love," I laugh under my breath, approaching the bar with Tiffany. Full bladder forgotten, I need a drink to really appreciate where I am, climbing on top of something squishy, which I have to steady myself on before ordering us both the house cocktail. Underneath, my feet feel something lumpy, almost moving, steadying myself again, holding onto the bar as I wait for our drinks. Above, a tv screen is playing full-on porn, looking around, embarrassed to see if anyone else is watching. The men onscreen lick and touch each other everywhere, a young, naked, handsome man, who looks to be close to my age, writhes in false ecstasy as he's felt up by a much older naked man who looks to be enjoying the experience more. I'm not sure whether I'm slightly turned on or off by it, but I can't stop watching the older man as he positions the young man just in front of a mirror so he can watch from all angles. Engrossed, seeming to be the only one watching, I'm a little flustered, shifting from one foot to the other, my high heels digging again into whatever I'm standing on. Quickly checking my shoes to see what they are stuck in, to my amazement I'm standing on a dirty rolled-up carpet.

"What the fuck? Why in God's name is there a fricking carpet at the bar? How weird."

Digging my heels to get some sort of balance, a sudden howl from below makes me jump. Tiffany, who's been watching, laughs in my ear.

"Don't worry about Ralph, darling. He just gets off on people standing on him, especially the heels. The harder you dig, the more he cums."

"What the fuck?"

Looking down, a bright-purple bald head pops out the end of the carpet; Ralph looks up at me in ecstasy, blowing me a kiss. Nearly falling backwards in shock, grabbing my drink, and unrigging my heels, I dismount from the moving carpet.

"Crazy mother fucker."

Luckily, there is no blood on my best heels, moving away from Ralph, who is still blowing kisses at me while I stand gulping my Hot Flush cocktail. Not prepared for the brain freeze, my head starts to pound, and even worse, my throat, which now feels like I've just swallowed an iceberg, hurts like hell. I've only picked another cocktail I shouldn't have. Rubbing my neck vigorously to try to warm it up, I'm wondering what the hell they put in my drink. Ralph winks at me before popping his head back into the carpet as another unsuspecting woman stands on top of him. Popping my glass back on the bar, carefully sidestepping Ralph, my weak bladder reminds me it needs to be emptied. It's been the same since I was a young girl putting it down to the anxiety of wetting my pants only once, but once was enough. My mother had never let me forget it, periodically bringing it up at dinner parties whenever she felt like humiliating me. My father hated her for hurting me so much. It had mentally scarred me more than my mother knew.

The thought of that day now at the forefront of my mind, the long queue triggers my anxiety, willing my bladder to hold, standing at the back of the waiting line with the others, searching for Tiffany, whom I'm unable to see in the crowds. Watching people to keep myself distracted, the Marilyn Monroe queen approaches me from out of nowhere, looks me up and down and blows me a kiss, breasts still exposed. Looking at me she says, "you're hot," staggering through the toilet door as men all around touch her breasts as she walks past, which she looks happy for them to do.

Weird how they touch a man dressed as a woman but aren't interested in touching real breasts.

From the speakers, 'Divine' sings, 'You Think You're a Man but You're Only a Boy,' the high squeals of different queens' voices piercing my ears as they approve and start to sing along. Two men at the bar watching the porn, feel each other up as others around them watch them feel each other up. It feels like any minute there might be a full-on live show. The place is so full, the different voices all blending together, amazed anyone can hear each other. The reverberation of the combined noises is making my head buzz, or the drink is working its magic.

My nose, suddenly coming alive, picks up the scent of cheap aftershave and cum combined, although it is much stronger than I'm used to. Attaching itself to me like an invisible cloak, I smell myself, already stinking of it. I will definitely need a shower when I get home.

Still in line for the loo, bladder now growling at me, a man in normal clothes approaches holding an extravagant silver tray. On top sits a little silver box, following his finger, seeing his eyes and mouth don't seem to be in time as he struggles to talk over the noise.

"COcaiiine, ecstasssy, criiistal Meth?"

"What."

"COcaiiine, ecstasssy, criiistal Meth?"

Have I heard that right? Is the man offering me class A drugs? Mouth hanging open, I sheepishly look to the people beside me who are also waiting for the loo. Smiling wide, one man nods his head vigorously at me, the other, a young, very thin ugly girl in heavy eye makeup, smirks, basking in my discomfort. Hand to my heart, I'm shocked at the openness of the drug deals, quickly looking over to two policemen who stand close by, choosing to ignore what's going on.

"What the hell?"

Shrugging my shoulders, buying a couple of ecstasy pills, I swallow one saving the other one in my bra if I should need it later. The vigorous head shaker whispers in my ear from behind.

"Don't mind the Pigs. They're not even real. Just like to freak people out. You'll be alright."

Smiling, I can't keep up with his shaking head and eyes that are bobbing right out of their sockets. Whatever he's on, it's strong stuff.

Bladder now ready to burst, I'm next in line for the loo, trying not to pee on the spot. Unprepared for how busy it is in the restroom; Marilyn Monroe kneels on the floor in the corner blowing the same young man who sat at her table. Winking at me, smiling, she continues to go down on him as people around her laugh in conversations of their own, all oblivious to the different things going on around them. No one seems interested in using the toilet for anything other than snorting, having sex or talking. Pouncing on a cubicle when it finally becomes free, I quickly clean the toilet seat with tissues and ease myself onto the seat, reflecting on what I've experienced in the last hour. I can almost hear my bladder sigh in relief below, listening to the sounds around me as the pill starts to take effect. It's like being in my own little toilet soap opera, nearly giving myself away snorting with laughter.

"I'm gonna cum."

"Not in my mouth, you filthy boy. Here wank over my tits."

"Arghhh."

"Now you gotta clean me up, darrrrrling. Ha, ha, ha."

"Girrl, you gotta try the E's. They are strong tonight. I'm cumming in my pants as we speak."

"I need to vomit. What's my girlfriend gonna do when she finds out?"

"Oh, darling. Every man gets sucked off once in his life."

Laughing, loving the buzz of being high, there's not a worry in the world. Fifteen minutes later, exiting the loo, hugging all the angry faces waiting to use it, I head up some stairs to another room, looking for Tiffany, who seems to have disappeared.

Blondie's 'Atomic' opening riff suddenly blasts from the speakers and a whole room of people dressed in nothing but black, dance like sardines squashed together with no room to move. I'm hot, feeling like I've been hit with a nuclear blast and it's making me feel almost faint watching their arms wave about and sweat hit each other; all I want to do is get in there and dance.

Vampire look-alikes from every angle give me funny looks as I push my way into the centre, not sure whether to be scared as they all circle around me smiling. Envisioning holes in the ceiling opening up and spraying me with blood, will they pounce on me and suck every last bit of blood out of my body?

Screaming, the vampires laugh, pushing me back and forth from one vampire lookalike to the other until I can't take anymore. I'm a fish out of water, this is another world, a complete contrast to what is happening only a few feet away downstairs. The DJ welcomes me over the loudspeaker, and the vampires, who all stare at me like food, turn and circle me again. Hardly able to breathe, I only last till the end of the song. My dry throat is screaming for water, hardly able to swallow.

Laughing, the DJ waves goodbye and smiles, sure I see fangs.

Making my way downstairs to look for Tiffany, the place looks to have filled up with even more people. The bar is so full people are finding it hard to move. Even Ralph the carpet guy has decided to call it a night, standing at the bar covered in purple spike marks all over his pale body and what looks like cum stains all over his pants. He's talking to the two deaf queens and spots me, winking, mouthing 'thank you,' blowing me a kiss, meanwhile the porn is still playing above his head, and the guy selling drugs is still doing the rounds. Marilyn Monroe looks to be having a row with the girlfriend of the bloke she blew, and Delirious, the owner of the bar, is being photographed with a celebrity I can't remember the name of.

Now completely out of it, I need my bed, deciding to call it a night. I have my limits, and this is one party too bizarre, even for me.

Slipping away without saying goodbye to Tiffany, who is still on the missing list, I can't believe what a fantastically surreal night I've had. I'll be sure to thank her next time I see her. My arms hardly able to go around the bouncer hug him hard as I leave, him helping me into a waiting cab.

"Say goodbye to Tiffany for me," blowing kisses to him and everyone smoking outside who laugh and wave me off.

"I love you all."

Sitting back, the seat feels like rock against my back, wincing, quickly asking the driver to stop at the first open takeaway place he can find. Donna's Dream Donuts is still open, buying six sugar-glazed donuts, finally arriving back at my flat at four in the morning, coat-less. The cab driver doesn't want a hug, or a donut, quickly driving off to his next job. Cold and not really wanting to walk up the three flights of stairs, I fling my heels off nearly falling over picking them up off the ground. Steadying myself, holding onto them for dear life, I tell them to move onto the steel stairs, welcoming the coldness on my soles. Tingling with delight, my feet are nearly as excited about eating the donuts as my stomach, drawing the last bit of energy I can muster to run up the stairs, nearly falling, twice. Jingling the keys out of my handbag, which takes everything I have to focus, the door helps me balance while I open it, calling to my couch like it understands what I'm saying.

"Couch, where are you? I'm fucked."

Swaying, throwing the donuts in the kitchen on my way to the sitting room, I fly through the air jumping onto my little two-seater, happy to be somewhere comfortable. My donuts. Where are they? I'm sure I just had them in my hands.

Groaning, lifting myself off the couch, my feet moan in protest, finally finding the donuts in the kitchen. How the fuck did they get there? I must be more drunk than I think.

"Coffee, you can't have a donut without coffee."

Staggering to the couch, flopping down with my box of donuts; nearly spilling hot coffee all over myself. My fuzzy eyes watch the girls who are still on the corner, my mouth orgasming as one of the donuts melts in my mouth. Scoffing one after the other, reflecting on my night, asking myself if it was even real, I can't believe that I wasn't hit on, not even once by anyone. Marilyn Monroe told me I was hot, but that was it. Never had I experienced that before. Ever. It's the only place I've ever been where men weren't interested in me at all. Not one. What a night. I couldn't have dreamt it up.

Waking the next afternoon, the phone ringing sounds like an alarm, my head is thumping, hardly able to swallow. Looking around, slits for eyes see I'm still lying on the couch in my clothes from the night before, and sticking to one of my breasts, is a half-eaten donut and the spare ecstasy tablet, peeling them off, listening for the beep of the answer phone. Sticking the donut in my mouth, it's a little hard but still delicious, stopping in mid chew, nearly choking as my mother's voice echoes through the tiny room.

"Zoe. Zoe. Pick up the phone or I'll bloody come over and pick it up for you. You'd better have a job. Ring me."

Remembering the pill's effect, my worries now well and truly back; I pop it into my mouth without hesitation, lay back and wait for the magic to begin again.

Chapter Thirty-Two

Meeting Tiffany the following Tuesday at Hot Flush, I'm not surprised to see Delirious looks as extravagant as ever in a tiny electric-blue sequin dress. Today, though, she has a full-on bright-orange wig which perfectly matches her now bright-orange beard. As she talks, her face moves like it is dancing, laughing when I tell her about my night and how I had to go home because of how hot I was.

"Daaarling, you should've gone up to the fridge room to cool off. Isn't that what women want when they have a 'flush'? It's not called 'Hot Flush' for nothing. Ha! You would've been fine in no time."

How could I have not noticed the fridge room? Gliding off to the same guy selling the E's, Tiffany and I watch as Delirious stops at the bar and shoos him off to another corner where it's more discreet. Tiffany doesn't like him, and neither do I, telling her how pushy he was the night I came with her. Luckily for me, she says she knows a dealer that some of her friends use and happily passes on his details, explaining she's heard he has the 'best shit' in town.

Handing me my coat, thankful she picked it up for me, I hug her close, ordering some drinks, chatting about our respective nights.

Very soon the chat changes, and just like that, we are opening up about our lives, Tiffany telling me about her early life in Fiji. The youngest of four children, she didn't have it easy; it's like I'm back there, witnessing it first-hand.

"One disastrous night Happy, my brother, caught me playing with some My Little Ponies under my sheet and dragged me to our father who burnt the lot of them in front of me. I was only seven. Can you believe, he tried to beat the 'gayness' out of me, even took me to the local church to be exorcised, but of course it never worked. My mother tried to accept it, but when I asked to be called 'Tiffany,' at the age of sixteen, the family just couldn't cope anymore saying I was bringing shame to it. They kicked me, and my belongings, including the ponies I'd managed to save, to the curb. I lived on the streets of Suva with the other 'embarrassments' and even managed to find a job at a local corner shop after giving the owner a blowjob behind the bins one night. Two years, and at least a thousand blowjobs and my virginal butt later, the same owner helped me apply for a passport and a ticket to fly to Wellington, where I've been ever since."

"God, that sounds awful. Why are parents so fucking awful. Mine have given me six months to get a job or I'll be kicked out. I love my father, but my mother is a bitch with a capital B. I'd do anything never to see her again."

"Don't say that, baby. Family are all we have. Do you have any brothers or sisters?"

"Nope. Just me. I was adopted. Only found out two years ago. My mother saved that grenade for my sixteenth birthday. She didn't tell me in private like most parents would. No. She told me in front of everyone at the restaurant we were at. I didn't cope very well with it. I'll never forgive her. Anyway, I don't want to talk about it. I want to know about you. What did you do once you moved to Wellington. That must've been so scary."

"I'm so sorry, baby. If you ever need to talk, just let me know."

Her big arms wrapped right around me; I'm shocked at how close I already feel to Tiffany. She's like the big sister I always wanted.

Urging her to go on with her story, her soft lips brush my cheek as she hugs me again before continuing with her story.

"It was scary as hell coming here. Getting to Wellington nearly never happened, though. Joni, my other brother, who I kept in contact with when I was still in Suva, reluctantly helped me steal my birth certificate from my parents so I could get a passport, and very soon he followed me to Wellington using the excuse he was going to play rugby for a local team. It turned into reality once he arrived. He was scouted at a local match and was asked to play, and the rest is history. I don't think he plays much these days due to an injury. I'm sure my mother asked him to follow and keep an eye on me. I know Joni isn't happy with my gender change or choice of work, so I don't really see him much at all now."

"That's so sad, Tiffany. Do you miss him?"

"Yeah, a lot. But what can I do? He won't see me unless I'm dressed like a man. That was the only time I ever dressed as one. To see him. I hated it, but that's the price I paid for loving him. I'm sure Joni hates me because I was the reason he had to give up on his dream of becoming a doctor back in Suva. He was the only one who'd get on a plane and come over. Our mother wouldn't have let him live if he hadn't. I can't see him ever coming around. He hardly loves me as a man, so actually loving me as a woman is out of the question. I bumped into him one night when he was out with his rugby mates. It was after he injured himself and they took him out to cheer him up. They came into the bar I was working in at the time. I didn't know what to do. I knew he'd freak when he saw me because I was dressed like a waitress, so I asked one of the others to cover my table, but they fucking refused saying they were going on a break. I had to take these guys orders and try not to make eye contact with Joni. One of the other guys took me aside pretending to add something to the order, but he hit on me, asked me to meet him outside. So, thinking he was into that, I told him to meet me out in the alleyway for a 'quickie.' When I arrived, a few of them were waiting. They'd obviously been told by someone that I wasn't a girl and he and the rest of them each took turns beating me up, including my brother. He was the worst. He snarled into my face and called me a faggot right before punching me in the head."

"What an arsehole!"

Brushing a tear from my cheek I'm amazed at how emotional Tiffany's story is making me feel, softly squeezing her arm, encouraging her to go on.

"Total opposites we are, my brother and I. He's huge, handsome, plays rugby and is everything a family, especially a Fijian family wishes their son to be. I'm tall, thin, wiry, pretty, and would spend my life dancing and singing. He sends money to my parents every month making sure they're looked after, and still goes to church every week. I've made money and would send it if I knew they'd take it, but he's told them what I do for a living. They wouldn't touch it with a bar of soap. Not even if it was pure gold. To them it's money that's been made by the devil. I'm an embarrassment, shameful. I know that much. I heard they made up some story about me leaving, told the villagers I'd run away. Those people weren't dumb. Most of them knew what I was, but no one ever had the guts to confront my parents, actually tell them they knew I liked boys. Not even the dads who came looking for me out in the field, who took me aside discreetly and touched me. So many asked me to suck their dicks in the bushes, for Christ's sake. None of them helped me, though, because they were too embarrassed to admit what they were. They threatened to beat me if I ever told anyone. If only my parents knew, especially my father. Ha!"

"Why can't we all just live the way we want. Parents, people are such bastards, aren't they? If I was gay my mother wouldn't cope! Sad how we can't be who we want to be."

"Are you trying to tell me something, honey? Ha! You're way too pretty to be gay. Anyway, Mum tries to contact me every so often. She knows where I live through Joni, who I haven't seen since that night. She's softened over the years, but my father still refuses to have anything to do with me. He won't accept he's lost a son and gained a daughter. Carole, my sister, writes and has even said she'd come visit one day, but I know she won't. As for Happy? He's disowned me, like my father. He can't accept that this is who I want to be. His loss. Joni works close by at a club as the doorman. I go down and watch him when he's not looking, just to make sure he's ok. One day I hope he'll put the past behind us, move on and love me again. Until that day, though, I never want to come face to face with him. I never thought he'd ever hurt me as much as he did. I've forgiven him, but I'll never forget what he did."

Hugging Tiffany close, I haven't got the heart to tell her I know who her brother is. She doesn't need to know. I'm a little embarrassed I fancied him the first time I saw him. If I'd known what I know now, I wouldn't have looked at him twice. A song playing on the jukebox brings a tear to both our eyes. A man sings about leaving his family because he's gay. It's like the song has been played especially for Tiffany.

Stroking her cheek, the connection I feel towards her is extraordinary. Not in a million years did I expect this is what I'd be doing today; taking her hand in mine, squeezing it; urging her to go on with her story when she's ready. Wiping her tears away, the kindest eyes I've ever seen smile at me, breathing in hard, nodding, squeezing my hand back.

"I remember hearing 'Smalltown Boy' for the first time and crying my eyes out. It resonated right through to my soul. I'm lucky. I've made some good friends on the streets here in Wellington. Finally, I felt I belonged somewhere and had the family I always wanted where everyone looked out for each other no matter what. It felt different to Suva. I felt more accepted, freer here. Some nights, though, I feared for my life. There's one night I'll never forget. One piece of advice, honey. Don't ever get hooked on crack. Try anything else, just stay off the crack. I've been clean for a few years now and would never go back to it, ever. The dealers offer it to you for free and soon you're walking around and the only thing you think of is your next fix. Some days I couldn't even dress myself. I just stood there looking at the clothes, not able to even lift an arm to put on a shirt. Friends, strangers, I didn't care who they were, if I could steal off them, I did to get my next fix. I hung around the streets, filthy, dirty, stinking to high heaven, waiting for dealers to come by. One dealer, Spud, a nasty evil little bastard, near enough tried to kill me. I thank the Lord I came out of there alive."

"Oh, God. What happened?"

"He lured me to his apartment telling me he had drugs, the next thing I knew, he had a piece of wire around my neck trying to kill me."

"Fuck! OMG, what did you do?"

"Fuck alright. He kept me there for a whole day beating and raping me, and when I woke up, I'm sure he thought I was the living dead, the look on his face. He just let me get dressed and escorted me down the stairs and out onto the street again. Two months later, they found five women's bodies stashed in a freezer in one of his filthy rooms. All drug addicts."

"OMG! Are you serious? What a fucking lunatic!"

"I am serious as hell. I tried to tell the police the day he let me go, but they'd just looked at me like I was another crackhead. If they'd listened to me, then all those other women would still be alive. Fucking pigs."

"They're bastards. I remember going to see them when my friend, Jesse, went missing and they told me to come back when I was more 'useful.' They didn't help. They're bloody useless."

"They sure are. I don't even think they got into trouble for not listening to me. No-one came looking for me. Not one of them wanted to know my side of the story. The day I left that house was the day I came off the crack. It's the hardest thing I've ever had to do in my life, but back then I figured I wasn't going to get another chance at not being killed. Of course, it didn't last long. That's what crack does to you. It owns you, feeds off your need for it. My lowest night, when I was going to end it all, I met Gail. She saw me on a bridge and talked me down. She walked right up to me and spoke with a voice so soft; she made me feel valued, loved, relevant. I took her hand and let her take me to her place. She looked after me for weeks until I was clean. She was my gift from God, my saviour. I'll never forget what she did for me. I loved her so much and was very close to ending it all again when I heard she was gone. You see, I never got to say goodbye, tell her how much she meant to me. I carried so much guilt around for months because of it. If there's one thing I'd wish for, it would be a magic wand so I could see her just one more time, tell her how much I appreciated and loved her. Word on the street is she found a long-lost family relative just before passing. It probably killed her heart to finally find family. I know how much her heart bled after losing her two babies all those years ago. Bless that angel in heaven."

Crossing herself, kissing her hand, she places it next to her heart.

"My best friend, Jesse, you know, the one who works at The Orchard? She's Gail's niece. She still misses her, too. I really wish I'd met Gail. She sounded amazing."

"I think I remember your friend. I saw her at the funeral. What a small world. You'll have to make sure we all meet up. I'd love to see her again."

"I will, I promise. Anyway, what happened after the funeral? What did you do?"

"I was a mess. I still cry just thinking of her. She was my best friend, my street mother, and I still feel her loss. Every... single... day. After she passed I stayed clean, only for her. The first thing I wanted to do the day I found out she'd died was to find a way to numb the pain, but I stayed clean cause that's what she would've wanted. That's what she would've expected of me, and I sure as hell wasn't going to disappoint her, alive or dead."

"She really did sound amazing. I wish I had a mother like that. I would've loved to have felt loved by mine. All I ever felt from her was jealousy and after she told me I was adopted on my sixteenth birthday. Why do you think I want to escape from my life by getting high?"

"I understand, honey. It's awful wanting something so much knowing you're never going to get it. That's why I loved Gail. She was like the mother I always wanted. She would've protected me through thick and thin and would never have let a bully like my father hurt me. I really think she loved me like I was her child. She wasn't even that old. I'm sure living on the streets didn't help the way she looked. People thought she was a lot older than she was. For someone so young and especially the childhood she had, she was extremely maternal. She would've been an awesome mother. Everyone who knew her was heartbroken when she died. All I wanted to be was numb, so to keep my mind off the drugs, and her death, I became addicted to something else... sex. I started working the streets every night, finding as many men as I could. Black, white, fat, thin, tall, skinny, you name it. I didn't care as long as my mind was distracted from the hurt, and from myself. That was the only way to distract me from the crack. To start using another crack if you get my drift? Ha."

I'm amazed she can joke telling such a sad story, but I love her even more for it. Laughing along with her as she continues.

"One of my regulars, Roy, an ugly tiny Chinese man with the thinnest little chicken legs I'd ever seen, bought me an orchid every month. God knows where he thought I'd put it. Ha! He fell in love with me; I could see it in his eyes from the first moment I got into his car. He said he'd been watching me for months, but I already knew because I'd spotted him. I thought he was a serial killer or some pervert. Every time he came to the city, I'd see him sitting in his car, watching me. I thought he was waiting to kill me, and a few times I got scared, but he was just plucking up enough courage to come talk to me. He asked me at least six times to get into his car, but I wouldn't, not until I'd got some feedback from the other girls on the street. They told me he was harmless, that he was shy and just watching to see if I was ok. Anyway, after about six months of seeing him, he offered to take care of me, rent me a flat close by so he knew I'd be safe. The rest is history. I've been looking after him ever since if you get what I mean? Every month without fail a beautiful bouquet of flowers is delivered, and every so often, he'll surprise me with a different coloured orchid. I'm sure my angel in heaven sent him to me."

Watching Tiffany absentmindedly roll her finger around the rim of her glass, she talks about Gail some more, the grief in her voice the same as when Jesse has spoken of her. Suddenly she turns towards me and stares right at me, gently taking my hands, looking me dead in the eyes. There is a seriousness to them, but they are still kind, even in grief.

"I realise just how lucky I am. Life really is precious, Lola. You just don't know when your time is up, and lucky for me someone up there had other plans for me."

Pointing her eyes to the ceiling, crossing herself again, she kisses her hand when she's finished.

"Thank God for Gail, and Roy, and of course, our Lord Jesus. Without all of them, I wouldn't be here now, telling you anything. I'd be rotting in the ground, or worse, cut up in Spud's freezer. Roy knows I still work the streets, that I still need the distraction every now and then, but he's happy for me to do it, just not when he's in town, which suits me fine. It's all thankfully worked out for me. Gail, bless her soul, would've been so happy to see me settled. I wish my brother could be happy for me, too, but I figure, you can't have everything. I really hope he comes around one day, but I'm not counting on it. I think hell will freeze over first. I avoid any regular bars for fear of bumping into him, that's why I come here, and the place you met me. Remember? A seedy little gay bar to watch a bloke review chippies and beer. He's straight by the way, but nobody else will hire him. Hee, hee. My brother would never go there, or come to Hot Flush. Not in a million years. He lives close, though. I just don't know where. God, wouldn't it be hilarious if he turned out to be gay, too?"

"I wasn't going to tell you, but I know who your brother is. Jesse and I go to the club he works at practically every Wednesday. I'm a little embarrassed to say I thought he was hot the first time I saw him.

I won't be so nice to him next time I see him, that's for sure. Wait till I tell Jesse. She thinks the sun shines out of his arse."

"No, baby girl. Please, don't tell Jesse about this conversation. The only people who know any of this is Roy, and my angel in heaven, Gail. I don't know why, but I feel the same kind of connection with you as I did with her. I really don't want anyone else to know, even Jesse. Please, keep it to yourself. Promise me?"

Pinky promising, I know how hard it's going to be to keep my mouth shut about Joni, but I don't want to lose Tiffany as a friend, so will just this once keep my promise. Staring hard into my eyes, Tiffany's eyes smile, her kissing my hand and placing it on the table in front. Remembering what we were talking about five minutes before, I can't stop giggling.

"That guy reviewing the chippies and beer. He was such a crack up! Who was he again?"

"Oh yes! Charlz Reviews is quite unique. Guzzle time is always my favourite time of the night."

Laughing, we hug, both a little teary.

"I bloody wondered why I wasn't being hit on in that place. Usually men are lined up in front of me acting like puppies. I'm so glad I decided to go there that night. Never did I imagine I'd meet someone like you. Honestly, you're inspiring. You should write a book. I'd read it. Might be the only book I'll ever read. I could listen to you for hours."

Hugging again, she's buys another round of drinks and we toast to Gail and new beginnings for myself.

"Be careful though, baby. Remember what I told you about crack? Don't even be tempted. Just keep to the soft stuff. Promise me?"

Promising, I know my reliance on drugs is increasing, and Tiffany knows it too having been around enough people on drugs for most of her life. She knows the signs. This is another promise I'll keep. I can't lose her as a friend. They are few and far between. No-one, except Jesse, and now Tiffany, knows how the thought of heading straight back to my parents is sending me off the edge. I need something to keep me going.

Nothing seems to be going right for me. My looks and body are only scoring me cheap thrills and free pills, taking whatever I can, using the only thing I have to score shit for free, but even I know my looks and body will only last so long.

I need a job, or someone rich, but neither seems to be coming my way. To make it worse, the shit I'm scoring only keeps me high for a short amount of time, which isn't enough. I need more.

Setting up a meeting with the dealer Tiffany gave me, I'm curious to know if his shit is as superior as all of Tiffany's friends say.

Arranging to meet the following night in an alleyway downtown I know very well, I'm a teeny bit scared. I don't know this guy from Adam and have to trust Tiffany wouldn't set me up with anyone dangerous. I haven't told anyone, not even Jesse about it. She would only judge me and tell me not to do it, and right now I need people around me who won't tell me what to do. I need my escape from my pathetic life, and if he can give me what I need, I'm all for it. You never know, he might be gorgeous. I'm hoping he is because God knows all the men I've been with lately have looked like gorillas.

The following night, waiting in the alley, my distorted reflection on a metal sheet nailed to a broken window stares at me with anxiousness. I hope the dealer, who I now know is called Brett, likes what he sees. I've made more of an effort to look gorgeous tonight, hoping he might give me the shit for free if he likes what he sees.

Walking up and down like I have pins and needles in both feet, I'm nervous, watching people pass giving me dirty looks. They know why I'm here. I wish Brett would hurry the fuck up.

Fifteen long agonising minutes later, wondering whether to just call it a night and go home, I hear him before I see him. Sounding like a horse sauntering up the alleyway, his black cowboy boots clip clop in a steady rhythm as the silhouette of his big, curly, frizzy hair, comes into the light and stops. He looks like he has a halo around his head, but I can see he is anything but godly. Continuing forward, his thin face and lips are smirking, and his long horse-like chin and spindly little limbs, walk towards me in tight blue jeans, plain, white, slightly soiled *Led Zeppelin* t-shirt, and black tatty-leather tasselled jacket. Coming to a stop right in front of me, he taps his steel-heeled cowboy boots on the ground, whistling like the cat that got the cream. I'm praying to God he is *not* who I'm waiting for.

"You Lola?"

No! I hate myself.

For a dealer who earns a lot of money, he is not what I expected. I've dressed up, for Christ's sake. If I'd known he'd turn up looking like *this*, I would've worn track pants and no makeup.

Nodding at him, glaring, he knows I'm pissed off. The darkness of the alley casts shadows over his long face as his tiny, squinty black eyes framed in round John Lennon look-alike glasses, smile at me while his head scans my whole body up and down. His two front teeth hanging out of his mouth, gape at me; his long nostrils suck air in and out of his thin nose, snorting, making me feel like I'm actually having a meeting with a horse rather than a person. In his case a horse might be too nice a comparison, more like a mule.

The type of guy who wouldn't have a chance with anyone like me in real life, the look on the little dweebs face tells me he thinks the same, waiting for his thin lips to start moving, quickly beginning to think the meeting is a big mistake.

"I got all the best shit in town. Whatever you want, I can get, you just gotta give me twenty-four hours' notice and ring me on this phone number. Code word, 'sweet cheeks.' The other number is only for emergencies, got it?"

Smirking, licking his lips, one of his unmanly hands passes me a grubby piece of paper with what looks like leftover food on it. Taking it with two fingers, not hiding my disgust, I put it in my pocket, retrieving a tissue to wipe my hand, watching as he walks around me, whistling. My neck hurts from twisting, him stopping and bending down close to my ear, hearing his low nasally voice utter the words I so desperately don't want to hear.

"I'm sure you and me can come to some sort of 'arrangement' about payment."

Arching his right eyebrow, not leaving me guessing what he means, I'm stiff as a post, flinching as he reaches into his pocket to pull out a long fat joint.

"I ain't gonna hurt you, darling. No need to flinch."

Licking the joint seductively with his tongue, he's repulsive, watching him light the end and suck hard, letting the smoke escape from his mouth and swirl through the air.

"I got a lot of people growing this stuff. You'll like it."

Sucking hard, holding his breath, and pursing his lips, he waits to exhale as his eyes point to what he is holding, speaking before he does.

"This little lady is made with only class A female heads. The best for the best, aye?"

Leery, hungry eyes scan my body again stopping at my breasts, where they feast on my cleavage. Pulling my jacket across my chest, kicking myself again at my choice of clothing, I'm shivering as he closes in abruptly and wraps a thin hand around my neck. Pulling me close, I hold my breath, nearly passing out as he speaks.

"The best high you'll ever get. Smooth and easy on the throat, too."

Trying to blow some of the smoke into my mouth, his breath is rancid, quickly taking the joint from his hand and placing it between my lips. His spit on the end of it makes me gag, forcing myself to think of something happy as I suck hard, feeling the wetness on my lips. Holding my breath, within seconds it feels like I've swallowed the sun, the warmth radiating through my body, spreading to every limb. Swearing I can hear my heartbeat on the brick walls, the smoke surrounds us like a cocoon.

I've used this alley for all kinds of business in the past and know which corner is most discreet.

I wish I'd chosen a more public space.

Heart pulsing out of my chest, I hear every beat as his weedy little body closes in on me; the muffled sounds of people yelling and traffic stopping and starting fading into the background. Hyper focused on his warm breath on my neck, I hear him breathing in and out. It's like an alarm in my ear that's warning me to get the hell away. I want to run, escape from him, and am sure as hell he knows because my body can't help itself, twitching at every breath, every movement of his thin fingers. Hating that I don't know what will happen next, it's like a knife to my skin every time he touches me.

Like all the men before him, he's hardened at the sheer touch of me, but this feels a lot different from the rest. The other men looked for me, needed me to get them off, to make their sordid fantasies real, which I was more than happy to oblige. This man? Brett? He doesn't need me the same way. I need him more than he needs me, and he knows I wouldn't have chosen him if he was the last man on Earth. He only wants me because he can, because he's fully aware what someone reliant on drugs will do.

I hate myself.

Eyes boring into each other's skulls, I know he knows what I'm thinking, which makes it worse.

His repulsive body is even worse to touch, feeling his hardness against me.

I want to be sick.

Close to his chest, nearly passing out from the stale smell of his body odour, I reluctantly let my hand slip underneath his t-shirt to his back, balking as my fingertips feel hundreds of bumps, some bigger than others. Fighting to breathe, my lungs try to filter out the smell as my fingers touch the coarse bumps on his back. Too big for goosebumps, the skin around them is wet, almost greasy, and some of the bumps are crusty and hard, scratching the tops like I'm reading braille up and down his back. Rubbing my fingers together, feeling like I've put them in a big pot of oil, it's disgusting, quickly pulling my hand out and wiping my fingers on my dress, pushing away from him abruptly.

Looking up at the sky, the full moon shines directly down the alley onto Brett's partially exposed neck, and not giving me enough time to see, he suddenly lifts me from underneath and places me on his spindly hips, the last place I want to be. Quickly taking my chance and peering over his shoulder at his exposed neck, one packed pussy pimple bursts, landing on my fingers.

I want to vomit, quickly jumping from his grip, wiping the pus off my fingers onto his shirt. How can he be so filthy? I don't want to see or feel any more of his skin, pulling on his shirt, but my hand slips, feeling the grease through it, panicking, shifting my hand to his face.

Close up, his face is full of blackheads and boils, not sure I can take anymore. Praying to myself, focusing on the image on his t-shirt, he takes my chin and very slowly directs me up to his dark beady eyes which are glaring, threatening me to say anything. Wild, dirty, greasy, frizzy hair waves in the breeze; I'm crying, coughing, choking, suffocating, struggling to breathe. Pulling him away, giving myself some much-needed air, I don't know if his shit is worth all of this.

Gasping, feeling like I'm in a room with no air, his angry arms draw me deeper and deeper to his stench and mouth, which is daringly close to mine. I'll be dead before I let that happen, quickly turning my head to the side, successfully avoiding his mouth, feeling his face land in my hair. Falling to my knees before he has a chance to try again, my bones crack on the cold cruel concrete, straight away questioning why I wore a dress? Trying to position myself, my eyes, now level with his groin, bulge seeing the outline of his dick which I wouldn't have given him credit for.

A big woman and tiny man walk into the alley, seeing me on my knees, laughing. Staring at her with pleading eyes, I beg the universe she sees me and knows I need help.

"This one's already being used, honey. Let's go somewhere else."

The universe hates me.

Above me, Brett steps back, resting his hands on the wall, reading the graffiti out loud.

"Suck... my... cock. Now that sounds like a good idea, don't it?"

Wincing, unzipping his filthy jeans, I don't want to go near his filthy underwear or dick, but if I want his shit, I have no other choice. Hand inside his jeans, my two front fingers take out his filthy dick, balking as I direct it to my mouth. Suddenly letting rip a fart, it's so loud my knees jump, hurting them all over again.

What kind of monster is he?

Coughing, gagging, trying to stand, his hand holds me down.

"You got some business to finish first, babe."

Deceivably strong, he pulls me down to the hard concrete again, gagging, trying not to breathe any of his fart particles in. This is so not what I was expecting to be happening right now. I thought I'd be with some gorgeous hunk of a man, back at his flat, exploring each other's bodies, halfway to heaven. Instead, I'm with one of the most repulsive human beings I've ever met, about to gag on the most revolting smelling dick I've ever had the misfortune of putting anywhere near my mouth.

Killing him with my eyes, glaring up to his ugly face, he's smirking.

"You filthy bastard. You do that again; I'll be doing more than suck."

Grabbing his balls, squeezing them just enough to let him know I mean business, he grunts as I gently guide the tip of his dick into my mouth. The taste, a cross between onion and bleach, is too horrific for me to continue and my gag reflex involuntarily takes over, having to remind myself his stuff is too good to pass up. Remembering I bought mouth spray, I retrieve it from my jacket pocket spraying my mouth until his taste is gone, and lifting my head, stretching my neck muscles, he seems to be enjoying my pain.

"I fucking hate you. Your shit better be the best of the best."

Closing my eyes, thinking of anything other than what I'm doing, I give possibly the worst blowjob of my life, and one inglorious minute later, pulling him out just before he sprays all over me, some of it lands on my face, making me gag for the fourth time tonight. Frantically wiping my face, chest, and hands with tissues from my pocket, I don't want any part of him left on me.

Wait until I tell Tiffany.

Heavy breathing above me suggests he is more than happy with what has just happened, zipping up his jeans, grinning from ear to ear as he extends a grimy hand to me to help me up.

"You can do that whenever you want, babe."

Brushing myself off, paying special attention to my throbbing red knees, I bend down, gagging for the fifth time, spraying whatever is left of my mouth spray everywhere. Laughing, he dips his hand into his pocket and hands me the biggest bullet I've ever seen. Grabbing it, he suddenly grasps my wrist, holding it tight; his leery eyes looking straight into mine.

"No charge."

Bewildered, looking ahead like a statue, I'm ready to burst.

"I should bloody well think so, you filthy bastard."

Running like I have air in my feet, I pass another couple having sex, ignoring them and everyone else as they combine into a blur in front of me. The only thing on my mind is my bath, filling it to the brim as soon as I get in, sitting in the water for hours, scrubbing every part of my skin, hair, and mouth until I'm satisfied I can no longer smell, or taste, any part of him on me.

Lucky for Brett, his shit is the best I've ever had, striking up some sort of deal where he's willing to let me try anything I want for free, as long as he gets what he wants. I have to make sure I profit from having to touch his revolting body, eventually getting him to agree to coming to my flat where at least I'm able to lure him into the bath before we get down to business.

Undeniably the worst thing I've ever done, it's not long before I decide I need to find another dealer, panicking that the inevitable will happen and I'll have to have sex with him. Just the thought of it makes me want to be sick, not able to imagine his dick in any place other than my mouth, and that's bad enough. There have to be other dealers out there.

If Jesse, or my parents, especially my mother, knew what I was doing, they'd have a fit. The thought of their disapproval though, is the only thing that keeps me doing it.

Puff too weak, Opium too strong, pills are only good for a moment of fun and mushrooms send me loopy. I've tried Acid once, deciding once was enough after walking down Cuba Street and seeing every single person walking towards me with devil horns on their head. I'd thought I was in hell. People had tried to help, but I'd screamed in their faces and made the sign of the cross, running from them like they were all devils.

My worst trip to date wasn't Acid, but a lovely white and purple flower that grows everywhere. Datura had sent my hallucinogenic powers off the scale...

One month earlier

Out with Tiffany and one of her friends at a bar down Vivian Street, I listen as her friend retells a story of how she tripped for twelve hours after drinking Datura. I've never heard of it, intrigued to find out more. Apparently, it's a flower that grows wild, and it's everywhere.

Asking her friend where to find it, I'm shocked to discover that I walk past the flowers almost daily, picking some from a bush the next night, pretending I'm on a walk so no-one will suspect what I'm doing. Tucking them in my bag, quickly taking them home, I boil them in a pot of water, as per instructions, and wait until only a green liquid remains. Carefully sieving the liquid into a cup and placing it in the fridge. I impatiently wait for it to cool, unable to wait too long, drinking the whole cup lukewarm, screwing my nose up at how sour it is.

An hour later, ringing Brett, I'm sitting, playing my imaginary guitar, looking up at my imaginary posters of Jimi Hendrix and Axl Rose on my wall, laughing to myself.

Brrring, brrring.

"Yeah, what do you want?"

"Hey baby, it's me, Jimi wants me to play a G, Jimi's talking to me."

"Who the fuck is this?"

"It's me, baby. Lola! I'm here with Jimi Hendrix and Axl Rose. Jimi wants me to play a G on my guitar, and *Axl* wants me to sing with him. It's crazy. Come meet them."

"Lola, what the fuck are you on now? I told you never to ring me on this number unless it was for some sweet cheeks. *Jimi Hendrix? Axl Rose*? Talking to you? For fucks sake, stay where you are, I'm on my way round."

Twenty minutes later, Brett arrives to find the door already open.

"Lola, where are you? Lola? Lola?"

Hiding in a wardrobe in the bedroom, I hear him and scream, terrified.

"Help. Help me. The Klu Klux Klan are trying to find me."

Opening the wardrobe, finding me crouched underneath a blanket, hiding, he lifts the blanket off me and I scream up at him, running out and down the stairs onto the road, which I think is as soft as a meadow.

"Oooh, look at the lovely fresh green grass."

Rolling about on the road, the imaginary grass underneath me feels soft and floaty and a car coming nearly hits me, beeping loudly.

"For fucks sake, Lola! That's some strong shit you're on. Whoever sold you this is gonna hear from me. Get the fuck up before you're killed."

Picking me up, carrying me inside to safety, another car honks in protest having to swerve out of the way. Hours later, sober, and very sore from where Brett has had to clean me up, I'm thankful it was early morning and the roads weren't that busy...

Still highly amused by that epic trip, whenever I hear Jimi Hendrix or Gun's n Roses on the radio, I remember that trip of all trips, and the only time I let that mother fucker cum in my mouth.

Chapter Thirty-Three

The drug I finally settle on which allows me to have fun and doesn't make me go mad is cocaine.

Retelling my stories to Jesse one night, explaining how the come-down of taking coke isn't so nice, I tell her how I counteract it by taking speed to make sure I'm always high. Horrified, the lecture I'm expecting starts.

"The harder stuff will have you hooked in no time. Just bloody well stick to the weed."

Jesse's started doing the odd bit of puff and doesn't seem as uptight and nerdy, but she still refuses to try anything stronger. She's been the same forever. I find her so boring in that sense. I wish she'd just let her hair down and try different things. The new friends I'm making are much more fun, and easier going.

A few of the girls I've met through Jesse at The Orchard often tell me I'd make thousands a month with my looks. They say I should talk to Sharon and that she'd take me on in a second. They aren't too keen to socialise with me though, making excuse after excuse every time Jesse and I invite them out with us. It's been the same for as long as I can remember. Girls just don't want me around them, especially if it means the attention they want will be taken away. I'll show them. I'll work at The Orchard and they won't have any choice but to socialise. Two can play at that game.

Determined to catch Sharon's eye, every time I visit Jesse at work, Sharon's not there, which pisses me off. Gonzo, the big, brutish, bald security guy Sharon's hired, doesn't start till late, so is never there, which is a godsend. He'd never let me in. His huge nose is so crooked, he really does look just like something out of the Muppets.

I need Sharon to be there when he's not. Sharon needs to see me in the flesh for my plan to work. I'm getting desperate, and my nightmares of living back with my parents are getting more and more horrific. If I dream of another saggy arse, I swear, I'll go fucking mad.

At this moment in time anything will do, and I figure if the girls are as confident as they are about me, then I shouldn't have a problem. I just need Sharon to be there.

Gigi, the cleaner, is always there, but that doesn't help. She stops me every time, and like a record, tells me the same thing.

"You remind me so much of my old friend, Gail. She worked here, too. Used to be gorgeous, like you. She had men queuing up. Easy money."

Intrigued to hear more about Gail from a different pair of eyes, I ask for more information about her.

"How old was she?"

"I think she was the same age as you, about eighteen or nineteen."

"Gail? I've heard of her now from two friends of mine. Jesse, you know, and Tiffany, a prostitute she helped get off drugs who said if it wasn't for Gail she would have died. Do you know her? Came from Fiji? Did Gail work here, too, as a working girl? I'm hearing all sorts of stories."

"Yes, Gail did work here like that, but not for long. Said she'd rather go out onto the streets and help people in need. She must've saved hundreds of girls over the years, it's hard to keep track. I don't remember meeting Tiffany before, but maybe I did. Gail never went back to normal after she lost her two babies. She was only sixteen.

Very, very sad. Took her a long time to get over them. I think Sharon saw her on the streets one day and offered her work. Gail never looked back. Sharon had lost her mother years before and had never had children so she sort've took Gail under her wing. They became inseparable; almost ran this place together. Gail never wanted to live here, though; always said she was more comfortable on the streets which killed Sharon. She ended up getting lots of girls to come work here and took a bit of the profits for herself. Good little set up. I remember meeting Sharon and Gail for the first time and thinking they looked a little weird together. I remember knocking on the door of The Orchard to ask if Sharon needed a cleaner. I knew what the place was and thought I would try my luck. No one else would hire me. My family just moved from Lebanon, so my English was not so good, but Sharon's English was bad, too. The interview was so funny. Both me and Sharon spoke in our broken English and Gail had to help, but we soon came to a deal and the rest is history. Sharon's looked after me ever since, and Gail did too when she was alive. We all looked out for each other, were the best of friends, but we also gave each other the space we needed, too. It's rare you have friends like that. I see you and Jesse are good friends. Keep it that way. Don't let anything come in between your friendship. Nothing. Not men, not money, not possessions. Do that, and you'll have a friend for life. Jesse's a good girl. She's had a bit of a hard life, too, but she's here, and we are looking after her. Sharon and I. We're looking after her like she's our own because she's Gail's niece. I'm sure that's what killed my beautiful friend, finding out she had family after all these years. We were so heartbroken when we heard she suddenly passed. We just couldn't believe it. Everyone loved her, especially Jesse. Hit her real hard."

Taking Gigi's hand, squeezing it tight, her eyes are glassing over, near enough making me cry, too.

"I couldn't believe it when Jesse told me Gail was her aunt. Jesse's mother was such a monster, it would've killed her to have lost Gail that quick after finding her. I'm glad you and Sharon were here."

Staring into my eyes, Gigi looks confused, like she's questioning her own thoughts. It doesn't take her long to let me know what she's thinking.

"Gail had the same beautiful eyes as you. Unusual colour you do not often see. You remind me of her a lot. She was curious like you, and boy did the men love her. She wasn't the same though after the babies, I've been told. Sharon knew her for the longest time. Said losing the babies was the single worst thing that happened to her. I know that if Gail could've had anything in the world, she would've wanted to meet her babies again. Anyway, that is not going to happen. You've got a chance to make something of yourself, Lola. I know Sharon would hate for me to say this, but don't waste your time here. Don't listen to them girls. You are different from the rest of them, you already know. Stop doing the drugs, and get a proper job. One you are proud of. Get off the shit, keep your looks and fly, like you're supposed to. You are beautiful now, but you soon won't be if you keep putting all that crap into your body."

Rolling my eyes, smiling at Gigi, I raise my eyebrow in question.

"Maybe Gail's my long-lost mother. Now wouldn't that be a turn up for the books. Two generations working at The Orchard. *Ha!* I've got a plan, Gigi. Don't you worry your pretty little head."

Tapping my nose, winking at her, laughing, she shakes her head.

"If Gail is your mother, I'm the Queen of England. Ha! Get off with you."

Sick of 'entertaining' Brett to fund my drugs, I've now got to the point where I would rather pay than have to touch his spindly body anymore. The last blowjob had sealed it for me, swearing he'd had an infection of some sort. The taste of bleach had not left my mouth for days, and no amount of mouthwash had worked.

Enough was enough!

Taking matters into my own hands, I start investigating The Orchard behind Jesse's back. Hiding in a bush outside, watching the men come and go, the same people frequent the place, wondering if their wives or girlfriends know what they're up to. Normal to look at, they all seem pretty decent, not one giving me, or Gonzo any reason to be worried. These men don't look as seedy as the ones on the street. One bloke, though, an ugly little oldish guy with a goatee beard and tiny eyes, gives me the creeps. Never entering the premises, he watches from his car scanning the joint for hours, seeming to wait for women to leave who I've noticed all have the same particular look. Breasts not too big, their hair is short, dark and bobbed, and they look miles younger than they are. Unbeknown to them, he follows them in his car until they catch a cab or disappear into the city. A pervert for sure, it has me wondering more often than not if he has a daughter of his own. The poor girl if he does. Just watching him sends shivers down my spine, and Gonzo seems to have his eye on him too, which worries me. It's like I've seen him somewhere before.

Slimy and revolting, he reminds me of the perv who used to touch up Jesse, and even though I know I'll get into trouble, I can't keep it to myself and tell her about him the next time she comes to visit.

Still clearly affected by her abuser, she begs me to stay away.

"You don't need to be doing that shit, Lola. Waiting outside in a bush, watching the men. Are you crazy? There's a reason why we have Gonzo on the door. That creep in the car might see you, and then what will happen? If you want to know, just ask me. I know them all. Just do some glamour modelling, get your portfolio made, and actually try to get some work. You know you'd be great. Putting strangers' dicks in your mouth? You're classier than that."

Swallowing, her emotions start to elevate, but I pay no attention to them. I know what I need to do, and glamour modelling won't keep my drug habit funded, or help me keep the lifestyle I'm accustomed to. It's that, or go back to my mother, and I know what I would rather do.

"It's *my* mouth and my life to do with as I please. It's easy money and means I don't have to suck Brett's dick, which believe me is the most repulsive dick you're ever likely to put anywhere near your mouth. A homeless man's dick would be cleaner than that little geeks. That's all I can do for the time being until I get into your place."

Jesse's dagger-like glare is all the communication I need to let me know the conversation about me working at The Orchard is finished. Showing her the door, practically pushing her out, I don't even say goodbye, slamming it in her face. Blood boiling, watching her from my window as she crosses the road and walks off in the direction of The Orchard, I stare until she is out of sight. Face on fire, I'll bloody show her. What Lola wants; Lola gets.

Deciding to try my luck the following night, I'm still furious with how Jesse spoke to me. I need to show her I'm still in charge of this relationship, and if that means pissing her off by going into her work and demanding to see Sharon, then so be it. That'll show her. Dodging Gonzo though will be tricky. I'll have to wait until he's on his break, which could be anytime between ten and twelve am.

Standing in the doorway to my room, staring at the rail of clothes hanging from my wardrobe, a conversation Jesse and I had about Sharon springs to mind. She'd said that for any girl to even be considered, Sharon would have to think they look like a million dollars. A million dollars?

Walking forward, letting my right-hand flick over different coloured hangers, it finally stops on a tiny gold dress which screams to be worn.

"Of course! Gold! What looks more like a million dollars."

Remembering the last time I'd worn it, the super clingy fabric had made it seem like it'd been painted on, and most importantly, it had showed off every curve to perfection.

Tonight, I'll make sure I walk in looking like an expensive jewel.

Slipping it over my head, the super smooth silky material feels like heaven on my skin, patting it flat over my body, pulling up my breasts and gently rubbing my nipples so they are seen through the fabric. Every little detail must be perfect. Happy with how it looks, I walk quickly to the bathroom, grabbing my half a comb from my dresser on the way. Wiping the grubby mirror, I get to work gently back-combing my thick blonde hair, brushing some unteased hair over my crown, finishing off the whole look with some spray, emptying most of the contents onto my hair, nearly choking myself in the process. Backing away from the mirror, gagging, trying not to pee on my dress, I collapse on the toilet until the coughing subsides. Thankfully, I've not yet put on knickers or make-up, panicking I've peed on my dress, checking the back of it, relieved to see it's stain free. Peering at myself in the mirror as I flush the loo, I'm glad to see my hair has been spared. That's what I get for using too much hairspray.

Grabbing my makeup bag, quickly walking back to my room, I lay everything I need on the vanity unit before me. Tonight I need to look the most beautiful I've ever looked; nothing can be off. Dabbing my eyes and drying them before I make myself up, I pay special attention to my eyes which are by far my best feature. Frosting my lips with the tiniest bit of gloss, I stand in front of my full-length mirror admiring my work.

"What shoes? They need to finish the whole look off so that when Sharon sees me, all she sees are dollar signs above my head."

Glancing towards my shoes, my eyes decide before I do, leading me to killer gold heels which I slip on with ease. For just a moment I imagine this is what Cinderella must've felt like. Applauding my good work, gazing at myself, I fall a little more in love with my reflection. If this doesn't get me work, I don't know what will. Deciding my good work deserves a reward, I rush to my bedside drawer not sure I can wait for my fix. If I'm totally honest, I need a little bit of Dutch courage to get me through the next couple of hours. I'm more nervous than I thought I'd be. Hand inside my bedside drawer, I bend down to see where my stash is, seeing it's stuck at the back against a little white box, having to cram my hand in as far as I can.

"Fuuuck."

Burning in pain, my hand feels like it's been stung by a bee, desperately trying to pull the drawer with my free hand but I tug it a little too hard and catch my skin between the two boxes. Kneeling, wishing I hadn't put on my shoes, one of them catches on the carpet nearly making me fall backwards, steadying myself, trying not to pee, my knees digging into the carpet while I try to peek into the drawer to see what is making my hand stuck. As if by luck, a chopstick from a takeaway looks up at me, picking it up and using it to manoeuvre bits of paper out of the way until I'm finally able to free my stuck hand.

Rubbing it hard, checking for bruising or broken bones, I'm lucky to have come out with only a few scuffs. Beyond pissed off, the drawer comes off second best as I yank it hard, making it slip off its hinges and nearly hit me in the face. Finally finding the box I seek, I quickly search for my tiny bag of white powder, placing a little line under one of my fingernails and sniffing, making sure there is no residue left around my nose when I'm finished.

Melting against my bed, I look up to the ceiling feeling like ice in the sun, tingling, a lot less stressed. My drawer, which now sits beside me, is full of stuff, the little white box that caused all the trouble right in the middle. Without even thinking, I scoop it up, placing it on top of my bedside table, willing myself to look inside. I've still not found the courage to open it and doubt I will tonight. Trembling, willing it open of its own accord, I'm desperate to see what the necklace my birth mother left me looks like, but I'm still not quite ready for the emotional journey it's bound to take me on. I'll never forgive my mother for what she did. She'd wanted me to suffer and still wants it, reinforcing it every time she calls me.

"Have you seen the necklace yet? Isn't it beautiful? What? You haven't even opened it? Why on earth not?"

I can't open it. I know it's only a stupid necklace, and it's not like I knew my birth mother. But I'm scared to take a look. I'm scared of what I will feel when I see it.

This is not how I want to be feeling before going to The Orchard, throwing it back in my drawer and backing away, nearly tripping on my high heels again. I simply can't concentrate on it tonight. My mother would be so happy to know how it's making me feel, but I won't let her, or thoughts of her, spoil my night.

Snorting one more line for good luck, replacing the drawer and slamming it shut, I brush myself, and my knees off, deciding I'll open the box with the necklace when I'm ready. One thing is sure. I won't tell my mother. At least I'll have control of that one.

Grabbing my full-length Zebra coat from behind the door, wrapping it tightly around my shoulders and scooping up my gold clutch, the universe better bring me some luck tonight because I need this more than I've ever needed anything before.

Blowing my flat a goodbye kiss, crossing myself for more luck, I carefully navigate the steep steel stairs, hitting the pavement two minutes later. Gliding in the direction of The Orchard, hundreds of lustful eyes follow my every step, but I ignore them all. Tonight, nothing will stop me from getting a job, not even Jesse.

Fifteen minutes later, storming through the door, not giving Jesse enough time to react, my loudest voice demands to see the Madam and, unprepared for my dramatic entrance, Jesse's mouth hangs open in shock as I wink at her, waiting for Sharon, who, right on cue seconds later, marches out to see what all the commotion is about. In less than ten seconds she is welcoming me into her office, dutifully following her, winking at Jesse again as I pass while some of the other girls and clients come out to see what's going on. Gonzo looks from the door, panting. The universe has definitely helped me tonight. The rest is history.

Chapter Thirty-Four

Persuading Jesse to agree to me working wasn't easy at all. She didn't speak to me for weeks after my surprise visit and I'd actually worried our friendship was in real danger, but after explaining that the decision to get off the streets and work in a place that was a lot safer, was the best thing for not only her, but our friendship too; she eventually thawed and forgave me.

Never in a million years did I expect I'd ever have to ask for her forgiveness for anything.

A few months later, around mine, Jesse and I have decided to stay in for a change and order a pizza. After downing a few vodkas, the conversation veers towards that eventful night.

"I thought you were going to kill me. The look in your eyes. You looked so much like your mother. I wish I'd taken a photo."

"Don't say that. Ever. I'm not like her, and never will be. I wasn't prepared for your sudden visit; you knew I didn't want you working there. After all the stories I'd told you about the men, you still bloody ignored me. You wouldn't have even made it through the door if Gonzo was there. I'd already told him not to let you in. He had to be late that bloody night, didn't he? Now look what you have to deal with? Pervy men who touch you up and probably think about you when they go home and have sex with their poor wives or girlfriends who don't have a bloody clue. I'm surprised you don't freak out when you see some of them at the club. I'd bloody run a mile."

Listening to the music playing in the background, I know what she's saying is true. Still, if it means never having to suck Brett's dick ever again, I know my decision was the right one. He hadn't been happy when our little 'arrangement' had ended.

"At least the men who come into The Orchard are vetted and clean."

Eating our pizza, killing each other with our eyes, I'm not really in the mood for one of her lectures tonight. Her music isn't helping either. More in the mood for some rock, she's playing some folky shit by a band she loves from the sixties who are singing about dreaming in California.

"What crap are you getting me to listen to now, you freak? I prefer your harder stuff. Not really feeling this. What else have you got?"

Watching her walk towards her bag, I have to admit, I'm happy she's still around. I wouldn't have a job for one, and my parents would still be ringing if it weren't for her. Now I actually have some breathing space, they only ring every other week, more than happy to hear I'm finally making money. Making up some cock and bull story about modelling for a company overseas, they'd believed me, not even curious when I'd told them they'd probably not be able to see the pictures. They pretend to care, but I'm not convinced, especially where my mother's concerned. She's definitely turned my father's neck well and truly away from me, now. He used to ring every day and chat about anything, always telling me at the end not to tell her. He only rings me once in a blue moon, and that's if I'm lucky. He gives some dumb excuse about having to work longer hours. He's never worked long hours, ever. I'd do anything to hear his voice more often. I miss him. Swallowing the lump in my throat, I won't think about it too much. If he was my real father I might not forgive him, but as he's not, I'll let him love me just that little bit less. Jesse's the only one who's stuck by me, even when I know she hasn't wanted to. I'm grateful for at least having her still in my life.

Handing me a CD, smiling while I read the front cover, my eyebrows question her choice.

"*Wonderful Life*? This looks interesting. Who's the guy on the front? He looks like a right geek."

"Wait till you hear his voice. You'll fall in love. This song will make him a millionaire for years to come. Not my favourite track, though. The final song will have you melting."

Popping the CD into the player, the opening riffs aren't too bad, scanning the cover again, thinking he doesn't look like someone who'd have you melting. And then he starts to sing; his deep melodic voice grabs me, totally getting what Jesse means. Listening to the lyrics, I hate to admit, I quite like it.

"So, do you think your life is wonderful now? A place to live, a job and me back in your life?"

The grin on her face says it all. I can see she is the happiest she's ever been. Asking her to tell me about her job when she started, I'm curious to know what The Orchid was like back then.

"It's not Orchid, it's Orchard. There's a difference. I think Sharon likes to think of you girls as her own Orchard of love, so to speak."

"Orchard of love? Where the hell do you think these things up? Just tell me what it was like."

You really want to know? It could take a while."

"Wait, let me fill up my drink and go for a pee."

Running to the kitchen, grabbing the vodka, and handing it to her to fill us up, I quickly run to the loo and settle back down on the couch, wrapping myself in a blanket. Grinning from ear to ear, Jesse's staring at me like she's about to unload the world's biggest secret.

Just as she's about to start, an almighty crash right outside the window startles us, running to see what has happened. Staring at each other in shock, we can't hold in our giggles.

Pointing to the street outside, I'm in stitches, crying with laughter.

"No way! No - fucking - way! It's a sign, Jesse. It's a mother fucking sign."

To be continued...

Acknowledgments

Writing is always something I wanted to do. I just had to find the right time. That came when I was 45. One day I had this clear vision and knew it was time to start. Don't ask me why.

Writing *Secrets* was hard both emotionally and physically. Writing some of the scenes bought back a lot of unhappy memories; having to relive them through my words. But it was cathartic and healing at the same time, if that makes any sense. I'd like to think that some of my memories have been released from my mind, to my hands, to the pages of the book and released to the world. There's a lot to be said for writing things down.

Throughout my journey I've been quite vocal about my experiences. My partner, children and friends have listened, even when they've listened a hundred times before to the same thing. Their undying love and encouragement have kept me going.

Thank you Andy, Neil, Charley, Heidi, Cam, Steven, and Max. You have always been my biggest supporters. I love you all.

Thank you to Sian Phillips. Your editing skills and patience are second to none. I'm very grateful for everything you do.

Cameron McNally, your creativity in creating my covers, shines. You are brilliant inside and out.

Thank you to Romie Nguyen for typesetting.

I'm so lucky to have all these wonderful people in my life.

Thank you to every last person who buys my books and believes in me. I'm so grateful to you all.

About the Author

M.A. McNally writes page turning dark suspense in her second novel from the series *Broken*. In *Secrets,* the characters she created in her first novel will continue to have readers invested as they turn page after page. Part fact, part fiction, her stories are inspired by her early fascination with reading anything about true-life crime which started in her early teens, living in Wellington, New Zealand. Her earliest wish was to amaze the world with her rock star voice, but as that didn't work out, she finally let go of that dream and decided to focus on another. Writing. She's better at that - just.

Spending her days trying to inspire college students to love

English language through writing, it's much harder than she thinks, but she's sure she's getting through to some of them. Early in the morning, sitting at the kitchen table, she grabs an hour to write before work and clicks away on her keyboard while watching the sun say hello.

Currently living in Hampshire, England, she loves to sing (karaoke queen), go to gigs and the odd festival, but most of all she likes to catch up on the latest must see on television with her partner. Oh, and she loves all her kids.

Printed in Dunstable, United Kingdom

77866039R00143